HERO OF METALHAVEN
METAL AND BLOOD
BOOK 1

G J OGDEN

Copyright © 2023 by G J Ogden
All rights reserved.

No part of this book may be reproduced in any form or by any electronic or mechanical means, including information storage and retrieval systems, without written permission from the author, except for the use of brief quotations in a book review.

These novels are entirely works of fiction. The names, characters and incidents portrayed in it are the work of the author's imagination. Any resemblance to actual persons, living or dead, events or localities is entirely coincidental.

Illustration © Phil Dannels
www.phildannelsdesign.com

Editing by S L Ogden
Published by Ogden Media Ltd
www.ogdenmedia.net

PROLOGUE

The world as it had been ended in the year 2065 with the collapse of civilization and the ruin of Earth. The Last War and its devastating consequences left ninety percent of the planet uninhabitable. Fewer than two hundred thousand people survived.

Then the Authority rose.

Founded by oligarchs, dictators and sovereigns with the means to escape the devastation, Zavetgrad became Earth's last and only nation.

Maintaining oppressive control over any survivors who arrived hoping for salvation, the Authority enforced work in return for food and shelter in the relative safety of what was once northern Canada.

In the 266 years since the disaster, Zavetgrad has developed into a nation of one million, spread across nine work sectors.

Population and procreation are controlled. Women capable of giving birth are segregated for that function alone, while all men and women with viable seed or eggs must donate or face death in the Trials – brutal gladiatorial events held for public amusement under the façade of justice.

The Authority's strict rules are for the greater good. Nimbus, the orbital citadel and seat of the Authority's power, is humanity's future, far away from the rot of Earth's past.

But in the toil of the reclamation sector, known to its workers as Metalhaven, a chance for a better future will be forged from the iron will of Metal and Blood.

1
SOMEONE HAS TO

The crackle and hiss of the hundreds of laser cutters operating in Yard Seven was a symphony that Finn Brasa had grown to love over his many years in the reclamation sector, known to its workers as Metalhaven. It was just about the only thing he enjoyed about life in Zavetgrad, beyond the company of his friend and worker buddy, Owen. Burly, but not in a brutish way, and gentler than the snow that was constantly falling on their heads, Owen was a green shoot of goodness in an otherwise barren and bomb-blackened world. In contrast to his friend, Finn considered himself to be more of a cockroach – a survivor who had adapted to life in Earth's last, lonely pocket of civilization, not by choice, but out of habit.

"We must be well ahead of quota by now," Owen said, shouldering his laser cutter and carrying a tombstone-sized chunk of tank armor over to their trailer.

Finn disengaged his beam and checked his work logger. "You're right, we're ahead by two hundred kilos," he replied, with some measure of surprise. "In that case, we'd better slow down, otherwise the foreman will just increase our numbers."

"I'm on-board with that idea," Owen replied.

Finn's friend hurled the slab of metal into the trailer before mopping his brow with the back of his hand. It didn't seem conceivable that a man could perspire in bitter, freezing outdoor temperatures, but the hard graft combined with the searing heat of the lasers made reclamation work hotter than a workout in a sauna.

Finn also dropped a slab of metal into the trailer, causing the rear axle to dip by another few millimeters, then activated the controls to send the automated hauler back to the processing facility. It trundled away along the dirt road, politely waiting to allow another hauler to join the track ahead of it. Then, as if by magic, a foreman turned from its regular patrol route and began stomping toward them. The robot was wearing a reflective high-vis jacket and a hard hat, both in a gunmetal chrome, which was the designated color of Metalhaven.

"Oh shit, here we go," said Owen, drawing Finn's attention to the machine with a subtle nod of his head.

Finn sighed and pressed his hands to his hips. "That has to be a record. We only downed tools for what? Like, two seconds, before that hunk of crap singled us out?"

"He's just doing his job, I guess," Owen shrugged. "It's not his fault; it's how he was programmed."

Finn smiled at his friend, marveling at how he always managed to find the good in any situation. Then the looming presence of the six-foot humanlike machine wiped the grin off his face. He studied the foreman, recognizing it as a Gen-VII design, the latest in robotic middle-management. Gen-

VII's were equipped with AI speech modulators that allowed them to sound suitably gruff and dictatorial, while thirty mechanical 'muscles' allowed them to convey a wide range of facial expressions. Generally, the only ones they ever bothered to use were variations of 'angry' and 'disappointed'.

"Finn Brasa and Owen Thomas, why have you stopped working?" the foreman asked, articulating one of its crude metal eyebrows to mimic suspicion.

"We just sent the hauler away to the processing facility. We're taking a break," Finn replied, squaring off against the machine.

"You have not logged that you are taking a break," the foreman replied, sternly.

"That's because you were already on our assess before we had a chance to." Finn raised his left wrist and tapped the command into his work logger. "There, happy now?"

The foreman narrowed its manufactured eyes at him, then leaned in closer. "You have ten minutes Worker Brasa. I will be watching." With that, the foreman stomped away to pester another worker duo, though Finn knew the machine would be back on the dot of ten minutes to make sure they didn't exceed their allotted break time.

"What gets me is that the Authority makes them wear hard hats," Owen said, sliding a packet of cigarettes out of his overalls. "I mean, they're made of metal. How much protection does one of those things really need?"

"Their electronic brains are actually quite sensitive," Finn said, sitting down on a caterpillar track that they'd previously removed from the tank they were working on. "Given how expensive those machines are, it makes sense that the golds in the authority sector would want to protect their investment."

"Unlike us," Owen added, rapping his knuckles against his unprotected head before dropping down next to him. He removed a cigarette from the packet and tapped it against the tank track. "When's the last time you saw a hard hat on the head of a Metalhaven worker?"

Finn scowled at the stick, which was now stuck between Owen's lips. A second later, it was lit and the heady smell of tobacco, nicotine and narcotics wafted past his nose.

"You won't need a hard hat if you keep smoking those," Finn said, making sure to clearly convey his disapproval. "They'll melt your brain from the inside."

Owen snorted then cursed and accessed his work logger. "Shit, I forgot to enter that I was taking a break."

His friend tapped away at the device for a couple of seconds, then relaxed and took a long draw from the cigarette. The effect was immediate, and Finn could see the big man's muscles relax and the tension bleed away from his smoke-blackened face.

"I don't care what they put in these things, they make me feel good, and that's a rare thing," Owen said, allowing the smoke to billow from his mouth and nose as he spoke.

"You should care, because they make you feel good for a reason," Finn replied, choosing instead to revive himself with a drink of water from his flask. "It's just another way for the Authority to keep you compliant and dependent on them."

"Why do you always have to fight the golds?" Owen nudged him with his broad shoulder. "All it ever gets you is grief."

Finn shrugged. "Because fuck them, that's why."

Owen snorted again and shook his head, before taking another long draw from the cigarette. He held the smoke in his lungs for several seconds then let it swirl out through this nose like a dragon about to breath fire. Already, the man's eyes were glassy, like he was in a waking dream.

"Most folk from Metalhaven don't live to see forty, and we're already well over half-way there," Owen added, drowsily. "I say take what small pleasures you can get, while you can get them, before we end up on the scrapheap, like all the crap in here."

Finn managed a half-hearted laugh and nudged Owen right back. "That sort of shit logic is the *reason* we don't live past forty."

Owen didn't answer, which was par for the course. Unlike Finn, his friend didn't enjoy confrontation, but their argument, though good-natured, had already left Finn feeling brittle and on edge. The appearance of another foreman striding toward them only caused his hackles to rise further.

"Get back to work," the robot demanded.

Finn pushed himself up and squared off against the machine, just as he had done against the previous mechanical manager. This model was an aging Gen V, which was less sophisticated than the robot which had confronted them earlier. It lacked the ability to produce complex facial expressions, and its synthetic speech modulator was more stunted and aggressive, like its logic circuits.

"We're on a break, buzz off," Finn snapped, and straight after he heard Owen's resigned sigh from behind him.

"Worker Finn Brasa, your tone of disrespect will not be tolerated," the foreman replied. "One hour has been added to tomorrow's work shift. That makes two extra hours in total for tomorrow's shift."

Finn was about to tell the robot where it could stick its

extra hours, when Owen appeared at his side and bustled him away from the machine.

"Sorry, Mr. Foreman, it's been a hard day," Owen said, smiling at the robot, whose metal face did not smile back. "But, if you'll check our logs, you'll see we're ahead of quota, so it's all good, right?"

The robot's crude mechanical face scowled then it grabbed Owen's wrist and plugged itself into the man's work logger to download the data. A second later it detached, and the scowl was gone. "Good work, Owen Thomas. Your quota for next period has been increased by five percent."

The foreman then about-turned like a regimental Sergeant Major and stomped away.

"I told you so," Finn said. He'd blurted out the words before his better judgement took hold and stopped him from making the smart-ass remark.

Owen was understandably less than impressed by his impulsiveness, but the sound of a commotion from deeper inside the yard distracted them both. Finn moved away from their assigned scrap – a wrecked soviet tank – and looked out across Yard Seven, trying to spot the source of the affray, but the sheer density of junk impeded his search. Yard Seven was dedicated to military vehicles, ranging from the tanks he and Owen specialized in, to aircraft and other fighting machines that were all casualties of the Last War, brought to Zavetgrad for reclamation. The vehicles were piled so high in places that some stacks blotted out the low winter sun.

"It's Jonas and Warner again," Owen said. His friend had gone in the opposite direction and was standing on the chassis of the tank. "Those two knuckleheads are always at each other's throats."

Finn climbed up beside his worker buddy and saw Jonas and Warner pushing each other and yelling in each other's faces beneath the wing of a Chinese fighter jet. "Damn it, those two will miss quota again if they don't stop fighting, then the entire yard will get slapped with a fine, and everyone will get extra shift hours."

Finn set out toward the squabbling worker duo but Owen grabbed his arm and held him back.

"Why do you always have to be the peacekeeper?" Owen released him then folded his powerful arms across his chest. "Besides, you weren't bothered about getting extra shift hours when you were being a dick to that foreman..."

"What I get for myself is my lookout, but not everyone in this yard can physically handle any more hours, and that's not right," Finn countered. "Besides, someone has to protect them from their own stupidity."

Finn resumed course toward Jonas and Warner, who were now trading blows, stomping his heavy boots into the snow more heavily than the foremen. Owen defiantly stood his ground for a second or two then cursed under his breath and ran to catch up.

"Admit it, you just like getting up in the face of the Authority and poking it in the eyes," Owen said, jogging to his side.

Finn feigned a look of shock. "Me? I'm a model citizen, I'll have you know...."

Noting that a foreman had taken interest in the scuffle, Finn quickened his pace to reach the warring duo before the mechanical middle-manager did. Jonas now had his worker buddy in a headlock, while Warner flailed wild punches at his partner, to little effect. It was like a bar brawl but without the alcohol, or the bar.

"Break it up, that's enough!" Finn said, grabbing Jonas' arm and physically unfurling it from around Warner's neck, before pushing the man back.

Jonas was irate and lashed out with a wild haymaker that connected flush with Finn's jaw and sent him reeling back. Owen stopped dead, as did Warner and Jonas, who had the petrified look of a man who'd just accidentally cursed at his mother.

"Shit, sorry Finn, I just lashed out," Jonas said, holding up his hands.

The red mist descended on Finn and he grabbed the man's overalls and pinned him to the fuselage of the jet fighter. His other hand was balled into a fist, ready to strike. "That hurt," he hissed through gritted teeth, desperately trying to rein in the urge to flatten Jonas' already drawn, gormless face.

Owen coughed to get his attention and Finn saw the foreman rounding the corner. He released Jonas and stepped back, much to the worker's relief.

"Nothing is going on here, understood?" Finn said, not taking his eyes off the foreman. "Owen and I are on a break, and we came over to give you some pointers on cutting away this wing. That's all."

"You got it, Finn," Jonas said, sheepishly.

"Yeah, sorry Finn," Warner added.

Warner's comment didn't confirm that the man had understood his instructions, but the foreman arrived before Finn could make certain. He was glad to see it was another Gen VII, which meant that he at least had a chance of talking themselves out of the hole Jonas and Warner had put them all in.

"Why are you not working?" The foreman asked. The machine's tone was calm yet its question was delivered in a manner that made it abundantly clear the robot believed they *should* be working.

"My work partner and I are on a break, so we thought we'd help out Jonas and Warner here, by offering to help them with this wing." Finn hooked a thumb toward the burned-out fighter as he said this.

The foreman looked at the wing, then at Jonas and Warner, then back at Finn. Grabbing his wrist, the machine accessed his work logger to confirm that he was being truthful about being on a break, then took a pace back. "Get back to work," the robot said, before resuming its rounds.

Owen let out the breath he'd been holding and Jonas and Warner looked similarly relieved. Then the look Finn shot them both made the men stand tall, as if they'd been called to attention.

"Are you trying to get people killed?" Finn said, jabbing a finger into Jonas' chest. "If you don't make quota then we all get extra hours next period, and there are guys in here that are worked half-to-death as it is. Some are close to being sent to trial. Is that what you want?"

"Yeah, I get it, Finn, I'm sorry," Jonas said, hands up again. The man then pointed to two different parts of the wing. "I said we should cut there, and Warner said we should cut there, and it just got a little heated is all."

Finn shook his head then grabbed Jonas' laser cutter. He set the device to low power then scored lines across the wing in the places where the men actually needed to cut.

"That's where you cut," Finn said, shoving the tool back into Jonas' hands. "Anywhere else and this wing will have fallen on your heads and killed you both."

Both men went as white as the snow and their argument was suddenly overshadowed by the realization they'd dodged a bullet – or a falling wing, at least. Finn then reached into his pocket and pulled out two ration chits for drinks at the local Recovery Center, which was the Zavetgrad euphemism for a bar.

"Here, work it out later over a few beers," Finn said, slapping the chits into Warner's hand. "Until then, keep your shit together, okay?"

"Hey, thanks, Finn!" Warner said, closing his fingers around the chits and shaking his fist, like it contained a winning lottery ticket. "Despite what people say, you're okay, you know that?"

Warner realized his slip of the tongue and desperately tried to backtrack, though Finn wasn't offended. It was no secret that most people either didn't like him, or were intimidated by him, or both. He hooked a thumb toward another ruined vehicle that was assigned to the troublesome worker duo.

"Work on that fuselage section instead of this jet," he said, changing the subject. "It's easier to cut down and it might mean you actually hit quota this shift."

Jonas and Warner made their apologies again then hustled over to the lump of wreckage that Finn had highlighted, laser cutters slung over their shoulders like pickaxes.

"You could have bought me a drink with those chits," Owen said, slyly.

"I was actually hoping you'd buy me one," Finn replied,

smiling at his only true friend. "Besides, I have some extra chits for cigarettes that have your name on them."

Owen laughed and slapped him on the back, which almost knocked him over thanks to the man's uncommon strength. Finn's work logger then bleeped to signify they were coming toward the end of their ten-minute break.

"Shit, we'd better get back before that other foreman returns and finds us gone."

Finn cancelled the alert and was about to head off when he saw the glint of something metal on the ground. He knelt down and ruffled his fingers through the snow-covered dirt, uncovering a number of electronic components that had been buried in the shallow grave, like lost treasure. Looking in all directions for the watchful eyes of the foreman, he then slid the components into his boot and stood up, as if he'd merely been tying his laces.

"Never mind anyone else, you'll get sent to trial if they catch you with those," Owen warned. Naturally, his friend had seen everything.

"Then it's a good job they won't catch me," Finn replied, unrepentant.

Suddenly, the tortuous shriek of twisted metal split the air, as the weight of snow on its wing caused the old Russian fighter jet to become dislodged. Finn tried to dodge aside but his boots slid in the loose dirt, and the aircraft wing came crashing toward his head. Owen was there in an instant, bracing the weight of the wreck with his colossal strength, and allowing Finn to scramble away. Then Owen jumped aside and the wing thudded into the ground and broke free, like a biscuit wafer snapping in two.

"Thanks, my friend," Finn said, blowing out a sigh. "I'm glad you always have my back."

Owen snorted a laugh and pushed himself up, dusting down his hands on his overalls. "Someone in this godforsaken place has to..."

Another rumble split the air, but this time the sound wasn't the result of collapsing metal. The roar of rocket engines blanketed Zavetgrad like a thick covering of snow, and soon the billowing exhaust plume of a powerful spacecraft was tracing a path through the grey sky. Finn and Owen both looked up toward the rocket's final destination – the titanic space citadel of Nimbus. Nimbus was the seat of the Authority's power, and it was humanity's future – though not for people like Finn and Owen, or the hundreds of thousands of other workers in Zavetgrad. Nimbus symbolized everything Finn hated about the Authority and it tore him up inside that he could do absolutely nothing to stop its influence from dominating the lives of workers like himself and Owen.

Then an alarm signaled the end of their ten-minute break, and he tore his eyes away and grudgingly returned to work.

2

POKING THE BEAR

A ROCKET LAUNCH like the one Finn had just watched was not an uncommon event in Zavetgrad. One of the nine work sectors was entirely dedicated to the production and deployment of the Nimbus spacecraft and their cargo, and launches happened on a weekly basis. It had been that way for decades, and in that time the Nimbus Orbital Citadel had expanded to such a degree that it was clearly visible from the surface. Finn could hold up a thumb at arm's length and just manage to blot out the massive structure, which by the Authority's own boastful figures was considerably more than ten kilometers in diameter.

Unlike the space races of the old world, Nimbus did not exist merely to highlight Zavetgrad's power as a nation, since there was no-one left to compete with. It had been built as humanity's refuge in the stars, away from the creeping rot of the broken planet. Even in the cold heights of what was once northern Canada, Zavetgrad was not immune to the radioactive fallout from the war. Nimbus was humanity's salvation but Finn was painfully aware that it was not a place intended for the likes of him. Nimbus had been built for Zavetgrad's genetically-pure offspring, who were bred and farmed like salmon for the sole purpose of populating the new space-based civilization. Even the golds – the privileged members of the Authority Sector – were unlikely to ever set foot there, with the exception of the Regents and their families. The Regents were direct descendants of Zavetgrad's founders and were effectively royalty. Each work sector had its own Regent, though these aristocrats rarely showed their faces, preferring to live in luxury in their sub-oceanic villas, away from the blistering cold of the city.

"What do you think it's like up there?" Owen asked, while slicing through another chunk of tank armor with his laser cutter.

"What does it matter? We'll never see it," Finn answered, removing his thumb from over the citadel and returning to work.

"I'm just interested, that's all," Owen continued with a nonchalant shrug. "I bet it's like the great cities of the old world, like New York or London."

"New York and London are nothing but blackened wastelands," Finn said, continuing in a grumpy mood, though he couldn't quite put a finger on why he was so sour. "There's nothing good about the old world that we should aspire to, and Nimbus is no different."

"Well, I'd like to see it one day," Owen replied, refusing to be dragged down by Finn's foul temper. "I bet it's nothing like as bad as you make out."

Finn snorted. "And why the hell would you think that?"

Owen stopped cutting and grinned at him. "Because

nothing is ever as bad as you think it is. You just enjoy being pissy and morose."

"Bullshit, I am *not* pissy and morose!" Finn said, shouldering his cutter. He felt set upon and needed to defend himself.

"It's true!" Owen laughed. "You could get spoon-fed honey by beautiful, naked women and you'd still complain that that life wasn't sweet enough."

Finn tried to protest but all he could do was laugh at the image of himself, reclined on a chaise longue like a Roman senator, while being fed honey by oiled-up, naked concubines.

"I think that says more about your perverted mind than it does about me," he finally managed to answer.

"Workers Finn Brasa and Owen Thomas, come here."

Finn glanced to his left and saw the Chief Foreman standing on the dirt road, staring at them with its mechanical eyes. Neither he nor Owen had noticed the robot arrive. Owen immediately looked like a schoolkid who was being called to the principal's office, but Finn's reaction was the opposite. His instinct was to push back.

"Why don't you come over here?" Finn called over. "We're the ones carrying heavy laser cutters, not you."

"You will do as instructed," the Chief Foreman replied. It was another Gen VII, though as the Chief Foreman, it was programmed to be even more of an asshole than the regular robotic whip-crackers. "Set down your cutters and come here. That is an order."

Finn was set on continuing his defiant refusal to comply when Owen submitted and rested his laser cutter against the side of the tank. He scowled at his friend but Owen didn't have his rebellious streak, and Finn realized that continuing to antagonize the foreman would probably just get his worker buddy into trouble too. Even so, rather than setting down his cutter as he'd been ordered to do, he approached the robot with the tool sloped over his shoulder, like a soldier on parade. It was a minor act of defiance but still enough to sate him.

"What is it? We're busy," Finn grumbled.

"Reclamation Yard Seven is two-percent under quota for today. You will be required to work an additional hour."

The foreman then grabbed their arms and plugged into their work loggers to update the new shift-end time, and their updated quota. Finn snatched his arm away from the machine and read the update, before cursing into the snowy air.

"This is bullshit, we already smashed our personal quota ten minutes ago, and now we have another two hundred kilos to cut out and load up before we can clock off?"

"That is correct," the Chief Foreman replied, in an untroubled tone of voice that perfectly conveyed how little it cared for their predicament or protests.

Finn felt anger swelling inside him and his mind raced, thinking of a dozen arguments for why it was unfair to lumber them with the burden but, in the end, he spoke none of them out loud because there was simply no point. Foremen felt no compassion and could not be negotiated with. And fairness was just one of many principles that had died in the nuclear fires of the old world. In Zavetgrad, workers had no choice other than to comply or die.

"Fuck you, you metal heap of shit," Finn said, resorting to venting his anger. Owen sighed and tried to intervene, but he was too mad. "You can tell the Regent of Metalhaven to come down here and cut the extra sections himself."

"For your insubordination, one additional hour has been added to tomorrow's shift," the foreman replied, unmoved by Finn's tirade. "That makes three additional hours in total for tomorrow."

"Oh yeah? How about we go one better and make it an extra four hours tomorrow?" He knew he should give up, but he couldn't stop himself. "Even better, how about you pucker up those metal lips and kiss my ass?"

"Two additional hours have been added to tomorrow's shift, making four additional hours in total," the foreman replied, calmly. "Be warned that any further insubordination will result in two additional shift hours for every worker in this yard."

Finn was about to talk back again but the prospect of landing other workers with more shift hours made him clamp up tighter than the robot's metallic ass cheeks. He cared little for the consequences to himself but he wouldn't burden others with extra work because the harsh truth was that many could not survive it.

"Are you quite finished, Worker Brasa?" the foreman asked, and the machine actually smiled at him.

"We're done, aren't we, Finn?" Owen cut in, looking at him imploringly.

Finn sighed and shook his head. "Yes, we're done," he hissed, before adding, "Thank you so much..." as sarcastically as he could manage.

The foreman's mechanical smile faded. "Now get back to work."

Finn felt like turning the laser cutter onto the robot and

slicing the machine to pieces, but even his rebelliousness had limits. It was one thing to vent his frustrations at the robotic managers of Metalhaven, but causing criminal damage to one of the expensive machines was something else entirely. Such an act of vandalism came under the remit of the prefects, Zavetgrad's authoritarian police force, all of whom were golds from the Authority sector. At best, the prefects would simply give him a beating then lock him up in solitary for the night, before releasing him back to work with more shift hours that he could ever hope to recoup. At worst he'd be sent to trial, where he would be hunted to death in the crucible for the amusement of the mob.

Finn glanced at Owen, who was giving him a well-practiced judgmental look, then both of them set off back toward the tank to continue their newly-extended shift. They hadn't gotten far before the foreman called out to him again.

"Finn Brasa, remember that you have an appointment after shift at the Gene Bank to donate a seed sample, as mandated by the Seed Material Contribution Directive." Finn again had to fight the urge to tell the foreman where he could get off. "In light of today's extended shift hours, I will arrange the appointment to be put back by one hour. Do not miss it."

The prospect of having to visit the Gene Bank to 'donate' a sperm sample appealed to Finn about as much as having his teeth drilled. Most people carried out the duty happily, since the act itself was at least fun, but to him the legally mandated requirement to hand over his genetic material was the worst violation of basic rights that he could imagine. They were basically stealing his DNA to produce offspring that he'd never know or even see, since they were all blasted up to Nimbus to kick-start the new human race.

"Can't you postpone the appointment till tomorrow?" Finn asked, knowing that the chances of the foreman granting his request were almost zero.

"No," the foreman replied, flatly. "You will attend and donate, as scheduled. Failure to comply will result in forced extraction of your seed."

"He'll be there," Owen called out. Finn scowled at his friend, but Owen was not in the mood for any more of his nonsense. "Isn't that right?"

Finn growled a sigh then rolled his eyes at the foreman. "Sure, whatever. There's nothing I enjoy more than jacking off into a plastic cup after a hard day's work."

Owen choked down a snigger but the humorless foreman simply turned and marched away, and Finn was never gladder to see the back of one of the mechanical managers. He was so worked up that he was genuinely afraid of doing something stupid enough to merit a visit from the prefects.

"Why do you have to keep poking the bear?" Owen asked, once they were almost back to their assigned work area. "All it ever gets you is grief, and more work."

"You already know the answer," Finn replied, a dark cloud following him as he walked. "Because fuck them, that's why."

This time, however, Owen was not placated. "I know you hate the Authority, and I can't say that I like them too much either, but this is our lot, Finn, and we just gotta deal with it," Owen hit back. "This anger is gonna eat you up inside and I worry that one day it'll get you killed."

Finn was shocked by Owen's outburst, which was almost

unheard of from his normally mild-mannered friend. He took a breath then stopped and held his hands up.

"You're right, Owen, and I'm sorry," Finn said. The apology was sincere, as was the guilt he was feeling for dragging his friend through the mud with him. "Some days it just gets to me more than others, and I guess today is a bad day."

Owen considered the apology for a few moments, mulling it over to work out if Finn had meant it, or if he was just paying lip-service, before deciding that it was genuinely heartfelt. Then, in line with his hatred of confrontation, he dropped the matter and moved on.

"I hope you saved some drink chits for yourself, because winding down with a few beers after shift is exactly what you need right now," Owen said. "Hell, I know I do."

"Owen Thomas drinking beer?" Finn said, feigning shock and surprise. Owen was not only a big man but a big drinker too. "Now that is unusual…"

Owen laughed, and it was good to see his friend back to his usual self. Then the man's face fell, and the color drained from his features, as if the blood in his body was being siphoned away.

"My laser cutter is gone!"

3

SOREN DRISCOLL

Pulse racing, Finn ran over to where Owen had been working, desperately hoping that his friend had just forgotten where he'd placed the valuable tool. Like the robotic yard managers, laser cutters were costly pieces of equipment, and every worker in Metalhaven was solely responsible for their own unit. Losing or damaging a laser cutter was a serious offence, the consequences of which were no less severe than assaulting a foreman.

"It has to be here somewhere," Finn said, searching around the part-dismantled tank, in case the tool had just slipped and gotten buried in the snow. "Where did you stand it up?"

"It was right there," Owen answered, pointing to a section of the tank. Finn could see the dimple in the snow where the butt of the tool had been resting on the ground. "Someone must have taken it. There's no other explanation."

Owen's last comment made Finn think and he stepped away from the wreckage so that he could better survey the yard in the vicinity of their assigned work area. His gaze briefly fell upon Soren Driscoll, another worker from Metalhaven, and a first-class asshole. Soren quickly looked away, but not fast enough that Finn couldn't see the smirk on the man's face.

"Enter into your work logger that you're taking your final ten-minute break of the day, then follow me," Finn said, inputting the break into his own device at the same time. "I know who has your cutter."

Owen frowned but input the command into his logger without question before following in Finn's wake as he carved a path through the virgin snow to the adjacent work area. Soren and his worker buddy, Corbin Radcliffe, were casually reclining against the side of an APC, smoking cigarettes and pretending not to have noticed him. The duo were notorious in Metalhaven, both loathed and revered in equal measure. Soren Driscoll was a classic bully who stood up for the Authority, despite everything the regime did to drag workers like them through the dirt. Soren did this because he loved to wind people up, Finn most of all. The man got away with his behavior on account of his imposing physical presence and the fact he could be genuinely entertaining, so long as you laughed along and lapped up his bullshit. If you didn't then Soren would quickly turn cruel and even violent, which was why most people kept their heads down in his presence. Finn had never been one of those people, and Soren hated him for that.

If Soren was a comic book villain then Corbin Radcliffe was his loyal sidekick and man-at-arms. Easily led and none-too-bright, Corbin was a heavy-set bruiser who was rarely not by Soren's side. Anyone who challenged Soren would quickly find themselves in Corbin's sights, and the man was not subtle in his methods of dealing with dissenters. Despite this, Finn never wavered in his presence, and this occasion was no different.

"Give it back, Soren, and we'll say nothing more about it," Finn said, looking the man dead in the eyes, despite the fact the bully was doing his level best to pretend Finn was invisible.

"Give what back?" Soren replied, plucking the cigarette from his smirking lips, and extracting a chortle from his loyal sidekick.

"This isn't a joking matter, Soren, you know what happens to workers who lose their laser cutters," Finn snapped. He'd worked hard to put his anger back in the bottle after Owen's outburst, but Soren Driscoll could wind up him like no other man alive, and his composure was hanging by a thread.

"Oh, has someone lost their laser cutter then?" Soren replied, drawing another muted chuckle from Corbin. "That's a shame, isn't it?"

"Come on, you've had your fun," Finn continued. "Now just hand it over and we'll all get back to work."

Soren snorted then pressed a finger to one side of his nose and rocketed a globule of snot onto the snow in front of him. It was green, like the man's eyes. "Say please," Soren said, placing the cigarette back into the corner of his mouth.

Normally, Finn would have plucked the cigarette from the man's mouth and fed it to him, but on this occasion he had to play Soren's stupid game. He couldn't risk flying off the handle while the prospect of a beating or even a trial loomed heavy over Owen's head.

"Please..." Finn said, straining to form the word.

Soren's sneer tested the limits of his restraint and for a moment it looked like the man was about to direct Corbin to fetch the cutter. Then the worker's smile twisted into something closer to a grimace, and the darker side of Soren Driscoll took hold.

"I don't know what you're talking about," Soren said, tapping ash from his cigarette onto Finn's boot. "And I don't rightly care for the accusations you're making either."

Finn managed to hold his nerve then carefully surveyed their surroundings for a foreman, but none of the mechanical managers were in range. This gave him some much-needed leeway, should things turn ugly.

"Anyway, why isn't that fucking pussy asking me for the cutter back instead of you?" Soren added, pulling Finn's focus back to the bully, who was now glowering at Owen. "Do you wipe his ass and tuck him in at night too?"

Finn finally lost it and swung a haymaker at Soren that smacked the cigarette out of his mouth and sent it cartwheeling into the snow, where it hissed like an angry cat. He landed another hard punch before Soren could retaliate, then Corbin threw his sizable mass into the middle of the fight and tried to pull them apart. Owen may have despised conflict but he was no pushover and he always had Finn's back. His friend intervened, slamming Corbin to the ground and allowing Finn to land an uppercut that smacked Soren's head against the side of the wrecked APC, sounding a chime like the clang of a gong.

Soren's rage was unleashed but while he was the bigger man he was also clumsy, and the wild punches he threw in retaliation were easy to evade. Owen held Corbin back while Finn hammered a punch into Soren's gut that dropped the man to his knees. Gasping for breath, Soren pressed his hands into the snow and spat blood. Then the bully's eyes sharpened and Soren rocked back, pulling a jagged metal shard out of the snow and clutching it in his calloused hand like a knife.

"You're going to fucking pay for this!"

Soren angled the shard at Finn and was about to lunge when Corbin suddenly called out the man's name with the abruptness of a starter's pistol. The bully's eyes flicked in the direction of the dirt road and Soren dropped the shank like it was on fire. Finn also spun around and saw the Chief Foreman stomping toward them, mechanical eyes glowing hotter than Soren's fury.

"The cutter, Soren," Finn hissed, turning back to his opponent. "Now!"

"Fuck you!"

Finn choked down his anger. "If Owen goes down then you go down with him. Don't think I won't do it!"

"You'd rat me out?" Soren growled.

Finn nodded. "You know I would."

Soren snarled then nodded to Corbin, who was no longer being restrained by Owen, and the man reached inside the APC and retrieved his worker buddy's laser cutter. By the time the Chief Foreman had arrived, it was back in Owen's grasp.

"What is the meaning of this?" the Chief Foreman barked, employing its AI-synthetized assertiveness to maximum effect.

"We're on a break and just talking," Finn replied, this time wisely choosing not to stoke the flames by being short with the robot. He then looked to Soren. "Isn't that right?"

Soren plucked a fresh cigarette out of the packet in his overalls pocket and shoved it into the corner of his mouth. "Yeah, that's right," the man mumbled, while lighting the stick.

The Chief Foreman was about to say more when another commotion in an adjacent work area stole its attention. It was Jonas and Warner again, and never had Finn been happier to find the two morons at each other's throats.

"Break's over, get back to work," the foreman ordered, before turning and picking up speed to deal with the affray.

Owen moved back to Finn's side and at the same time Corbin shuffled beside his leader. The two men were still spoiling for a fight, and Finn was more than in the mood to give them one, but he'd caused enough trouble for one day.

"This isn't over, Finn," Soren growled, jabbing the lit cigarette at him. "Just you wait. I'll get you for this."

4

SCRAPS!

FINN PAUSED outside the Gene Bank and stared up at the neon green sign, which was a simplistic line-art design of a baby inside a womb. To someone with no knowledge of what actually occurred inside the facility, the sign might have inspired feelings of hope and new life but for Finn it simply made him feel sick to the stomach. And it wasn't like he could easily ignore the place, either, because the Authority, in their sadistic wisdom, had located it directly opposite the block of apartments where he lived in Metalhaven's claustrophobic and snow-covered residential district. This was precisely to make it easy for men like him to 'donate'.

"Donate..." Finn said, snorting a laugh at the word, which fogged the air as he exhaled it. "Like I have a choice."

One of Zavetgrad's key laws was that all men and women with viable seed or eggs had to donate a sample once per month, and sometimes more frequently, depending on the quality of the donator's DNA. Men like Finn were bracketed according to the purity of their seed, with the rating ranging from zero, which was effectively sterile, to five, which was deemed 'completely undamaged'. Finn rated five, a score that fewer than one in two-thousand men across all work sectors had, and this required him to donate far more frequently. It was also, as Owen was often keen to point out, the only reason that Finn had thus far managed to escape being put on trial, since he was considered extremely valuable to the Authority, like a prize bull.

The simple truth was that most men were either sterile or their sperm was damaged beyond the point of repair due to the insidious effects of background radiation and environmental toxicity. To some degree, damaged DNA at level two or three could be edited in the Authority Sector's gene labs so that it could still produce viable offspring, but those children would be raised in compounds to become workers like Finn. Seed ratings of four were used to produce gold sector workers, while pure, undamaged genetic material was reserved to create the precious cargo of babies and embryos that were transported to Nimbus, to kick-start the new human civilization in space.

Finn checked the time on his work logger and saw that it was 20:00 hours, the allotted time of his appointment. He sighed and lowered his arm to his side. He knew he should go in and just get the deed over and done with, but the day's events, not least his confrontation with Soren, had left him in an even more uncooperative mood than normal.

"Fuck them," he said, his words again fogging the air, then he put the Gene Bank to his back and crossed the narrow street to his apartment block.

Reaching the door to the building, his cold fingers fumbled for his keycard and he dropped it into the snow. Cursing, he bent down to pick it up, and at the same time he heard the familiar crunch of jackboots treading the icy sidewalk behind him. Straightening up, he made a point of not looking at the prefect patrol and slid his ident card through the lock scanner, hoping that the uniformed thugs would march past. They didn't. True to form, the prefects were unable to pass up an easy opportunity to antagonize an innocent worker.

"What are you doing loitering out on the street?" one of the two men asked.

Finn turned to face the man and held up his ident. "I'm not loitering, officer, I just dropped my ident card into the snow." The tone of his voice was at least somewhat respectful, since Finn wasn't stupid enough to give attitude to a prefect. That was a surefire way to get an electrified nightstick rammed into his face.

The officer snatched the card out of his hands and scowled at the holographic mugshot embedded into it. He grabbed Finn by the chin and maneuvered his head to the left and right, while at the same time comparing his true visage to the image on the card. Despite the forceful invasion of his personal space, Finn allowed it to happen, since to refuse or struggle would be to invite a beating.

He waited patiently, observing the officers as they went about their tyrannical work. They were dressed in black riot armor with a silver-grey chest plate to indicate Metalhaven, and gold shoulder pauldrons to denote that they were citizens of the Authority Sector. Besides their electrified nightsticks, all prefects also carried powerful sidearms and were fully authorized and willing to use them. Prefects needed little justification or motivation to discharge their weapons, and there were rarely any consequences for shooting a worker dead, even in cold blood. At least in this regard, Finn was safer than most because of his rare genetic rating.

Not satisfied with a visual confirmation, the prefect released Finn's chin then ran the Ident through his computer. The prefect system was called C.O.N.F.I.R.M.E, which stood for Centralized Observation Network for Forensic Identification, Registration, and Monitoring of Entities. The system revealed everything about Finn to the officers, from when he was first deemed a viable embryo to when he was born and in which compound he was raised. Finn had always found it darkly amusing that the prefects didn't even consider them to be people – mere 'entities' would suffice.

"You have an appointment at the Gene Bank," the prefect said, handing back his ID.

"Yeah, I just came from there," Finn lied, hooking a thumb to the building over the road. "I managed to get in a little early, and it doesn't take long to jerk off into a plastic cup, am I right?" He smiled and laughed, but the prefect didn't find his attempt at humor to be funny. This also wasn't surprising – prefects were selected at age thirteen and indoctrinated from that point forward to become the soulless, humorless, violent law enforcers that stood before him now.

"Either get inside your apartment or head to the Recovery Centre," the prefect replied, sternly. "Loitering on the street is not permitted."

Finn felt like reminding the officer that he'd already explained he wasn't loitering, but instead he just smiled and nodded. "Yes, officer. Thank you."

The prefect grunted and continued his patrol, barging past Finn in the process, not because he was in the way, but just because the man could. Sucking in a deep breath of the ice-cold air to cool his volcanic blood, Finn ran the card through the lock then pulled open the door to his apartment block and stepped inside. Like all the other blocks in Metalhaven, it was a basic mid-rise unit, and Finn's apartment was on the top, tenth floor. There was no elevator but he was pleased to discover that maintenance had at least gotten around to replacing the lightbulb on the stairs, so he could see where he was going.

Reaching apartment 1001, Finn used the same Ident card to unlock his door and slipped inside. His place wasn't much to look at, but it was the only place in Metalhaven where he could let his guard down. Like all other apartments in the block and others like it, his unit was two hundred square feet and open-plan, besides a small a bathroom cubicle. Inside there was a sofa bed, currently in its sofa configuration, a bistro table with one chair, since everyone in Metalhaven lived alone, and a simple food storage and heating station. It was the definition of minimalist, and everything in the apartment was built and finished to a bargain-basement standard, but Finn didn't care. It was private and it was his.

"Hay-wo!"

Finn almost jumped out of his boots then spun around to see a little robot built from the body of an oil-can and other junk parts sitting on the sofa, waving at him.

"Scraps, what the hell? I told you to stay hidden!" Finn said. Heart thumping in his chest, he checked to make doubly sure that he'd closed the door behind him, then hurried over to his little robot buddy and sat beside him on the couch. "If anyone saw you, we'd both be in deep shit, do you understand?"

The robot scowled and aimed a little finger at him, in an accusing manner. "U sweared!"

"Sorry, pal, my mistake," Finn replied, in a gentler tone. "But if the prefects knew I'd stolen these parts, especially the FLP from a foreman, I'd be on trial faster than you can say capacitor.

"Capacitor!" Scraps squeaked.

Finn laughed. "Exactly. Now do you understand?"

The one-foot-tall robot waddled over to Finn and jumped onto his lap. "Scraps understood..." The robot replied, dolefully. "Scraps careful..."

"I know you are, pal, I just worry, that's all." The little robot looked so sad and Finn felt awful for snapping at him. Then he remembered the components that he'd salvaged from the reclamation yard and fished them out of his boot.

"Here, I found some new bits and pieces for you," he said, picking up Scraps and carrying the robot over to the bistro table. He set down the bot and the components and sorted through them. "These should help to fix your defective rotor system," he added, pointing to some capacitors, resistors and integrated circuits, "and this computation chip can be programmed to interface with your Foreman Logic Processor." He smiled and waggled his eyebrows. "It should give you a boost in smarts, not that you need it." The bot chuckled as Finn ruffled its imaginary hair.

Finn moved to the far wall and shoved the sofa aside, so that he could get to the compartment in the wall that Scraps usually resided in, along with the rest of his contraband. Over a period of many years, Finn had not only salvaged electronics but also tech manuals and old-world data devices that had helped him to learn the language of computers and robotics.

His most valuable find was an FLP – a Foreman Logic Processor – which now resided inside Scraps and gave the bot his unique charm.

Finn had stolen the AI chip from a scrapped Gen III foreman, and while it wasn't the most sophisticated neural CPU in existence, it was still hyper-advanced tech. To have one found in his possession would mean instantly being sentenced to trial, but Finn didn't care. It had taken him seven years to learn how the FLP worked, so that he could erase the asshole foreman persona and replace it with a personality that was much more amenable and friendly.

Finn removed a programming module from the cubby – another device that would land him on trial if a prefect found him with it – plus a few more components, then returned to the bistro table. "Here, open wide!"

Scraps opened his mouth and Finn fed him six discrete components, a couple of simple ICs, plus the computation chip. A rumbling whir emanated from inside the robot's oil-can body then it burped, which was a running joke between them that always made Finn laugh.

"Okay, let's configure this new chip," Finn said, plugging Scraps into the programming module and setting to work.

An hour of intense concentration was interrupted by the rumbling of his stomach, which made Finn realize how famished he was. He finished writing the code then executed it and headed over to his bijou food preparation area.

"Now that you've been fed, it's time to do the same for me," Finn said.

No-one in Metalhaven cooked. Food was supplied from the production and manufacturing sector, more commonly known as Makehaven, and was ready to heat and eat. It consisted of engineered proteins that were like tempeh in taste and texture, along with a simple bread made from defatted algae powder. There was also a prebiotic drink prepared from fungi and, when they were really lucky, a selection of deep-friend insects.

He finished heating the engineered protein and small pot of insects then carried the food to the bistro table, along with his flask of prebiotic goop. Scraps was tapping his foot on the table, waiting for the program to finish running, and Finn filled the time by eating his dinner and reading about laser physics on a rectangular data device he'd found inside a wrecked jeep. The device contained a database with a natural language interface that allowed Finn to ask it pretty much anything he liked, so long as it referenced information and events prior to the year 2064. Unfortunately, a large portion of the database was corrupted, but it still offered Finn insights into the old world that weren't common knowledge, at least for the worker class. Learning about everything from science to literature was how Finn survived the daily grind without going insane.

"Ouch-ouch!"

Finn looked up from the device, concerned that Scraps was in pain. Instead, the bot wore a mechanical frown and was pointing at Finn's head. He touched a spot above his eye and realized that he'd suffered a few scrapes in the fight with Soren.

"Oh, it's nothing, pal, just an occupational hazard of working in the reclamation sector," Finn replied, setting the robot's artificially-intelligent mind at ease. He then carefully placed the data device onto the table and focused on his mechanical companion. "Did we talk about Zavetgrad and the different sectors yet?"

Scraps shook his head. "Nope-nope!"

Finn cleared his throat and prepared to give the robot his daily lesson. He could more easily have just uploaded the information, and for a lot of things that's what he did, but he enjoyed the process of teaching the bot verbally, not least because it was nice having someone to talk to, besides Owen, who invariably just ended up berating him for pushing the Authority's buttons.

"Okay, so there are nine work sectors in total," Finn began, before taking a slurp of his prebiotic, which was as revolting as usual. "Metalhaven you already know, because that's where we are now. Our color is chrome. Then there are the algae-farming greens from Seedhaven, the trawlermen from Seahaven, who are blue, and purples from Makehaven, who produce and manufacture everything from our food to our laser cutters."

"Lights?" Scraps said, pointing at the single incandescent lightbulb in the apartment.

"Right, electricity comes from Volthaven, on the edge of the city, where there are vast solar farms and chemical fuel production plants. They're the reds," Finn continued, thankful for the prompt. He sometimes forgot what the different sectors were since he'd only ever seen Makehaven. "Then there are oranges from Stonehaven who construct buildings, and the browns from Autohaven, who transport everything from one sector to another, and the whites from Spacehaven who handle all the rocket launches."

Scraps smiled then pointed to the ceiling. "Nimbus!"

Finn recoiled a little. "How do you know about Nimbus?"

"CPU!" Scraps replied, patting his belly.

Finn looked at the programming tool and saw that his code had finished running. The program had been successful and the IC he'd salvaged was now interfaced with Scraps' FLP, not only increasing his processing power, but also his access to information.

"Looks like you're smarter than me now," Finn said, patting his bot on the head.

Scraps giggled then suddenly looked sad. "Tell Scraps about sector nine. Golds..."

Finn blew out a sigh. "I'm not sure I could do that without swearing again." Scraps shuffled closer, undeterred. "What the hell, I guess you're old enough to know, but I don't really feel like talking about it, so I'll upload the data directly."

Finn accessed the programming tool and updated Scraps' database with a more complete picture of Zavetgrad and its various departments. The little robot assimilated the information in the space of seconds then looked glum.

"I know, pal, it sucks, right?"

"What Wellness Workers?" Scraps asked. "Scarlet with gold stripe."

Finn blew out another sigh. The question Scraps had just asked was akin to an adolescent child asking his parents the dreaded question, 'where do babies come from? ...'

"I think you might need to be a little older for that one, pal," Finn replied, chickening out.

Scraps shook his head. "Gene Bank where you give sperm. Wellness Centre is same?"

Finn's face burned brighter than a laser cutter. "What the hell? I think I've taught you too much!"

The robot continued to stare at him, and he realized that Scraps wasn't going to take no for answer. He considered how best to answer the question, in the shortest possible number of words, to spare his own blushes. The stark truth was that 'Wellness Centre' was simply a euphemism for brothel. Attendance was required by law since the Authority considered that regularly getting your rocks off was a great way to quell civil disobedience. The centers were staffed by men and women who were sterile, and who were unable to usefully fulfill a function in any of the other work sectors. In some cases, they were physically disabled, or had a serious or even terminal illness, where working was a requirement to receive life-sustaining treatment. In other examples, people were sent there merely as a punishment. Refusal to work meant certain death in a trial, and the sad reality was that many chose this path, rather than prostitute themselves.

He was about to explain this to Scraps when suddenly his door opened, and a figure stepped inside. He panicked and knocked his metal plate off the table, which crashed to the bare concrete floor and scraped and rattled like a drumkit that had been kicked over.

"You have a death wish, do you know that?" Owen said, hurriedly shutting the door behind him. "If I could just walk in then so could a prefect."

"It's a good job it was you then," Finn replied, peevishly. His friend shot him a dirty look and he backtracked. "I know, I'll be more careful in the future." He gathered up the remaining components and the data device, and concealed them in the secret compartment behind his sofa bed.

"If they catch you with this stuff, especially Scraps, you'll be sent to trial," Owen added, twisting the knife, "and even your top-level worker and genetic ratings won't save you. They'll feed you to the prosecutors in the crucible and not give it a second thought."

"I get it, Owen," Finn said, scooping up Scraps and carrying him to the cubby. He placed him inside and smiled at the bot. "Stay in here and process your new data, okay pal?"

"Okays! ..." Scraps replied, cheerfully.

Finn closed the cubby and pushed the sofa back into position, then picked his plate up off the floor. "What are doing here anyway?" he asked, placing the plate in the tiny sink in the food prep area.

"Because there's a trial tonight, remember? And the crucible is Metalhaven, so attendance is mandatory."

"Attendance is always mandatory," Finn answered, peevishly again.

"Then it's even more mandatory this time," Owen said, giving as good as he got. "The Regent will be here, so you have to show your face, whether you like it or not."

There was a hammering on the door and the two friends froze like the icicles dangling outside the porthole window in the side wall. The door was then flung open, and three robot foremen stomped inside the already cramped apartment.

"Worker, Finn Brasa, you are late for your appointment at the Gene Bank," the frontmost of the trio announced. "You will come with us now and donate a seed sample."

Finn defiantly folded his arms across his chest. "If it's a donation then that means its voluntary, and I don't volunteer."

The foreman, which was a stubborn Gen IV, narrowed its mechanical eyes at him.

"It is a compulsory donation…"

"There's no such thing," Finn hit back. "So, how about you fuck off and leave me alone?"

Owen slapped the palm of his hand over his face so loudly that the apartment's solitary window almost shattered, but the deed had already been done. The trio of foremen advanced and grabbed Finn's arms, before forcibly dragging him out of the door.

"I guess I'll see you in the Recovery Centre later then?" Owen called out, as Finn disappeared out onto the landing.

"Yeah!" he called back. "Save me a chair… and a pint!"

5
T.E.S.A.

The robotic foremen roughly bundled Finn through the door of the Gene Bank, then two stomped away, leaving one of the robotic tyrants behind to stand guard outside. Finn considered making a run for it until he spotted two jackbooted prefects in the reception area, and hastily abandoned any notion of absconding. The foremen were not averse to rough-handling people, but when it came to administering a good, old-fashioned beatdown, prefects never delegated the responsibility to a machine.

Straightening his overalls, Finn stood tall and strode over to the reception desk, watched every step of the way by the two prefects. He smiled at the officers, who naturally didn't smile back, then rested his elbows on the reception counter. A woman wearing a gold blouse to denote her status as a citizen of the Authority sector sat at the desk, ignoring him. She was different to the gold that usually staffed the desk and Finn idly wondered what had become of her predecessor. He coughed politely and loudly in an effort to get the gold's attention, causing the woman to briefly glower at him over the top of her horn-rimmed spectacles, then she continued to ignore him while tapping away at her computer.

"Worker, Finn Brasa, reporting as ordered to beat my meat into a plastic cup," Finn said, drumming his fingers on the countertop. He never passed up an opportunity to be a smartass, especially to a gold.

"You're late," the woman said, without looking up.

"I had a meeting with the Regent of Metalhaven to discuss sector waste management policy, and it overran," Finn replied, ramping up the sarcasm.

The woman stopped typing, carefully removed her spectacles then rocked back in her chair, studying Finn like he was a lab specimen. "Am I going to have a problem with you?" she asked.

Finn heard the shuffle of heavy boots behind him and remembered that the prefects were not far away. "No ma'am, no problem," he replied. "I was just trying to break the ice and lighten the mood."

The woman sighed then hooked her spectacles back over her ears and dragged her keyboard closer. "Name..."

He scowled at the top of the woman's head. "I already gave you my name."

The receptionist looked at him over the top of her glasses again, before glancing off to his side. Finn heard the clack, clack of a prefect taking a few steps closer. "Finn Brasa," he replied, though he didn't understand why it had been necessary to repeat himself.

"Place your right index finger into the scanner," the receptionist said, dropping a device the size of a pack of cards onto the counter. It was attached to her computer by a wire that was so twisted-up and coiled that it barely reached.

Finn did as he was instructed and felt a sharp prick as the device punctured his skin with a needle and took a blood sample. He removed his finger and rubbed it to massage away the pain. A tiny globule of blood oozed out of the microscopic wound, which throbbed like a wasp sting.

"Finn Brasa, Metalhaven Reclamation Yard Seven," the woman said out loud, as the data populated on her screen. She then recoiled, pushed her glasses further up her nose and looked at him like he was on fire. "I can see why they're so keen to have you donate. It says here that you have a Worker rating of five *and* a Genetic Purity rating of five."

Finn shrugged. "My mama always said I was special."

His bullshit answer didn't bother the receptionist on this occasion, because she was too wrapped up in his personal file.

"Do you know how many double-fives I've seen?" she asked, and Finn shrugged again. "Zero, that's how many."

"That's because you're new here," Finn replied, breezily. Then he had a thought that genuinely made him curious. "Do you mean that you've never seen a double-five worker at this facility, or that you've never seen one during all of your Gene Bank assignments?"

The woman smiled at him, and suddenly she seemed vaguely human. "Never," she replied. "You're a genetic goldmine, Mr. Brasa."

Finn huffed a laugh. "If I'm so wonderful then why does the Authority have me risking my neck every day, slicing up old tanks?"

The woman seemed surprised, as if she considered his question to be supremely naive.

"It's not *you* who is important Mr. Brasa but your DNA, from which we can create hundreds, even thousands more like you." The receptionist then shrugged. "Besides, we are able to retrieve a sample post-mortem, so it makes little difference in the end."

It took a lot to shock Finn but the woman's statement rocked him so hard that he had to take a step back from the counter.

"You mean that you can take my sperm even after I'm dead?"

"Of course, we do it all the time," the woman replied, again making it sound like Finn was stupid to not already know this.

"Is this worker causing you a problem, miss?"

Finn glanced over his shoulder and saw one of the two prefects looming close by, nightstick in hand. The man was old for a prefect, perhaps twenty-six or twenty-seven, and wore a neatly trimmed handlebar mustache that didn't suit his youthful face.

"He's a wise-ass but I can handle him, thanks Tommy."

The receptionist had turned her shoulders to face the prefect and was smiling at the man while twirling her strawberry-blonde hair. Finn glanced at the officer and saw that his pupils had dilated and that his skin had flushed. He sighed and rolled his eyes. While the worker class were not permitted to engage in relationships, golds were encouraged to fraternize and procreate with as many people as they could.

"Do you have a problem, worker?" the prefect snapped, pressing his nightstick against Finn's chest.

"No problem, I'm just keen to get this over with," Finn replied, careful to maintain a respectful tone. Prefects didn't need an excuse to lash out, and he was in no mood for a beatdown.

A door was suddenly flung open further inside the facility and a woman in chrome worker overalls was dragged through it by two prefects. Finn's instinct was to rush to her aid, but the nightstick remained pressed to his chest, and he knew that if he tried to slip past then he'd only receive a clobbering for his trouble.

"No, I can still work, please!" the woman cried out.

Her face was streaming with tears, and Finn noticed that her right hand was mangled and burned. It was a common workplace injury caused by a malfunctioning laser cutter that had exploded during operation. Finn had personally witnessed accidents of this nature more times than he cared to remember. It was akin to playing Russian Roulette, and each time a chrome from Metalhaven picked up their cutter to start the day's shift, they worked in constant fear of a similar accident befalling them.

"Please, I can still work in the yard!" the woman protested, as she was dragged toward another door. "I can carry loads and work the trailers, or maybe use a smaller cutter? Please!"

Finn couldn't stand it any longer, and he tried to push past the prefect, but the officer merely shoved him against the reception counter and stabbed the end of the nightstick into his throat. One flick of the man's thumb would dump thousands of volts into his neck, burning his skin and paralyzing him for several minutes. As much as he wanted to help the woman, he knew in his heart that it was folly to try.

"What's her problem?" the prefect asked, still pinning

Finn against the counter. The man's tone was one of disgust, not concern.

"She was just tested and found to have creeping genetic defects that are too serious to fix," The receptionist said. She had crossed her legs and was swiveling her chair from side-to-side, as if the worker's torment were an amusing distraction. "Since her hand is useless too, she was reclassified as a double-zero, which means that she'll be sterilized and reassigned to the Wellness Center."

The worker was bundled through the door, which was then slammed shut, silencing the woman's sobs and screams like she'd been shot in the head. Finn was released by the prefect and shoved aside, though the officer continued to watch him like a hawk.

"She can't work or donate eggs, so you're just going to force her into sexual slavery, is that it?" Finn said, making his contempt for what he'd just witnessed plain.

The receptionist's expression hardened, and all traces of her earlier flirtatiousness evaporated like snow on a hot laser cutter. It was clear that she was not about to be lectured by a mere worker, even if he was a double-five.

"That woman is thirty-five years old, unable to operate a laser cutter, unable to provide viable eggs, and unable to carry a fetus to term," the receptionist replied, punctuating each use of the word 'unable' with the report of a gunshot. "And she is no slave. Her service in the Wellness Center is reimbursed by the provision of food and lodgings in Zavetgrad. It is an honest trade, and far better than being euthanized, wouldn't you agree?"

Finn laughed, drawing the continued ire of both the woman and the prefect. "Given the option of death, or being forced to spread your legs every day for the rest of your life, which option would you choose, Madame Gold?"

The woman clamped her jaw shut and Finn could see that he'd angered her. He knew it was unwise, but he simply didn't care. He hated the golds and everything about them, and he wasn't about to bite his tongue, even if it meant receiving a beating. The sound of electricity ionizing the air then fizzed past his ears, and the prefect raised his energized nightstick, ready to strike. Finn held his ground – he wasn't going to cower from the officer or make any attempt to protect himself. Owen would ask, "why?" and the answer was always the same.

Because fuck them, that's why...

The nightstick was swung at his head, but a call of "Halt!" boomed across the reception area, and the nightstick's path was arrested mere centimeters from the side of his head. The prefect stepped back and stood to attention as another jackbooted officer approached.

"What the hell is going on here?" the new arrival demanded, addressing the question to the prefect who had almost struck Finn.

"Gross insubordination and disdain for the Authority, sir!" the young prefect replied, stating the charges as if they were more serious than murder or rape.

"I see," the older prefect replied. Finn knew from the man's uniform that the officer was Metalhaven's Prefect Captain, and he forced down a hard, dry swallow, knowing how close he was to being sent to trial. "Has this worker donated his sample yet?"

"No, sir, he is being obstinate," the prefect replied. "He

was also late for his appointment and had to be escorted here by foremen."

"I see," the older man said again.

The captain marched directly in front of Finn and peered into his eyes. Standing two inches taller than him, and with a physique fueled by real food and healthy living, the officer was easily his physical equal, despite Finn's impressive strength, forged through years of toil in the yards.

"My name is Captain Viktor Roth, Head Prefect of the Reclamation sector, or what you lowlife worker scum like to call Metalhaven," the officer continued, spitting in Finn's face as he spoke. "But to you, I am God."

"Nice to meet you, your worshipfulness," Finn replied.

If Owen were nearby, his friend would have facepalmed so hard at that moment, he would have knocked himself out. Finn fully expected to get a punch in the face for his facetious comment but to his surprise, Captain Roth laughed. The officer then checked his C.O.N.F.I.R.M.E. computer and the man's laser-straight eyebrow hooked upward.

"A double-five," Roth said, though unlike the receptionist, he didn't sound impressed. "You believe that your rating means you can bend the rules, Worker Brasa, but you are mistaken. I don't care if you are genetically pure, or the best worker in this godforsaken sector. No-one is above the Authority. No-one is above being sent to trial. I advise you to bear that in mind."

Finn dared to meet the captain's eyes; an act that in itself could have easily been construed as impudent. "I understand perfectly, sir." He knew he was walking a narrow tightrope between insolence and obedience, but the urge to fight the

Authority was hard-wired within him, as instinctive as breathing.

"You will donate a seed sample, without further protest, or you will have me to answer to," said Captain Roth.

"I'm not going to jerk off for your amusement, or anyone else's," Finn replied, still walking the narrow tightrope of the law. "So if you want a sample, you'll have to take it yourself."

Captain Roth smiled. "So be it."

The officer gestured to the younger prefect and the man's partner who had dutifully remained in position to watch over the rest of the facility, and the two men advanced. Finn was grabbed by both arms but he shook off the prefects, intending to walk to the donation room voluntarily, before a blinding light flooded his senses. The next thing he knew he was flat on his back on the polished stone floor, with the metallic taste of blood in his mouth. Captain Roth stood over him, nightstick in hand.

"Take him..."

Too stunned to resist, Finn was dragged into a nearby donation room and strapped to a medical bed. Captain Roth entered, leaving the door wide open behind him, then a doctor blustered inside, looking as shaken up as Finn felt.

"Doctor, you will extract a sample from this worker using T.E.S.A.," the officer ordered. "There will be no anesthesia and no pain relief."

Finn felt a chill rush down his spine and he looked to the doctor, imploring the man to intervene.

"Captain, I must protest," the doctor began, speaking in a condescending tone of voice that was deeply unwise even considering the medic's gold status. "To perform the procedure without any form of anesthesia would be extremely dangerous, not to mention painful and..."

"Enough!" Roth aimed his baton at the doctor and electricity crackled. "You will do as ordered or be next in line to receive the Authority's judgement!"

Captain Roth's bark shut down the doctor in a heartbeat, and there was no further protest from the medical practitioner. Instead, the man nodded meekly and went about collecting the instruments he needed. Finn could see that the doctor's hands were already shaking. He briefly considered apologizing and begging the captain's forgiveness but his stubborn pride refused to give Roth the satisfaction of seeing him crumble under pressure. Instead, he clamped his jaw shut and stared at the clinical white ceiling tiles, trying to disassociate his mind from his body.

The two prefects cut away his pants and his face burned hot with shame and embarrassment as his genitals were exposed for all to see. The door had remained open – another act of cruelty by Roth. Then the doctor arrived at the foot of the bed, gloved and holding a long needle in his hands. Sweat beaded on the man's brow and his hands continued to shake, making the needle dance like a conductor's baton.

"I will now insert this needle into your testes and extract your sperm," the doctor said, voice shivering with fear. "Without anesthesia, you will experience significant discomfort and pain. Please, try not to move; it will only make it worse."

"Just get on with it, doc..." Finn said before biting down so hard he feared his teeth might shatter.

He chanced a look at Captain Roth, but the man was smiling as if his torture was merely a game which, he realized, it was. To the golds, the torment and killing of lowly workers like him was the highest form of entertainment, and it was the reason why the Trials existed at all. In that moment, Finn would have rather faced a dozen prosecutors in the crucible than endure what was about to come next.

"I will begin," the doctor said.

Finn stared at the ceiling and waited. Then the needle pierced his right testis and he screamed.

6

A PINT AND A FIGHT

OWEN WAS WAITING for him outside the Recovery Center when he finally arrived, an hour later than expected. His friend didn't look especially concerned since this wasn't the first time Finn had antagonized the golds in the Wellness Center and been made late as a result. Owen couldn't have known how close to a trial Finn had come on that particular occasion, and he made sure to hide any suggestion of concern from his tired expression.

"What did you do this time to merit being detained?" Owen asked, arms folded across his chest. "More jokes about 'choking the chicken' or were you just generally uncooperative and annoying?"

"A bit of both, actually," Finn replied, smiling.

Owen snorted a laugh. "You're your own worst enemy. Why not just jerk off like us normal people do?"

Finn started to reply, "Because fuck them, that's why..." but Owen cut him off, knowing full-well what he was about to say. His friend then narrowed his eyes at him, suspiciously.

"You're looking very sprightly, considering you were under

anesthetic less than an hour ago," Owen said. His friend's scowl deepened. "Unless you actually did the deed willingly this time?"

"I did not, and I can promise you that I'm far from sprightly," Finn answered, shuffling his feet on account of the numb sense of discomfort he was still feeling. "I managed to piss off Captain Viktor Roth this time, and he made me undergo T.E.S.A. without anesthetic."

Owen's expression became even more doubtful. "Come on, that's bullshit. You wouldn't be able to walk if they did that."

"Trust me, twenty minutes ago it hurt to even breathe!" Finn replied, laughing.

Owen almost fell over with shock. "What the hell is so funny about having a needle shoved in your balls?"

"Absolutely nothing, but the doc took pity on me and gave me a hefty dose of pain meds while the prefects weren't looking, so I'm flying higher than Nimbus, right now!" He laughed again, though it was the drugs talking. The memory of the procedure was still raw in his mind.

"Should you be boozing as well then?" Owen asked. His friend had cycled through a range of emotions from skepticism to shock and now worry.

"Just you try to stop me," Finn replied, slapping Owen on the shoulder.

The pair were about to enter the Recovery Center, which was a dive bar by any another name, when the air shook and a rocket climbed above the horizon line. Finn recognized it as a Solaris Ignition IV, the latest starship design that was capable of carrying three-hundred metric tons of cargo to the Nimbus Space Citadel, before returning to Earth to be reused.

"Everything on that ship should have stayed here, for the people of Zavetgrad," Finn commented. The sight of the launch had soured his mood. "People like us break our backs to produce goods and supplies that get blasted into space for the benefit of some privileged assholes."

"Ah, shut your whining cake-hole, already!"

Finn turned away from the launch and saw Soren Driscoll on the sidewalk behind him, with his heavy-set sidekick, Corbin not far behind.

"You should be on your hands and knees, kissing the Authority's boots," Soren went on. "If it wasn't for the golds, you wouldn't have food in your belly or a roof over your head, you ungrateful fuck."

"What about choice?" Finn hit back. "We don't get to choose what we do, or where we live. We don't even get to decide what happens to our bodies. In this place we're little better than cattle."

"I've heard it all before from whiners like you," Soren replied, dismissing him with a waft of his hand. "The truth is you do have a choice. You can choose to live or choose to die, and in your case, I know which one I'd prefer."

Finn knew that Soren was only trying to bait him. The man was the quintessential troll who loved to take the opposite viewpoint to everyone else just to start a fight, but Finn was in no mood for another squabble.

"Come on, Finn, let's get a drink," Owen said, carefully placing his substantial mass between Finn and Soren. "This piece of scrap isn't worth it."

Finn turned his back on Soren but the man wasn't done with him yet.

"Yeah, that's right, go get a drink with your boyfriend. You two losers deserve each other."

Finn spun around and was about to deck Soren where he stood when he saw a squad of prefects approaching, and quickly hid his closed fist from sight. The group of five officers was led by Head Prefect, Captain Viktor Roth, who wasted no time in confronting him.

"I hope that you're not planning to cause any more trouble, Worker Brasa?" Roth said, standing tall with his hands pressed to the small of his back.

"No, sir, I'm just here for a drink," Finn replied. He'd learned his lesson, at least so far as antagonizing Viktor Roth was concerned.

"This one is always causing trouble, sir," Soren cut in, shuffling closer to Captain Roth while grinning at Finn. "Only a minute ago he was bad-mouthing the Authority and arguing that the supplies on the rocket should have stayed here."

Roth turned his icy stare to Soren then a second later his hand flew, hitting the bully hard across the side of the face. The blow landed cleanly and the sound of Roth's gloved knuckles striking flesh and bone rang out in the night air like a whipcrack. Soren staggered back and pressed a hand to his face, and for the briefest moment the man glowered at Roth with a look that threatened the prospect of retaliation. Then four nightsticks were drawn and energized and Soren was quickly cowed into submission.

"Do not presume to speak to me, worker," Roth spat, staring Soren in the face, though the man did not meet the captain's eyes. "Do not *ever* presume to speak to me."

Soren nodded and shuffled away, eyes down like a scolded

child. Finn enjoyed seeing the man put in his place, but wasn't foolish enough to show it, knowing that it would make him the next target of Roth's flying hand.

"As you all know, Metalhaven will be hosting tonight's trial, which means that I will not tolerate screw-ups like you for making my sector look bad." Roth turned his attention squarely to Finn and aimed a finger at him like a dagger. "I am warning you directly, Worker Brasa. One more step out of line, and you will be next on trial, genetic purity ratings be damned."

Roth marched away with his entourage in tow and Finn found himself exhaling sharply. He'd been holding his breath without even realizing it. Given what Roth had just said, he knew he should have kept his head down and just gone into the Recovery Center, but he couldn't resist rubbing salt in Soren's wound.

"That looks like it might sting a little," Finn said, pointing to the developing bruise on Soren's face. He then smiled at the man. "I certainly hope so."

Soren roared and tried to grab him, but Corbin held the man back, whispering promises of future reprisals, such as, "not while Roth is looking," and "we'll get him later..." Finn was content to have the last laugh and entered the Recovery Center, leaving the red-faced duo on the sidewalk.

The bar was already jumping, on account of the looming trial, which always attracted a large crowd, and not only because attendance was mandatory. Humans had enjoyed the spectacle of blood sports throughout the ages, even during the relatively civilized period before the Last War, and the inhabitants of Metalhaven were no different. From the colosseums of Rome to the crucibles of Zavetgrad, humanity had always derived a peculiar pleasure from violence.

The Trials were more than just a bloody spectacle and welcome distraction from the mundanity of normal life, though. They were also an opportunity to win additional food and drink chits and, most coveted of all, reductions to shift hours. This was achieved by betting on everything from which prosecutor would get the first kill to the number of minutes that the various 'offenders' on trial would last inside the crucible. It was also an opportunity for the sector's Regent to lord himself over the masses, by making a rousing speech and tossing mystery prize bundles into the baying crowds. These also contained bonus food or drink chits and on one occasion, so long ago that was it was considered legend, one Worker had won an entire week off shift.

"Are you planning to place a bet?" Owen asked, sliding two pints of ale onto the table before sitting down opposite Finn.

"Yeah, I thought I'd bet on you making a wiseass remark within seconds of sitting down," Finn replied, pulling his beer closer. Owen knew that he despised the Trials so was just being facetious. "Looks like I won."

Owen snorted then took a long swig of his ale, downing almost half of the pint in one gulp. The man then rested back in the wooden chair, which groaned under the strain of his muscular mass.

"Someone will lose the shirt off their back tonight, you can guarantee it," Finn added. "First, maybe you only bet a half-hour or two. Then, before you know it, you're down an entire shift's worth of hours and you have to work yourself to death to make up the time."

Owen snorted a "pish" sound at him. The man had already drunk his pint.

"I say this as your buddy, Finn, but you've got to lighten up a little. Most people end up in the green by an hour or so, because that's how the Authority wants it. They want us to have a good time and enjoy the Trials. Don't be so uptight all the time."

Finn tapped his friend's glass. "Sounds like the beer talking, if you ask me."

Owen "pished" him again then got up. "Speaking of which, I'm going to get another pint. And I'm getting one for you too."

"I haven't even started this one yet!" Finn protested.

"Then you'd better drink up..." Owen vanished, making a hole the through the crowd with ease on account of his bulldozer-like frame, leaving Finn smarting.

"I'm not uptight," he grumbled to himself, while scanning the room for people he knew.

Most everyone who met his eyes sharply looked away, as if they feared that Finn would slide over and berate them for betting or smoking or drinking, or even just breathing. He then looked to see if he could find Jonas and Warner, the quarreling worker duo from Yard Seven, but the pair were conspicuous by their absence, and he felt annoyed they were not using the drink chits he'd given them to patch up their differences. He scowled and picked up his pint.

"Well, maybe I am a little uptight..." he admitted, before drawing the glass to his lips.

The ale was ice cold and had a uniquely floral taste, thanks to the use of rye, algae and local botanicals in the brewing process. It was also nuclear-strong, which was intentional. Recovery Centers were places where workers could blow out and let their hair down, mostly away from the prying eyes of prefects or the robotic scrutiny of the foremen. "A pint and a fight..." was the best way to wind down after a hard day's work, and the effects of hangovers were chemically mitigated by the disgusting probiotic goop that everyone drank the next day.

Owen returned a couple of minutes later with a pint in each hand and a cigarette dangling from his bottom lip. He dropped into the chair, almost causing it to collapse in the process, and slid the pint over to him.

"You're looking more miserable than usual," Owen said, removing the cigarette so that he could take a fresh swig of ale. "What has the Authority done this time?"

"Getting stabbed in the nuts with a five-inch-long needle will tend to make a man miserable," Finn replied. He was more than three-quarters of the way through his first pint but while the initial hit of alcohol had mellowed his muscles, his mind was still fraught.

"It's more than just that. I can tell, you know?" Owen replied, puffing a blanket of smoke into the air. "Something else happened in the Gene Bank, didn't it?"

Finn sighed and finished his first pint. He didn't really want to talk about the woman that he'd seen being dragged away but he knew that it would gnaw at him unless he did. And Owen was a sympathetic listener.

"While I was in the reception, I saw someone get downrated to a zero," Finn explained. "A woman."

"Ah..." Owen said, speaking the word as a sigh. He understood exactly what that would likely mean for the woman in question. "Was her Worker rating okay?"

Finn shook his head, and again Owen didn't need the gaps filling in to understand what the fate of the woman had been.

"As you know, I don't have any problem 'taking matters into my own hands' in the Gene Bank, but the Wellness Centers are another thing entirely," Owen said.

Finn smiled at his friend's tactful metaphor for the process that most people elected to undertake in the Gene Bank, then realized they'd never really talked much about the Wellness Centers. Like making seed donations, visits to the Wellness Centers were mandatory. As with most of the Authority's draconian laws, Finn had found ways to get around them and he wondered how Owen dealt with the place before realizing it was none of his business.

"I have an arrangement with a woman in Center C," Owen said, sensing the question that Finn wasn't going to ask. "Her name is Brianna, and we knew each other from before I was transferred to Yard Seven. We kinda had a thing going back then, so we both figured, 'why not', you know?"

Finn nodded and partially hid behind his pint. "How did she end up in the center?"

Owen stared into the bottom of his glass as if it were a lens into a former life that he'd tried hard to forget.

"It was a laser cutter accident. It blew and she lost her right leg, below the knee." Owen sighed then sank the contents of his second pint in a matter of seconds. "She was already sterile by that point, so as a double-zero, it was either the center or go to trial. She was going to pick the crucible but I talked her out of it. Sometimes, I wonder if I helped her or just condemned her to a living hell."

"She still has you, Owen," Finn replied, putting his pint

back on the table so he could look his friend in the eyes. "And some kind of true human connection has got to be better than death, right?"

Owen smiled and nodded, but Finn could see that his friend wasn't convinced and, if he was honest, he hadn't really believed himself either.

"What about you?" Owen asked, surprising Finn with the frankness of the question. "They might be able to strap you down and poke needles in your balls inside the Gene Bank but forcing you to… you know… do it… that's not possible, right?"

Finn swilled his ale around his glass then took a long gulp, partly because his mouth was dry, but also to give him time to think.

"I find ways around it," Finn answered, tactfully, realizing that he was essentially admitting to breaking the law. "You might be surprised to learn I'm not the only one."

Owen shook his head decisively. "That don't surprise me at all." The man then smiled. "It does explain why you're so uptight, though."

Finn laughed and raised his pint to his friend to salute his witty zinger. He was about to down the contents when he saw Soren Driscoll, surrounded by an entourage of drunk workers from Yard Seven that buzzed around him like flies circling shit. The bully had a twisted smile on his round face, and Finn's gut knotted as he realized that Soren had been listening in on their conversation.

"What a fucking pussy!" Soren bellowed, to ripples of laughter from his cohort. "You don't flog the dolphin in the Gene Bank and you don't get yourself some ass in the center. It's no wonder you're so sour!"

The group laughed again and Finn thought his face was going to melt. Soren then sashayed closer, reveling in his opportunity to drag him through the mud.

"Personally, I don't care if they're dying, missing an arm or a leg, or as ugly as sin. It gets me some ass, then I go back in for seconds."

As he was saying this, Soren was thrusting his hips and pretending to spank his imaginary partner, which only made his groupies laugh harder.

"In fact, it don't rightly bother me too much if they're already dead, so long as they're still warm!"

The roar was even louder, and ale sloshed from pint glasses onto the floor as the group jostled and joined in with their imaginary acts of carnal pleasure.

"It's a good job that you're a rating four worker, Soren, otherwise you'd be working as a piece of ass in the center yourself," Finn countered.

He knew it was a low blow to bring up Soren's genetic rating of zero, but he needed to strike a pain point in order to shut the man up.

"Fuck you, Finn, it ain't my fault my genetics are bad!" Soren said, switching from playful buffoon to bitter tyrant in the blink of an eye.

"No, but it is your fault that you're a worthless piece of shit."

Soren burst toward him, knocking over Finn's table and shattering their pint glasses on the floor. The bully's punch came faster than he was expecting, and two pints down, his reactions were dulled. The blow connected with his chin and sent him flying over the back of his chair. A cheer went up, and Soren surged forward but Owen sprang up and clotheslined the man before he could get close enough to put the boot in. He scrambled to his feet and dove into the fray, landing a punch on Corbin, who was trying to wrestle Owen aside. The door to the Recovery Center then burst open and a worker ran inside, red-faced and panting for breath.

"It's here!" the man yelled, stealing the focus of the room. "The crucible is going to be Yard Seven. It's going to be in our yard!"

There was a resounding cheer from the occupants of the bar, followed by a mass surge to the exit. If the trial was being held in Yard Seven, as the worker had claimed, it meant that everyone who worked in that yard, Owen and Finn included, would get ringside seats to the spectacle. Soren pushed himself up and dragged Corbin to his feet. For a second the bully considered continuing the fight, but like most of the other workers, Soren was obsessed with the Trials.

"Another time, Finn!" Soren yelled, aiming a broken pint glass at him. "This only ends one way, with you on the ground, bleeding, and me standing over you."

With that, Soren and Corbin ran for the door, shoving people out of the way enroute, and seconds later they were both gone.

7

METAL AND BLOOD

Finn picked himself up then tutted at the wet patches staining his overalls from ale that had spilled onto the floor of the Recovery Center. As rowdy drinking establishments, it was common for as much ale to end up on the floor as it did inside the worker's stomachs. Finn then noticed that Owen had already dusted himself down and was waiting for him by the door, appearing impatient.

"Come on, the trial is going to be in our yard!" Owen called out. "We might never get ringside seats like this again." The two pints of strong ale plus the brief scuffle with Soren and Corbin had clearly put him in the mood for more violence.

"You know that I hate the Trials," Finn said. He picked up someone's else pint that had been abandoned on a table and took a long drink from it.

"Just this once, can't you join in without making a big song and dance about how you hate everything?" Owen answered. "Besides, you have to be there, just like we all do."

Finn sighed then finished the ale and tossed the pint pot

over his shoulder. It smashed a moment later and the fragments disappeared into the mass of broken glass that was already littering the floor. The Recovery Center staff didn't complain, because they too had already run outside to watch the Regent arriving.

"Fine, what the hell," Finn said, boots crunching glass underfoot as he approached his friend. "Just don't expect me to like it."

Owen smiled and was outside on the street before Finn could catch him up. The bassy thrum of rotor blades filled the air and he caught sight of the Regent's convoy swooping in from the direction of the eastern coastline, which was where the governor of Metalhaven resided in his luxury suboceanic villa. Accelerating to a jog, Finn finally caught up with Owen in time to see the convoy of skycars landing inside Reclamation Yard Seven. One mile squared and with a tall, electrified fence around the perimeter, their yard was a ready-made crucible, full of dangers and places to hide. Not that there was any hiding from the prosecutors. The trained killers always won in the end, and the sentence they conveyed was always death.

"It takes a lot to get that asshole to leave his undersea retreat," Finn muttered, as the Regent exited his car to raucous cheers from the crowd, then approached a podium that had been hastily constructed to host his imminent speech. The cheers weren't so much for the man as for the prizes that everyone knew he was about to hand out. "What a charade…"

Owen didn't hear him since the man was pushing forward in an attempt to catch one of the flying packages that the Regent's staff had begun to toss into the crowd, like bread being thrown to the mob inside the Colosseum. One landed nearby and a group of workers descended on it like vultures, fighting amongst themselves to claim it. Then another bundle soared overhead, and Owen jumped, using his height and reach to pluck it out of the air before anyone else could get close. Several workers considered trying to wrestle the package from his friend's grasp before thinking twice. Attempting to take the package from Owen was like trying to steal food from the claws of a hungry bear.

"Yes!" Owen roared, tearing open the package and finding a collection of chits inside. "Four shift hours, two bonus food rations and ten ale chits! What a score!"

Owen wrapped his arm around Finn's neck and jumped up and down, half-strangling him in the process but Finn didn't mind. He was glad to see his friend happy, and he had to admit that his prize package was one worthy of celebration. Then Finn spotted Soren in the crowd a few meters away. The man had been involved in the scuffle to claim the previous prize bundle but had been unsuccessful. Instead, one of the men who'd been laughing and joking with Soren at Finn's expense in the Recovery Center had claimed it and refused to share its contents. Soren looked rightfully furious and Finn couldn't help but smile. *Fair weather friends are no friends at all...* he thought.

Finn was then distracted by a flicker of movement on top of the gate to Yard Seven. He shifted position to get a better look then his heart almost leapt out of his chest. Scraps, his homemade robot, was sitting atop the five-meter-tall gate post, watching the events as they unfolded. The robot had apparently used his newly-fixed rotors to fly out of Finn's apartment and do some exploring.

Get back inside! Finn mouthed to the robot, trying to shoo him away at the same time, but Scraps was too far away to see him. *Go home!*

Scraps suddenly spotted Finn and waved, as if it were all a game to the robot, but the machine didn't move from the fence post. Finn cursed under his breath and tried to make his way through the crowd, but it was too thick with activity and there was no possibility of reaching the perimeter. And even if he could reach Scraps and hide the bot inside his overalls, prefects were already standing guard at every entrance, barring people from leaving the yard. An electronic screech then startled Finn and was quickly followed by a weighty thump as the Regent's microphone was switched on and the man tapped it to test it was working.

"What's wrong?" Owen whispered.

Finn looked at his friend but didn't know how to explain, not that Owen would have been able to help, anyway. He threw his hands out to the side and shook his head in frustration before turning back to the fence post. Scraps was gone.

"Workers of Metalhaven, welcome to today's trial!"

The congregation cheered and surged forward, only to be pushed back by an army of robotic foremen. One worker managed to break through the ranks and made a run for a prize bundle that had landed short of the crowd, only to be beaten to the ground by prefects. Even the sight of one of their own being battered with electrified batons didn't deter the mob, who were clamoring for more.

"Today, twelve offenders will face two prosecutors inside the crucible, where they will be judged and sentenced for their grievous crimes against the Authority."

HERO OF METALHAVEN 71

The Regent's voice was amplified through speakers attached to drones that were hovering above the yard, making it sound like the voice of God speaking to them. The Regent then raised a hand and gestured toward one of two armored Skycars that had landed in the middle of the yard. "Bring forth the offenders!"

The crowd cheered as hatch doors on the armored Skycars were flung open and two groups of six men and women were marched outside. Each of them was wearing a one-piece jumpsuit in the color of their work Sector, with some additional padding on the arms and knees. The outfits were designed to make the offenders look 'ready for action' but in reality, the clothing offered little protection against the harsh climate, and no protection at all against the deadly weapons the prosecutors employed.

While the offenders were being marched to the podium, Finn turned his attention to the Regent. The man rarely made an appearance inside Metalhaven and Finn could only remember seeing him on perhaps one or two other occasions. His name was Gabriel Montgomery and he was a descendent of one of the Authority's founder members, an oil magnate from a time long before the Last War. The title of Regent was hereditary, passed down the line only to male heirs. Montgomery was an entitled, bloated, obnoxious aristocrat who indulged in everything to excess. Stories of his debauchery had been told in Metalhaven's Recovery Centers for decades. Whether it was sex, drink, food or the slaughter of his citizens in the Trials, the man was gluttonous in his appetites, and Finn hated him more than any other gold in Zavetgrad.

"Shit, Jonas and Warner are up there!" said Owen.

"What?" Finn turned his attention from the Regent to the offenders who were now being lined up on the podium, and sure enough, Jonas and Warner were there, dressed in the chrome color of Metalhaven. Both men were staring at their feet and looked petrified.

"Damn it, I told those two to be careful," Finn gasped.

His comment was lost in the growing murmurs of the crowd. The sight of Yard Seven's own workers on the podium had transformed the mood of the assembled spectators, and from the frenzied high of moments ago, the crowd was now anxious and unsettled. It was one thing to watch complete strangers get fed to the prosecutors for entertainment, but quite another to see the same fate befall people you knew and liked. For all their squabbling and stupidity, Jonas and Warner were good people and everyone knew it.

"I will now read out the crimes of these twelve offenders," the Regent announced, and the crowd went silent. "Josiah Lee, Construction sector. Grievous assault!"

The crowd chanted, "Guilty," which was all part of the theatre that surrounded the trial. Though it was required by law to participate, Finn never did.

"He probably just knocked into a prefect by accident," Finn commented, as the man in an orange jumpsuit from Stonehaven was led away. All the so-called crimes were really trumped-up nonsense charges, yet every single man and woman on the podium had effectively been sentenced to death.

"Liam Grant, Farming sector, Gross idleness!"

"Guilty!"

Finn shook his head as the thin, sickly-looking man from

Seedhaven was led away by prefects. The worker's skin was almost the same color as his green jumpsuit.

"What a joke..." Finn spat. "He probably just missed quota one too many times."

"Then the lazy fucker deserves to be up there..."

Unknown to him, Soren Driscoll had crept closer and now stood behind him. Finn knew why, and the bully's last comment was a perfect example. Soren wanted to get a rise out of him, and hopefully get Finn into trouble with the prefects.

"Sienna Bell, Power sector, Refusal to work!"

"Guilty!"

"Useless slut..." Soren snorted, as the woman in a red jumpsuit was led away.

Finn had to fight hard not thump the man in the mouth, but the latest offender had snared his attention, like an accident you couldn't look away from. The woman was from an unspecified Wellness Center in Volthaven and was an indentured sex worker in all but name. To Finn, she looked like she'd already given up on life long before being sentenced to trial. Refusal to work simply meant that she'd rather die than give up her body to be used as a sex toy, day in, day out.

"Jonas Hawley and Warner Murray, Reclamation sector, irreparable damage to authority property!"

There were a few murmurs of "Guilty" from the crowd but the announcement of the two workers from Metalhaven's Yard Seven was largely met with silence. Captain Viktor Roth then stepped forward and spoke into the microphone.

"You will answer the prefect in accordance with the law!"

Captain Roth's men energized their nightsticks and expanded riot shields, before forming up a line and marching two paces forward. The aggressive maneuver was shocking in its suddenness, like a Roman legion advancing, and it successfully intimidated the crowd into compliance.

"Jonas Hawley and Warner Murray, Reclamation sector, irreparable damage to authority property!" the Regent repeated, this time louder.

"Guilty!" the crowd chanted, and Soren most loudly of all.

"Those two useless fuckers deserve to die," Soren said, leaning in close to Finn's ear to ensure he heard clearly.

Finn spun around, fist clenched, but Owen held him back. He met his friend's eyes and Owen shook his head firmly.

"Don't do it," Owen said. "That piece of scrap isn't worth dying for."

Finn clamped his jaw shut and turned away from the grinning face of Soren Driscoll. He closed his eyes and tried to shut out everything around him but the announcements were simply too loud, and he had no choice but to hear the ludicrous charges that had been leveled at every one of the seven remaining offenders. The real reason most of them were on the podium was because they were too physically or mentally broken to work, or because they had publicly defied the Authority, as Finn often and unwisely also did. His exceptionally rare double-five rating had saved him on those occasions – the people in the crucible were not so lucky.

"They're bringing out the prosecutors," Owen commented, his mood also now heavily subdued. "Shit, they're bad ones too."

Finn took a deep breath then shifted position so he could get a good look at the two prosecutors who would hunt down and kill the twelve offenders. The first was a man called

Herman Hanson, though that wasn't his real name, and inside the crucible he was simply known as The Hammer. Like most prosecutors, with a few very rare exceptions, Hanson had been selected from within the ranks of the prefects or had been born and bred for the role. Brutal but charismatic, Hanson was a showman and a crowd pleaser. The man was massive, purportedly weighing two-eighty pounds of solid muscle, even before donning the reinforced ceramic composite armor that protected his substantial frame. Like rumors of the Regent's decadence, it was likely this figure had been embellished, but Finn could see for himself that descriptions of The Hammer's chosen weapon had been faithful. It was a massive twenty-five-pound sledgehammer with an electrified head that killed with a single strike.

Herman Hanson arrived on the podium and lifted his hammer to salute the crowd, who cheered in response, though their enthusiasm had already waned. Finn doubted that anyone would have cheered at all were it not for fear of reprisals from the prefects, who were still poised to weigh in with their batons should the workers of Metalhaven not play their part in the ceremony. Even so, Finn refused to make a sound, risking a beating if he was spotted staying silent.

The next prosecutor then climbed onto the podium and it was a woman who needed no introduction. The Shadow, Elara Cage, was famous not least because of her exploits inside the crucible, but because she had once been a Metalhaven worker, like all of them. That had earned her the lesser-used title, 'The Iron Bitch of Metalhaven', though no-one would dare call her that to her face. Elara Cage wore a special kind of light-reactive armor that allowed her to practically disappear in plain sight. She was armed with a crossbow-pistol using poisoned or electrified darts, though the assassin often preferred to get close and make her kills with a black-steel roundel dagger.

"She don't look like much, but that bitch is a killer," Soren said, reminding Finn that the bully was still close by. "Man, I'd love to get a piece of that ass. She's fine as fuck."

"Then go out there and punch a prefect," Finn said, glaring at the man over his shoulder. "With any luck, they'll just add you to the list and you can be offender number thirteen."

"Yeah, you'd like that, wouldn't you, pussy?" Soren replied. He could smell the man's sweat and feel Soren's ale-stinking breath on his neck. "She was from Metalhaven, did you know that?"

"Everyone knows that, you moron," Finn snapped.

"That bitch won her trial, outlasting everyone in the crucible and even killing both of the prosecutors. Do you know how rare that is? Less than one in every two thousand survive a trial. We should be proud of her."

"Sure, we should be really proud of the woman who killed innocent workers to save her own skin and was rewarded for murder by being made into a gold. What a hero."

Soren shook his head. "You're a fucking disgrace, Finn. Why do you hate us all so much?"

Finn shook his head at Soren in dismay. "I don't hate *us*, I hate *them*. Just whose side are you on, anyway?"

Soren dismissed him then continued to watch as the events unfolded. Unlike The Hammer, Herman Hanson, Elara Cage didn't play up to the crowd. She merely stood on the podium beside the Regent, stony-faced and silent, yet despite this she was still more intimidating than her co-prosecutor. It was like staring death itself in the eyes and Finn felt a shiver of electricity rush down his spine. The Regent then raised his hands to get everyone's attention, ready to start the trial, when a cry of "Metal and Blood!" erupted from somewhere in the crowd. There were confused and fretful murmurs, then a man broke ranks and charged toward the podium, holding what looked to be an improvised pistol in his outstretched hand.

8

THE TRIAL

A DOZEN PREFECTS rushed onto the podium and surrounded the Regent, shielding him with their own bodies. Then a gunshot rang out and one of the officers was hit in the shoulder and sent crashing to the ground. The crowd dispersed in a mad panic then the man who had fired the shot turned to the fleeing masses and raised his hands.

"We are all Metal and Blood!" the man cried, as four prefects wrestled him to the ground and tried to press their hands over his mouth. "Haven is real! Haven is..."

Electrified nightsticks stymied any further outbursts from the would-be assassin, then a metal bit was rammed into the man's mouth and strapped around the back of his head to gag him. It was a medieval device not dissimilar to a scold's bridle and Finn hadn't seen one used in years. Normally, they were employed on workers who had succumbed to intense mental breakdowns to prevent them from cussing or spitting on prefects, but in this case its use was more insidious, because it was intended to silence words of sedition and rebellion.

"What a fucking disgrace," Soren said, as the assassin was

dragged away to a waiting armored skycar. "If the Regent calls off the trial now because of that selfish bastard, I'll be pissed."

"I'm the sure the Regent couldn't give two shits how you feel, just like the rest of us," Finn replied.

The bully shoved him in the back but the arrival of Gabriel Montgomery back on the podium quickly focus his and the crowd's attention. The line of robotic foremen had remained steadfast despite the excitement, and now dozens more prefects were rushing into Yard Seven to reinforce the already substantial police presence.

"He's going to call it off, I just know it," Soren grumbled.

Finn hoped that Soren was right but the Regent looked oddly cheerful and composed, considering the attempt on his life. Like all politicians, Montgomery was an expert at twisting situations to his advantage, and Finn suspected that the aristocrat was about to turn the assassination attempt into an opportunity to bolster his unjustified popularity.

"People of Metalhaven, please be calm," the Regent said into the microphone, and his smooth voice was amplified all across the yard. "Thanks to the quick actions of the prefects, the mentally-deranged worker has been safely detained."

There were murmurs of appreciation but the crowd was still anxious to learn the fate of the trial. The fate of hundreds of shift hours and dozens of food chits rested on its outcome. Head Prefect, Captain Viktor Roth, then stepped onto the podium, escorting another officer, who had his left arm in a sling. Finn recognized the man as the prefect who had taken a bullet on behalf of Montgomery.

"Thanks to the courageous and selfless actions of Prefect Anthony Gorman, I am unharmed," the Regent said, inviting the officer to step forward. "It is therefore my pleasure to award Prefect Gorman with the Zavetgrad Medal of Valor, our highest honor for bravery!"

Captain Roth handed the Regent a device similar in appearance to a pistol but with a wide rectangular barrel. Montgomery pressed the object to Gorman's chest and there was a brief and blinding flash of light. When the device was removed, a shimmering golden star with a silver border was etched onto the prefect's armored chest plate.

"Workers of Metalhaven, show your appreciation for Prefect Gorman!"

The Regent began a round of applause and was swiftly joined by the other prefects and even the robot foremen, who all clapped in perfect time. A row of prefects closer to the crowd then aimed their batons at the workers and demanded they join in, and slowly a ripple of polite applause began to cascade through the ranks of assembled spectators. Once the Regent was satisfied, Captain Roth led Prefect Gorman off the podium and Montgomery raised his hands to quieten the crowd, though most people had already stopped clapping by that point.

"I give my thanks to Captain Roth and his superbly-trained officers for maintaining order and resolving a difficult situation with minimal disruption. I see no reason to curtail today's proceedings."

This announcement caused far more excitement and Finn scoffed under his breath. Only a few minutes earlier, the sight of Jonas and Warner on the podium had caused the workers of Metalhaven to lose all appetite for the trial. *People have short memories* he thought. While he had been focused on the Regent's latest announcement, Finn hadn't noticed that Captain Roth had returned to the armored skycar and was now escorting the assassin back into the center of the crucible. The man was still gagged with the bridle.

"And we will have one more offender to face trial!" the Regent added, as the assassin was shoved in line with the other twelve men and women. "I'm sure I don't need to remind you of this man's offense!"

The prefects laughed but the crowd remained muted in its appreciation for the Regent's gallows humor.

"Let the trial commence!"

Music blared from the same speakers that had carried the Regent's voice, and aerial drones released a cascade of fireworks that rippled across the sky above Reclamation Yard Seven. This piece of theatre was enough to recapture the crowd's interest and workers gawped upward, wowed by the dazzling display. The gates were then opened and foremen began to usher people outside the yard and toward stands that had been constructed beyond the five-meter-tall, electrified fence that surrounded the reclamation facility. Finn, Owen, Soren and Corbin didn't need to join the hustle and bustle because as workers of Yard Seven, they had VIP passes and reserved seats. And for the people who were not lucky enough to get a ringside view of the brutal event, vast TV screens were being raised high above the crucible by drones so that everyone in Metalhaven would be able to enjoy the spectacle in bloody, high-definition glory.

"Hey, Finn, what did that guy mean by 'Metal and Blood', and 'Haven is real'?" Owen asked, while they waited for the yard to empty of non-combatants. "I remember a guy from Yard Six mentioned Haven in the Recovery Centre some months back, but I never saw them again to ask."

"Haven is a rumored refuge outside of the city," Finn

replied. Ever since the gunshot had rung out, the assassin's statement had not been far from his thoughts. "It's a place where men, women and even machines all live free and as equals."

"Bullshit!" Soren snorted. "If you believe that fairytale then you'll believe anything. It's a story that weak-minded snowflakes like you tell each other to help you sleep at night."

"I wasn't asking you," Owen snapped, showing a rare flicker of anger. It did not go unnoticed by Soren.

"Well fuck, has Owen Thomas finally grown a pair?" Soren replied, grinning at the man. "I thought you let Finn do all the talking for you?"

Owen shook his head and turned his back on the bully. Despite the flash of anger, his friend still had far more self-restraint than Finn did.

"What else do you know?" Owen asked, keeping his voice low in the hope that Soren wouldn't overhear.

It was unusual for his friend to take an interest in anything illegal, which explained why Owen hadn't heard much of Haven before. Any talk of the rumored city that supposedly lay across the Davis Strait from Zavetgrad fell under the category of Spreading Seditious Lies, which was a serious crime, punishable by trial. Finn hadn't wanted to place his friend in a tricky situation and so had kept his opinions to himself. Yet, there were others who were willing to take the risk, such as the worker from Yard Six that Owen had mentioned. The fact this worker had suddenly vanished from the face of the earth after unwisely discussing Haven in a public place was not a coincidence, he thought. Finn had learned of Haven four years earlier from a Wellness Center worker who had claimed that agents from outside Zavetgrad worked in secret to free people from the oppression of the Authority. In truth, he hadn't really believed her, but it was a welcome distraction from his lived reality of the reclamation yard that made his visits to the center more bearable, until one day the woman had been reassigned, and he never saw her again.

"There's not much more to tell," Finn said, again choosing to limit what he revealed to Owen, for his own safety. "It's just stories, really, myths and legends borne out of the hope there's something better than all of this."

"It's also sedition, you stupid fucks," Soren cut in. Foremen were now leading them to their VIP area, which was close to where the Regent and the senior prefects, including Captain Roth, were seated. "If the prefects hear you talking about that bullshit place, we might all get in the shit, so for once just shut your fucking mouths!"

"I'm getting really tired of hearing your voice, Soren," Finn said, side-eyeing the bully as they made their way to the stand.

"Yeah, then why don't you try to shut me up?" Soren answered, pushing back. "I'd love to see you try, pussy."

Finn wanted nothing more than to bury his boot into Soren's foul mouth, but with Captain Roth so close by, he knew better than to rattle the hornet's nest. The Head Prefect was watching him closely, and the officer had already proven that he enjoyed making an example of people. Suddenly, a fanfare blared out of the hovering speakers, and the cinematic floating TV screens flickered on to show the thirteen offenders, gathered in the center of Reclamation Yard Seven, which had become a temporary crucible for the day. One TV screen was focused on the prosecutors, who were standing about thirty meters away from the offenders, weapons in hand.

The Regent, who had been seated at the top of the VIP stand, got to his feet and raised his hands to the crowd. "Let the trial begin!"

A horn sounded, shrill and biting like the icy wind that enveloped Metalhaven three hundred and sixty-five days of every year, and the offenders turned and ran. All but one. The failed assassin, offender number thirteen, stood his ground as the two prosecutors stalked toward him.

"What an idiot!" Soren laughed, pointing and jeering. Then the bully changed his tune. "Fuck, I bet one shift hour that the slut from the Wellness Center would get killed first; if that moron doesn't move then I lose!"

Finn tried to put the grating sound of Soren's voice out of his mind and watched, heart in his mouth, as the assassin wrestled with his bridle. Then to utterances of shock and revulsion from the assembled guests, the man tore out the metal bit, ripping open the corner of his mouth and shattering teeth in the process. The bridle was thrown to the dirt and the man turned to face the crowd, blood pouring off his chin.

"Workers of Metalhaven!" the man yelled, though his words were muffled and strained. "There is a place where all men and women are free. Haven is real. We are all Metal and Blood! We are all Metal and Blood!"

"For God's sake, kill him now!" Captain Roth roared, rising to his feet.

The Hammer, Herman Hanson, broke into a sprint and covered the distance to where the assassin stood in a matter of seconds. The enormous sledgehammer was raised high above the prosecutor's head then brought down with ferocious power, caving in the assassin's skull in a single, savage blow. The crowd reacted with mixed feelings. Some cheered and whooped, while others retched or turned their heads and closed their eyes.

"Fucking hell, that's two shift hours I'm down!" Soren roared, stomping his foot on the wooden stand like a toddler having a tantrum. "I also bet The Shadow would get the first kill…"

Corbin and Soren began to argue as to whether the assassin's death even counted as the first kill, since the man had been added late to the trial, and no-one had been able to place any bets on his outcome. Finn was grateful for their squabbling, because it meant that Soren was no longer bothering him.

"Look, Jonas is climbing onto that stack of crushed trucks," Owen said, pointing to an area just away from the center of the yard, close to where the offenders had been released. "That's actually pretty smart. They won't find him up there."

Finn spotted the worker and nodded. Jonas was using his unique knowledge of Yard Seven to his advantage.

"Where's Warner? Do you see him?" Finn asked.

Owen scouted the crucible for Jonas' worker buddy then shook his head.

"No, and I didn't see in which direction he ran, either," his friend replied. "But those two are never far from one other."

Finn nodded again then anxiously rubbed his face and forced down a dry swallow. Trials rarely lasted more than a couple of hours, and the prosecutors and Trial Controllers made sure of this. If the kills were coming too quickly then the hunters would toy with the remaining offenders to drag it out, like a cat with a mouse. On the rare occasions that anyone managed to survive longer than ninety minutes, Trial Controllers would begin to feed intelligence to the prosecutors and guide them to their targets. Sometimes, they would even unleash drones or foremen into the arena to herd offenders to designated killzones. It was for this reason that it had been so vanishingly rare for anyone to survive a trial. Not only did an offender have to avoid being killed, but they also had to take out two trained and heavily armed killers with nothing more than their wits and what they could find lying around in the crucible.

"The Hammer is moving away," Owen added, now pointing to the brute of a man. "Maybe Jonas will survive this!"

The Hammer, buoyed by his early kill, continued at speed deeper inside the crucible, using his tracking device to pursue the remaining offenders. The Shadow, Elara Kage, on the other hand, stood in the dead center of the arena, watching and waiting.

"What is she doing?" Finn wondered.

Owen shook his head then they both watched as The Shadow crept beside a wrecked howitzer gun. The woman's armor reacted to its new environment, taking on the color and texture of the rusted metal, and Elara Kage vanished like a chameleon.

"She knows that someone is near," Finn added, suddenly realizing what was happening. "She was from Metalhaven, remember? She knows these yards just as well as we do."

Finn spotted Jonas atop the eight-meter-high stack of

vehicles. The man had crawled out on his belly and appeared to be speaking to someone on the ground. Finn scowled then looked at one of the enormous TV screens, which was showing a blown-up view of Jonas and the area around the worker.

"Oh shit, he's calling out to Warner!" Owen said, understanding the situation before Finn had figured it out. "He's going to lead The Shadow right to them."

Finn's pulse was already so high he thought he might have heart attack but the sight of Warner, dragging his body out of a burned-out APC, nearly tipped him over the edge.

Run, you fools... Finn urged the two men. *Run!*

It was too late. Elara Kage stepped out into the open and her camouflaged armor reverted back to its usual, inky black state. Warner cried out but the bolt from The Shadow's crossbow pistol had already been fired and Jonas was hit in the neck. The worker fell from the summit of the stacked trucks and landed in a contorted heap directly in front of his worker buddy and friend.

"Damn it, Warner, get up and run!" Finn roared, shaking a fist at the TV screen.

His cries were lost in the tumult of the crowd, as hundreds more workers from Metalhaven implored the man to flee, but Warner didn't move. Instead, he collapsed beside the body of his dead friend and hugged the man to his chest, trembling and with tears flowing freely from his eyes. The Shadow approached but Warner was imprisoned by fear and grief.

"Run! Run you fool!"

Finn screamed his voice hoarse, but Warner had already accepted the inevitability of his death. The man simply looked into the eyes of Elara Kage and submitted. The Shadow drew a roundel dagger from a leather sheath, its black blade as cold as the woman's eyes, and plunged it hilt-deep into the man's neck. The crowd was as silent as the night, and even Soren and Corbin kept their mouths shut, as they watched their friend and co-worker die. The Shadow removed her dagger, allowing blood to gush and paint the snow red, then cleaned the blade on Warner's jumpsuit and returned the weapon to its sheath. She remained standing over the body for a few seconds before her armor shimmered and the woman vanished into the night like a specter.

"Fuck this, I've seen enough," Finn said, jostling his way off the stand.

"Don't be a pussy," Soren called out, and the man's voice rooted him to the spot like a ship's anchor. "People die, Finn. Get over yourself."

Finn was shaking with rage. He tried to ignore Soren and tried even harder to leave, but the bully was not about to let him go easily.

"If you duck out now then I'm telling the prefects you left," Soren added, jumping down from the stand to block Finn's path. The man stabbed a chubby finger into Finn's chest, and added, "We all have to watch, and you're not above the law, so sit the fuck down!"

Finn flipped. His fists flew and before he knew it, he was on top of Soren, raining blow after blow onto his face and body. Corbin darted into the mix and kicked him so hard to the side of his head that he almost blanked out. Owen sprang into action, instinct driving the man to defend his friend, and Corbin was rocked by a heavy right hand that sent the brute crashing into the stands. Then his friend was stabbed with an electrified baton and paralyzed with pain. Prefects piled in all around them and Finn felt hands grabbing at his arms and legs, but he shook them off and dove back on top of Soren, raining more blows into the man's already bludgeoned face.

"That's enough!"

Finn was pulled clear but he was still in the grip of rage and not thinking straight. He lashed out to his rear with his elbows and struck whoever was trying to restrain him. An electrified baton was thrust at his chest, but he caught the weapon and tore it from the prefect's grasp before spinning around and lashing out with the baton like a man possessed. In his blind anger, he struck Captain Viktor Roth, and the weapon scorched a jagged furrow across the officer's face, causing Roth to reel back and scream in pain. Finn dropped the baton and the realization of what he'd done hit him like a shotgun blast to the head.

"Arrest him!" Roth roared, cradling his wounded flesh. "Arrest them all!"

Dozens of officers piled in, and Finn and the others were restrained and placed in handcuffs. Then Captain Roth stormed toward him and grabbed him by the throat, gripping so hard he couldn't breathe.

"I warned you, Brasa!" Roth snarled. "Now you're all going to trial!"

9
REGRETS

THE SLIDING door was flung open, and Finn was dragged from the armored skycar by two prefects, one on either arm. The journey had lasted barely two minutes and from the buildings he could make out through the snowy darkness, Finn knew he was still inside Metalhaven, most likely at the primary Law Enforcement Hub for the Reclamation sector. Owen was bundled out of the skycar next, followed by Soren and Corbin, who had barely stopped protesting since their arrest. The tune they had been singing was a familiar one.

"I keep telling you, this isn't my fault!" Soren yelled as the prefects from the skycar handed them over to officers from the hub. "I was an innocent bystander! Finn Brasa is the one you want, not me!"

One of the new prefects hammered the end of his nightstick into Soren's gut, pressing the air from the man's lungs and causing him to bend double.

"The offender will be silent!" the officer snarled. The man was a supervisor, which meant he had at least ten years of experience, despite the fact the officer was barely in his mid-twenties. "Gag him…"

"No, no, please!" Soren protested, wheezing the words, but it was a waste of what little breath the man could muster.

Two officers held Soren's arms, while a third prefect forced a rectangular metal bit into the bully's mouth. A strap was passed over Soren's head and tightened so securely that Finn saw a bead of blood trickle down the man's neck. Soren's eyes almost bulged out of his head and he moaned and mumbled in an effort to speak but it was impossible. Finn almost felt sorry for the man before reminding himself that it was Soren who had gotten them into this mess into first place. Then his gut knotted with guilt and shame, knowing in his heart that this was a lie. Soren had played his part but so had Finn. If anyone was to blame, it was him.

"Wait here," the prefect supervisor ordered, before walking toward the main doors of the Law Enforcement Hub, which opened automatically as he approached.

Finn did as he was instructed because he knew there was no point putting up a fight, at least not yet. The Law Enforcement Hub was home to at least a hundred prefects and there wasn't the slightest possibility of escape. He also knew that no-one who had ever been sent to the hub had been returned to the yards, and as he cast his eyes across the courtyard, he understood that this would be his fate too. A golden skycar sat on the landing pad, ready to take them from Metalhaven to the Authority sector to await trial.

The doors to the hub slid open again and the Supervisor returned, nightstick in hand. The officer stood in the threshold to prevent the doors from closing again, then signaled for Finn and the others to enter.

"Move inside and wait on the gold crosses marked on the floor," the prefect supervisor ordered.

Finn went first with Owen at his side. The friends had barely said two words to each other since their arrest. Partly, this was because of the threat of a clobbering from one of the prefect guards, though it was mainly because Finn didn't know what to say. Owen had cautioned him against his insubordination more times that he could count, and often to the point of being a bore. Now, Finn understood all too well the consequences of defying the Authority. And, worst of all, he had dragged his best and only friend down with him.

The supervisor spoke to a female prefect inside the lobby of the Law Enforcement Hub then saluted, pressing two fingers of his right hand to the insignia of the Authority on his left shoulder. The insignia depicted a burst of golden light exploding from the desolate, rocky plains surrounding Zavetgrad and reaching to a city in the stars – the Nimbus citadel. Finn had never paid much attention to the emblem before, but the prominence of Nimbus gleaming above the ashes of Earth suddenly struck home. Zavetgrad, and everyone in it, were ultimately disposable, and he, Owen, Soren and Corbin were next on the list to be discarded. The prefect supervisor lowered his salute then stepped aside, and the officer promptly departed without giving Finn or the others a second look. To that particular officer, they were already as good as dead.

"My name is Lieutenant Holloway," the new officer announced, standing tall and looking down her nose at them. The woman was so severe she could have been roughly chiseled from granite. "You will obey my commands or be punished. I will not repeat this warning. Now, all offenders will follow me."

Electrified nightsticks were prodded in their backs but the charge was set low enough that it merely caused pain rather than paralysis. Finn and the others were marched through the Law Enforcement Hub as if making a walk of shame, then shoved into a cell that was little more than ten meters square. The door was slammed shut and locked behind them, then a crackle of electricity gripped the metal and the entire cell hummed like a swarm of bees. Lieutenant Holloway departed, along with the bulk of her prefects, leaving only two guards in the cell block.

Finn realized that the prefects had left the bridle on Soren and the man rushed to the bars, eyes still wide with terror. Soren grabbed the metal columns with both hands, desperate to get the attention of the officers, and a powerful electric shock rippled through his body. Muted screams leaked from the corners of Soren's mouth, which was as much sound as the metal bit pressing down on the man's tongue would allow. The current was briefly turned off and Soren collapsed to the ground, his body wracked with tremors. Soren lost control of his bladder and urine began to soak into his overalls and pool around him. Corbin pulled his friend clear and knelt down beside the incapacitated worker, before glaring up at Finn with vengeful eyes.

"Are you happy now?" Corbin snarled, though the man was smart enough to keep his voice down. "Soren always said you were trouble and now look at us. This is your fault!"

Owen stepped forward; his hammer-like fists clenched tightly at his side. "Soren pushing Finn's buttons is what got us into this mess," Owen hit back. "If you'd have just stayed away then we'd be back in the Recovery Center, getting drunk by now!"

Finn was grateful for his friend defending him, though in his heart he knew he didn't deserve Owen's loyalty. The blame certainly wasn't all his but he shouldered more than a fair share of it.

"Quiet!" barked one of the two prefects in the cell block, and Owen drew back, though his fists remained tightly bundled.

Finn turned his back on Corbin and positioned himself as a shield between Owen and the others. His friend had always been the embodiment of calm, the unwavering voice of reason. Yet, the weight of their circumstances had begun to chip away at his once unyielding composure, and he needed Owen's steadying influence more than ever.

"Take it easy, big guy, we need to keep a cool head," Finn said, speaking at little more than a whisper so Corbin couldn't overhear. "We're in trouble and we need to think clearly."

"You're telling me to take it easy?" Owen had reeled back and was looking at Finn like an enemy. It sent a chill racing down his spine. "How many times have I warned you about stepping out of line, Finn? *How many times?*"

Finn couldn't even look his friend in the eye. "I know, I know and I'm sorry, Owen, I really am. I don't know what else to say."

Owen shook his head and immediately climbed down. If anything, the man looked embarrassed for his outburst, even though the, 'I told you so...' speech had been more than justified. The big man's shoulders sagged and he shoved his hands into his overall pockets, already looking defeated.

"What does it matter now whose fault is was?" Owen said. "We're being sent to trial and that's that. In a few days, we'll be dead."

"Maybe not."

Owen glanced at Corbin who was still tending to Soren as best he could and wasn't paying any attention to either of them. He shuffled beside Finn and turned his back on the others, while also trying to hide what he was saying from the prying eyes of the prefect guards.

"What do you mean by that?" Owen asked. "Once someone is sent to trial the decision is never overturned. It hasn't happened once in the history of Zavetgrad."

Finn glanced at the prefects but the two men were chatting to each other and not looking in their direction. He angled the rear of his shoulder toward the officers and turned his head so that neither the prefects nor Corbin could see his lips moving.

"There's always Haven," Finn whispered.

Owen's broad shoulders sagged again. "But you said that Haven was a myth. Just stories that people made up."

Finn shrugged. "All myths have some basis in reality, Owen. I've known people who talked about Haven with absolutely certainty, as if it were no less real than this cell. A woman I used to visit in the Wellness Center even told me that she was getting out. Then a couple of weeks later, she was gone."

"Anything could have happened to her, Finn, you know that," Owen replied. "She could have been transferred, or sent to trial, or more likely just committed suicide. You know it happens far more often than golds would have us believe."

Finn sensed that his friend wanted to trust him, but he'd

given Owen nothing more to go on than hearsay; Chinese whispers at best. He wracked his brain, trying to think of a more concrete example but drew a blank. Owen was right, Haven was nothing more than a story, but at that moment the hope of its existence was the only thing he could cling to. The alternative was to admit defeat and accept that they were dead men walking.

"We either die in the crucible or die trying to escape," Finn said. In his mind, there was only one choice. "I know which I'd prefer."

Owen considered Finn's words then nodded his agreement but without any enthusiasm. A vain hope was better than none, Finn told himself, though like his friend, he did not feel any sense of optimism in that moment. Their arrest and sentence, all in the space of a few seconds, had left his mind reeling and body numb, like he was trapped inside a nightmare and unable to wake up.

The door to the cell block opened and Finn snapped to attention, concerned that their whispered conversations had attracted the attention of Lieutenant Holloway. Instead, Head Prefect, Captain Viktor Roth walked inside, and Finn's mouth went dry. The man's face was still scarred where he'd struck the officer with an electrified nightstick but even without the savage wound, Roth would still have looked fearsome and angry, like a sadistic executioner, ready to dispense his twisted version of justice.

Soren saw the captain and scrambled to his feet, helped by Corbin since the man was still unsteady because of the electric shock. Soren staggered toward the bars and almost grabbed them for a second time before catching himself and pulling his hands away. Finn could see that they were burned red.

Soren then proceeded to mumble words at the captain while making imploring gestures with his hands. Tears streamed down Soren's face and this time Finn's hatred for the man could not overcome his human compassion for a soul who was suffering greatly. Soren may have been obnoxious but he didn't deserve this. None of them did.

"The offenders will step back from the bars and remain silent," Roth barked, jabbing his nightstick in Soren's direction. It was like the officer had cast a spell and Soren was repelled as if struck by a magical force. "You have all been sentenced to trial, and nothing you say will change the outcome, so I strongly advise you to save your breath."

"What happens now?" Corbin asked.

Roth raised an eyebrow then stabbed Corbin through the bars with the electrified nightstick. The man screeched like a wounded cat and crumpled to his knees, smoke rising from his gut where the weapon had contacted his body.

"What happens now, *sir...*" Roth said, underling the requirement for their obedience and deference while in the captain's presence.

The officer marched to the right-hand side of the cell and looked Finn dead in the eye. The captain was so close to the bars that he briefly considered darting toward the man and pulling him against the electrified metal, but other than a fleeting sense of satisfaction from seeing Roth suffer, it would do them no good. Finn had to fight his natural urge to dissent and instead do something that he'd never done in his entire life – comply with the Authority.

"In answer to the offender's question, you will be transported to the Authority sector for processing," Roth continued, addressing Finn directly, even though he had not made the inquiry. "Once that has been completed, you will be sent to trial."

Nothing was known about how offenders were prepared for trial, at least not in the worker class, but from the way Roth had spoken, being 'processed' was not something Finn expected to enjoy. He knew he was pushing his luck to ask anything more, especially considering what had happened to Corbin, but he figured that Captain Roth would revel in detailing the specific ways in which Finn was going to suffer, so he took a chance.

"Sir, what does 'processing' involve?" Finn asked.

Roth laughed and the officer's narrow-set eyes widened with surprise.

"*Sir?*" the captain replied, mocking Finn. "It's a little late in the hour for you to have learned respect, Worker Brasa. If you had conducted yourself in a proper manner in the Gene Bank and during the Yard Seven Trial, then you would not be behind bars now."

"I understand that now, sir," Finn replied, swallowing his pride and the bile that had risen into his throat. "And I have accepted my fate."

Finn might have expected Roth's eyes to widen further but instead they tightened and became skeptical.

"I do not believe that for one second, Worker Brasa," Roth replied, his gruff voice thick with malice. "But since you have taken an interest in the process of the trial, let me explain what will happen to you."

Finn tasted bile in his mouth, but he swallowed hard and stood tall. His hands were trembling and he pressed them together behind his back in an attempt to hide his fear from the captain.

"The skycar that is being prepared for departure as we speak will take you to the processing facility in the heart of the Authority sector," Roth began, recounting the information like a judge passing sentence. "Those with viable seed will have a sufficient quantity extracted, since it would be a shame for it to go to waste, then you will be treated for any injuries or ailments that might impede your performance in the trial." Roth smiled and the look on the man's face turned Finn's stomach. "We must make sure you are fit to participate, otherwise it wouldn't be a fair trial, would it?" The guards to Roth's rear laughed and it seemed clear that this was an in-joke within the rank of the Prefecture. "Then you will be granted a period of recuperation and given some basic instructions before a skycar will transport you to the crucible and your trial will begin, in a little more that twenty-four hours from now."

"Are you able to tell us where the crucible will be, sir?" Finn replied. Bile again crept into his mouth as he spoke, but he managed to swallow it before the acidic liquid leaked over his dry lips.

Roth shrugged. "It does you no harm or good to know, so what the hell. Your crucible will be one of the under-construction launch facilities within the Nimbus sector, or what you plebians like to call Spacehaven."

Finn's heart sank. He had hoped for the Transport sector, which might have allowed him to steal a skycar and make a break across the Davis Strait to the east, where Haven was rumored to be located. Solid second choices would have been Volthaven or the algae farms, both of which were on the outskirts of Zavetgrad, and might present an opportunity to escape beyond the city limits, but the Nimbus sector was another matter entirely. Next to the Authority sector, Spacehaven was the most heavily-guarded and secure location in Zavetgrad. Finn sighed. His notions of breaking free of the Authority's grip had always seemed like a flight of fancy but now they were pure make-believe. Another officer then entered the cell block and spoke into Captain Roth's ear. Roth nodded and the man departed, rejoining a group of eleven other officers that Finn now noticed had assembled in ranks outside.

"Offenders will form up, two by two, with their hands on their heads," Captain Roth ordered. "Your skycar awaits and the clock is ticking. Twenty-four hours from now, you will all be dead and justice will have been served."

10

FOUR BECOMES SIX

Finn and Owen were marched out of the cell block side-by-side, with their hands pressed to the backs of their heads. Two prefects stopped them at the door leading onto the landing pad by pressing batons to their chests, while another officer slapped name tags onto their overalls. The cheap, sticky label was colored chrome to match their work sector and Finn's simply read, "Brasa", above a barcode that told the story of his arrest and crimes.

While they were being processed to leave, Finn spotted something flying around the courtyard. At first, he thought it was a rare sighting of a bird, but as he squinted his eyes to get a sharper view, he realized to his horror that it was Scraps. His little robot was employing his newly fixed rotor system to hop from location to location, using objects on the landing pad for cover. One moment, Scraps was hiding behind a fuel truck and the next he was peeking out from behind a bright orange hazard cone. Each hop through the air brought the little robot closer to the golden skycar that was waiting to transport them to the Authority sector

"Hey, are you okay? You look like you've seen a ghost," Owen asked, as the pair were shoved forward so that Soren and Corbin could receive their nametags.

"I think I saw Scraps," Finn replied in a hushed tone of voice.

"Scraps?" Owen said, blurting the word out before realizing his mistake and also lowering his voice. "You mean that little oilcan robot you built?" Owen started to look around for the machine but Finn was quick to stop him.

"Yes, but don't look now," Finn said, concerned that a prefect might also spot the robot or, worse, Soren. "If the prefects catch him, he'll be torn down for parts."

Owen nodded and abandoned his search for the machine though, ironically, by trying not to look suspicious, his friend ended up looking even more so.

"Are you sure it was him?" Owen whispered back.

Finn looked toward the orange hazard cone where he'd last seen Scraps, but the robot was gone, and he couldn't see him anywhere else outside. He suddenly doubted whether he'd actually seen Scraps at all and considered the possibility that it had simply been a figment of his imagination.

"I guess it could have been a bird," Finn admitted.

"A bird?" Owen snorted. "When's the last time you saw a bird?"

"Stop talking!" a prefect barked.

Finn and Owen both clamped their jaws shut and stared ahead. Suitably placated, it didn't take long for the prefect to lose interest in them, and Finn chanced speaking again.

"I hope Scraps did manage to get out of my apartment," he said, trying to talk without moving his lips, like a bad ventriloquist. "I can't bear to think of him alone, trapped inside that little cubby until his battery cells run down."

"I said stop talking!"

An electrified nightstick was rammed into Finn's back, pushing him on toward the skycar. He hissed as the pain of the electric shock flooded his body but didn't react, knowing that even looking at the officer the wrong way would likely mean he received another jolt, at an even higher voltage.

Reaching the skycar first, Owen climbed in, then shuffled along the bench to the far side. Finn pulled himself through the narrow opening next then realized that his friend was not the only other offender inside the vehicle. Two women, also from Metalhaven, were on the bench opposite and their nametags simply read, "Maeve" and "Khloe," with accompanying barcodes. Despite being from the same sector the women couldn't have looked more different. Maeve was stocky, but her mass was from muscle not fat. She had the aura of an angry volcano on the verge of erupting. The woman had close-cropped dirty-blonde hair, close-set hazel eyes and easily as many scars as Finn did, at least based off those that were visible on her arms and face. The woman was leaning her head against the skycar's porthole window, looking distinctly bored and not the least bit afraid.

Khloe was another matter entirely. It was difficult to be certain because of her slouched posture, but she looked tall and slender, with a swimmer's physique that was in stark contrast to Maeve's power-lifter build. She had fine red hair that was swept over her face like a veil, perhaps intentionally, but not enough that Finn couldn't see her eyes and read her expression. He was good at reading people, and it seemed clear to him that Khloe had already given up hope, and that she'd given up long before she was seated inside the skycar.

Corbin then grabbed the handrails and pulled himself on to the seat bench next to Finn. The two men glowered at each other, but despite his questionable allegiances, Corbin wasn't as stupid as the man he served like a loyal lieutenant, and he kept his mouth shut. Soren entered next and Finn noticed that the scold's bridle had finally been removed. He was in two minds as to whether this was a good thing. On the one hand, no-one, no matter how big of an asshole they were, deserved to be tortured with that medieval implement, but on the other hand, it meant that Soren was able to speak again.

"At least we're not the only fuck-ups in Metalhaven," Soren said, wasting no time in putting his liberated tongue to use by uttering a stupid comment. "What are you two in for? Refusing to spread your legs?"

Soren laughed and Corbin joined in, though without any real eagerness to participate. Soren's delivery had also been stunted in comparison to the man's usual brashly-confident manner of speaking, and it seemed clear that the bully was putting on a front. Soren was also aggressively rubbing his knuckles to disguise his shaking hands, and Finn figured that the wisecracks were just an attempt to mask the man's insecurities. Perhaps, he figured, they always had been.

"I ain't no whore from the center," Maeve replied, pulling her head away from the window to look Soren squarely in the eyes. "And you'd better watch your mouth, big boy."

"Or what, thunder thighs? You'll sit on me?" Soren answered, before guffawing another strained laugh.

"Quiet back there!" a prefect in the front of the skycar called out through the metal grate that separated the rear cabin from the cockpit section. To Finn's surprise and relief, Soren backed down.

"Why are you both here?" Owen asked.

Unlike Soren, Owen had an honest face and manner that effortlessly drew others towards him. He was the sort of person that people confided in, willingly sharing their thoughts and feelings, knowing they could trust him without reservation. Incredibly this natural charm even worked on Maeve, who had already demonstrated that she was not someone to be trifled with.

"I got this gig because I crotch-shotted some twat who wouldn't take no for answer," Maeve replied. The woman leant forward slightly and glared at Soren again. "You see, some guys just don't know when to shut the fuck up and back down."

Soren snorted with derision and shook his head. "Bullshit, you don't get sent to trial for kicking some useless schmuck in the balls. At most, you'd get a day or two in a cold cell."

Owen was looking pensive, then the big man snapped his fingers, his eyes suddenly bright. "Wait a second, you're Maeve Brockhouse from Yard One, aren't you?" Owen said. "I heard about what you did from the pint puller in our local Recovery Center."

Soren scoffed again. "Ringing some dumb tosser's balls is big news these days, is it?"

Owen shook his head at the man. "She didn't punch the guy in the balls, she went to town on him with a laser cutter and sheared his testicles clean off."

Soren went deathly quiet and blood drained from his face. Maeve smiled then winked and blew a kiss at the man before returning her head to the window and closing her eyes, as if she were trying to catch up on some sleep.

"I heard about that too," Corbin chipped in, but in contrast to Owen's vibrant curiosity, the man was angrier than a rattlesnake. "Did you know that the guy she cut on had a genetic purity rating of four?" Corbin snorted through his nostrils like a wild bull. "You should have been shot on the spot for what you did. Don't you know how valuable guys like us are? Without us, there's no future."

Maeve sighed and opened her eyes but didn't take her head away the window. "And what future is that sweet cheeks?" the woman asked. "You know as well as I do that there's no future for people like us. We work and we die. That's it. I'd rather take my chances in the trial. At least if I win, I get out of this shit life."

Finn suddenly understood why Maeve didn't look scared. The woman had wanted to go to trial, and it seemed clear she had every intention of staying alive, right to the very end. That meant she had guts, and it also meant she was dangerous.

"But even if you outlasted everyone and managed to kill or maim the prosecutors, they'd just make you one of them," Owen said, appalled by Maeve's reasoning. "Winning the trial means you'd become a prosecutor and have to spend the rest of your life hunting and murdering innocent people."

"I don't make the rules," Maeve shrugged. "And let's not be cute and pretend that any of us are innocent. The innocent all got slaughtered centuries ago in the Last War. We're just what's left. The cockroaches who refused to die."

Owen reeled back from Maeve, chilled by the callousness of her answer, and even Soren was unable to conjure up a witty or acerbic comeback. Finn also stayed silent though not because he was too shocked to talk. Maeve had revealed more than enough about herself and her motivations for Finn to not need any more answers. Prosecutors aside, he understood that Maeve Brockhouse was going to be the most dangerous person in their crucible. Instead, Finn turned to the only remaining enigma in the skycar, Khloe, keen to get some insight on how she would react under the intense pressure of a trial.

"What's your story, Khloe?" Finn asked, trying to channel some of Owen's charm and natural friendliness.

Khloe didn't answer and remained placid behind her veil of red hair. Finn frowned and glanced at Owen, hoping that he'd take over and give it another shot. Instead, Maeve answered on behalf of the other woman from Metalhaven.

"Her story is that she actually *was* a whore from a Wellness Center who refused to spread her legs," Maeve said, again surprising everyone with her callousness. "Not putting out is all it takes to get a death sentence in this shithole town, whether you're a man or a woman." She shook her head then stared out of the window again. "And you gorillas think that having a pair of balls makes you special."

Soren looked flabbergasted. "I honest-to-God don't get people like you. You'd rather be dead than lie on your back for ten minutes."

Maeve grunted a laugh. "More like one minute for you, big boy, and I doubt you can even manage that."

At one time, a joke at Soren's expense would have caused the bully to fly off the handle and launch a physical attack, but the man said nothing and did nothing. For all his big talk,

Soren's arrest had shown him to be nothing more than a scared little man, and Maeve had put him firmly in his place.

The skycar's four rotors spun up and the craft lifted off the landing pad so suddenly that Finn had to snatch a grab handle to stop himself sliding off his bench. The jolt of motion also caused Khloe's hair to sweep away from her face, but she quickly brushed it back over her eyes to reestablish her veil. Curiously, Maeve revealing Khloe's secret hadn't elicited a reaction of any kind from the plain-looking woman. She wasn't angry or embarrassed or distraught, and were it not for her physical presence taking up space in the skycar, Finn might not have known she was there at all.

Before long, the craft had reached its cruising altitude of one hundred and fifty meters and the ride had smoothed out. No-one said a word as they travelled toward the sector boundary that separated Metalhaven from the rest of Zavetgrad. None of them had ever ventured beyond the narrow, snow-covered streets of their home sector, so suddenly being able to see Zavetgrad in its entirety was a wonder that they all experienced in reverent silence, accompanied only by the thumping beat of the rotors.

The Authority sector was close to the eastern coastline of the Davis Strait, within easy reach of the sub-oceanic habitats that the Regents and their privileged families and staff inhabited. Finn took the opportunity to look out across the sea, hoping that he might be able to spot land on the other side of the strait, but there was nothing but violent, ice-cold water for as far as he could see. Despite wanting to keep faith with the idea of Haven, he was struggling to believe that anything could survive beyond the small pocket of civilization that was Zavetgrad. Outside the city limits, there was only an endless nothingness, barren, lifeless and as cold as his blood felt at that moment.

Soon, the skycar was passing over the Metalhaven reclamation yards and everyone craned their necks to get a look at their old home. Even Khloe took a break from hiding behind her mask of red hair to look down, but only for a few seconds, before she retreated back into her cocoon.

"I had no idea how big Metalhaven was," Owen commented. "Our ten reclamation yards must make up maybe a quarter of Zavetgrad's total area."

"What the hell are they breaking down over there?" Soren chipped in.

Finn peered out of the closest side window and saw a massive yard on the southern edge of the sector that contained hulks of metal twenty or thirty times the size of the tanks and APCs he and Owen were used to cutting apart.

"They're old naval warships and nuclear submarines," Maeve commented, in a bored voice. "That's Yard One, my old yard," she added. "Part of what we did was break down intercontinental and hypersonic missiles for parts that could be used in the Nimbus project."

"Sounds like dangerous work," Owen observed. He offered the woman a smile, but she shunned his attempt to build a rapport and did not return it.

"It was," Maeve replied, flatly. "The yards are numbered according to how dangerous the work is, with Yard One being the deadliest." She did then smile, but not to be friendly. "What yard are you boys from?"

"Seven," Owen replied, somewhat sheepishly.

"That's cute," Maeve said. "What was it that your boys

broke down in Yard Seven? Old laundry machines and toaster ovens?"

"Yeah, fuck you, Maeve," Soren said, twisting his body to put his back to the woman. "Plenty of workers die in Yard Seven. You're not the only one who's had it tough."

Maeve smiled again but she was content to let it lie on that occasion, and the group continued the journey in silence again until the sight of Volthaven's vast solar farms came into view on the horizon. Finn shifted in his seat to get a better look at the seemingly unending checkerboard of solar panels that stretched across the vast plains of what was once northern Canada. It was like looking out across a sea of shimmering mercury, and Finn found himself mesmerized until the panels gave way to an enormous plantation of ugly chemical fuel cylinders. While solar energy powered Zavetgrad's infrastructure, its fleet of skycars and ground vehicles still relied on chemical fuels, as did its burgeoning armada of Nimbus rockets. Finn watched as an electric freight train hummed away from the primary depot, carrying its precious cargo of fuel to the eight other work sectors along an intricate magnetic rail system. Compared to the rudimentary tools and facilities in Metalhaven, the most advanced of which were the laser cutters they used to split apart tanks and APCs, the rest of Zavetgrad appeared almost futuristic.

"You can just about see the factories of Makehaven over in that direction," Owen said, pointing northwest of their position. "And if you look that way, you can see the greenhouses that produce all the algae we eat."

"I won't miss that disgusting fucking goop," Soren cut in.

"I bet the golds in the Authority sector don't eat plant proteins and shit-tasting algae bread."

"Given the size of your gut, it doesn't look like you abstained much, fatso" Maeve said, teasing Soren with her sharp eyes.

"You can talk, thunder thighs," Soren hit back. It was like watching two kids squabbling in the playground. "If you ask me, you look like a man."

"That's funny, because if you ask me, you don't," Maeve countered.

Finn snorted a laugh and even Corbin struggled to hide his smile. Soren was desperate for a comeback, but the man had been soundly beaten. He cursed under his breath, turned his back on Maeve and returned to staring out of the window. Finally, Soren had met his match, and had there not been the small matter of a death sentence hanging over all of their heads, Finn might have drawn some measure of satisfaction from that fact.

"I thought it would be bigger," Owen said.

"That's what the girls at the Wellness Center say when Soren pulls his pants down," Maeve cut in. Finn laughed again, but Soren steadfastly ignored them both.

"Zavetgrad, I mean," Owen continued, smiling and kicking Maeve's foot with the toe of his boot. "We've almost flown across the entire city already, and most of it is just junkyards, algae fields and solar cells. Where are all the people?"

Finn pointed at the tinted glass canopy above their heads. "The folk that matter are up there," he said, aiming his finger at the Nimbus Space Citadel, which was an ever-present feature of the Zavetgrad sky, as immutable as the stars themselves. "They limit the population down here to a manageable level. The more our numbers increase the more mouths there are to feed."

"That ain't the reason," Maeve grunted, looking Finn in the eyes for the first time since he'd stepped aboard the skycar. "They keep our numbers low because the more we are, the harder we are to control. It ain't about food. It's about preventing an uprising." Maeve then turned her gaze toward Nimbus, but there was no wonder in her hard expression, and certainly no affection. "That's the future, up there, but we ain't ever gonna be a part of it," Maeve continued. "Every year we get fewer and fewer. You must have noticed it too? Eventually, Nimbus will have everything it needs to survive on its own, and when that happens, we'll be left to rot." The woman turned away and rested her head against the glass window. "I say we take what we can, while we can. It's every man and woman for themselves."

Owen physically shivered as a chill raced down the big man's spine, and Finn could see that even Corbin had found Maeve's hopeless assessment of Zavetgrad's future to be unsettlingly bleak. Finn was used to being the one who spouted off doom and gloom predictions of the future, which no-one paid any mind too, and to finally hear someone else echo his opinions wasn't comforting in the slightest.

The skycar suddenly shook as if it had flown through a patch of atmospheric turbulence, but the skies were cloudless and bright. Then a flash of light briefly illuminated the cabin and Finn saw a rocket arcing skyward from a launch site in center of Spacehaven. Everyone shifted position to get a better view, including Khloe, just for a few seconds before retreating back behind her curtain of hair. The rocket accelerated with a terrifying speeda, like a spear thrown by a god, and soon the spacecraft was encroaching on the boundary of space, headed for Nimbus.

"I think that must be our crucible," Owen said. While Finn and the others had been looking up, Owen had turned his attention to the ground, which was drawing nearer as the skycar continued its descent. "Just how many of those damned things do they need?"

No-one bothered to answer Owen's rhetorical question because they were all focused on their destination. It was a major construction project on the outskirts of the city, and Finn could see two part-assembled launch towers, along with a cluster of buildings in various stages of completion, and a fleet of heavy machinery. The area had been cordoned off by a tall, electrified fence and Finn could even see the beginnings of the spectator stands taking shape, along with the VIP area where the Regent of Spacehaven would preside over their slaughter. Hundreds of construction workers, seconded from Stonehaven, had briefly downed tools to watch as the skycar came in to land at the sector's Law Enforcement Hub.

'It looks like we have a welcoming committee," Maeve commented.

Through the porthole window, Finn could see what looked like an entire patrol division of prefects formed up on the landing pad, waiting for them. They were all wearing black riot armor with a mixture of white or orange chest plates, which suggested that the officers were a mix of prefects from both Stonehaven and Spacehaven.

The skycar touched down hard on the pad and the door was flung open. The roar of the rotors rushed inside, drowning out the barked commands that were being shouted at them by prefects on the ground, but Finn didn't need to hear the words to understand that they were being ordered to exit the craft. Corbin and Soren were practically dragged out but Finn jumped down without delay or protest and was spared the sort of rough handling that his Metalhaven compatriots had received. All six offenders were then lined up on the asphalt with their hands on their heads, and the golden skycar lifted off, kicking up a plume of dust that stung Finn's eyes and clung to his throat. An officer confidently strode forward through the haze, nightstick in hand. She was tall and her posture and iron expression exuded the strength and discipline of a gold who had been born and bred to prosecute the role of tyrannical oppressor. Her eyes were soulless blue-gray orbs, while her hair was bleached white like the color of Spacehaven and compressed into a tight, efficient bun.

"My name is Captain Mackenzie Withers," the woman announced, her voice as strong and as confident as her stature. "I am the Head Prefect of Nimbus Sector, and you will obey my commands or be disciplined."

The woman slowly walked the line of offenders, starting at the left with Maeve, who returned the woman's probing gaze without seeming intimidated in the slightest. Owen looked down as did Corbin and Soren, while the veil of hair shrouding Khloe's face meant that her reaction was hidden too. Then Captain Withers reached Finn and the woman stopped. Finn's heart started to race, and the sickly feeling of adrenaline swelled in his gut, but he continued to stare straight ahead, as if looking through the officer rather than at her.

"You are Worker Finn Brasa from Metalhaven?"

Finn frowned and nodded. "Yes, ma'am."

Captain Withers electrified her nightstick and punched it into his gut with breathtaking speed and force. The physical impact combined with the paralyzing electric shock knocked him off his feet, and he came-to moments later to find himself drooling onto the captain's mirror-polished boots. Withers grabbed a thick tuft of his messy hair and yanked Finn's head back so their eyes could meet.

"Captain Roth says hello…"

11

SIX BECOME TWELVE

STILL BLEARY-EYED from the effect of the stun baton, Finn was scooped off the floor by two prefects and hauled to his feet. The officers released their holds as suddenly as they had accosted him, and Finn would have collapsed on the spot had Owen not been there to catch him.

"Shit, Finn, are you okay?" Owen asked.

Finn would have laughed if he had the energy to do so, because it was self-evident that he was far from okay. Even so, he didn't want to present the appearance of weakness, in front of either the prefects or his fellow offenders.

"I'm okay, buddy, thanks," Finn said, though he was still unable to take his full weight onto his shaky legs.

"As touching as it is to see you Metalhaven folk bandy together in support of one another, I urge you to abandon your allegiances," Captain Withers said. "There is only one chance to survive a trial, which is to be the last man or woman still alive when it ends. Not a single one of you can hope to achieve that by helping another."

"We're not going to turn on each other just for your amusement," Owen snapped.

Withers lashed out with her baton and struck Owen across the back of his hand, forcing him to release Finn's arm. His strength had returned enough that he didn't fall flat on his face, but he was barely holding on through force of will alone.

"That was a warning, Worker Thomas," Withers said, aiming her nightstick at the man. "Speak out of turn again, and I will have you muzzled like a dog."

An armored ground vehicle pulled up and a sliding door was flung open. Captain Withers stepped back and nodded to a prefect supervisor who advanced with a dozen men.

"Get inside the vehicle," the supervisor barked, shoving Finn forward while the other officers shepherded Owen and the remaining offenders toward the armored ground car.

Finn staggered through the door and welcomed the chance to sit down, despite the seat inside the vehicle being harder than granite. The others were bundled inside in short order then the door was slammed shut and the vehicle set off at speed. The streets of Spacehaven were soon flashing past the windows, and despite the metal grates that obscured his view, Finn could still see how radically different the sector was compared to Metalhaven. The building designs were sleek like marble and the streets were wide, clean and cleared of snow. It was like they had been transported to another time as well as another place, a time when people lived in comfort and luxury, freed from the hardships of daily life that Finn was used to.

After a few minutes the armored ground car slowed to a stop at a checkpoint and prefects wearing orange-colored riot vests waved them through. The futuristic streets of Spacehaven disappeared and instead Finn was confronted by a vast construction yard, shielded from the Nimbus Space sector by a ten-meter-tall wood-paneled wall. This was the work zone managed by the Construction Division, known to its workers as Stonehaven. Unlike all the other sectors, which had permanent locations, Stonehaven was nomadic, moving from sector to sector, depending on where the next major construction project was.

"This place doesn't look all that different from Metalhaven," Owen commented as the vehicle trundled across the stony, unmettled road.

Finn noticed that many of the workers had downed tools in order to watch the armored car make its procession to the Law Enforcement Hub. The faces of the workers were dirty and drawn, and many were marred by past injuries that had left them physically disfigured or disabled in some way. Finn had known hard work his entire life but he never expected to find a work sector that was more brutal on the body and mind than Metalhaven.

"If you ask me, it looks worse," Finn commented. "Many of these people look worked half-to-death already."

"Our work wasn't exactly easy, either," Soren chipped in. His natural tendency to be an argumentative dick was reasserting itself. "These folk are no worse off than we were."

The vehicle rumbled past a Wellness Center, which was an incongruously-sterile slice of the Authority in the middle of a grubby construction site.

"Hey, big boy, why don't you ask the driver to stop, so you can pay a visit?" Maeve bellowed, hooking her thumb toward the center. "I'm sure it will only take you a minute to blow your load, so it's no real holdup."

Maeve laughed at her own joke and Soren gritted his teeth and turned away, blood rushing to his face, which was burning hot enough to melt the ice on the car's narrow windows. The brothel quickly slipped out of view then the armored car drove past a Recovery Center, which was full to bursting with drunk, off-shift Stonehaven workers. A group spilled out into the streets, laughing and joking, and the driver honked his horn at them aggressively, but the men either ignored the warning, or were too inebriated to hear it. The brakes were slammed on, the doors opened and four prefects jumped out. Nightsticks were electrified and the men were beaten so severely that blood from their wounds colored the snow red. Their bludgeoned bodies were dragged onto the sidewalk and dumped, and the prefects returned to the armored car, which resumed its journey as if nothing untoward had occurred. From that point on, until they arrived at the Law Enforcement Hub, no-one said another word.

Finally, the armored car arrived at its destination and they were roughly manhandled out of the vehicle and into the building through a side entrance. The barren room had only two sets of wooden benches, one on either wall to the left and right as they entered. Above the right-hand bench, strung up on hangers attached to the wall, were six jumpsuits, all in the steel-gray color of Metalhaven.

"Remove your work garments and change into these, then line-up in front of the door at the far end of the room," the prefect supervisor ordered. "Your names are written on the uniforms."

Finn found his uniform, which appeared to be in the correct size, then realized that it was hung up next to the uniform designated for Khloe.

"Hey, aren't there separate changing spaces, or at least a screen?" Finn asked.

"Just shut up and get changed," the supervisor growled, angling his nightstick at Finn.

"What's up sweet cheeks, are you shy?" Maeve said. She had already removed her overalls and was nude from the bottom half down. "A nice-looking lad like you shouldn't be afraid of getting naked."

"I reckon he's got a crooked one," Soren added, glad that Maeve was finally picking on someone else for a change. "Either that, or he just has a really tiny cock!"

It was now Finn's turn to feel his cheeks burn hot, as Maeve, Corbin and Soren all burst into ripples of gaudy laugher. Oddly, the Prefect Supervisor didn't intervene. If anything, Finn thought the man was hoping they'd all set upon each other like wild animals and was encouraging this through his inaction. Then he remembered Captain Withers' recommendation that they abandon allegiances, because it was every man and woman for themselves, and he understood the supervisor's motive. The Authority wanted them at each other's throats, because if they were fighting amongst themselves then they weren't fighting against the prosecutors. Besides, it also made for a more exciting show, he figured.

Finn got changed, keeping his back to the others, but there was no possibility of privacy. Maeve wolf-whistled as he removed his pants, and Soren cracked more jokes about the inadequate size of everyone's manhood compared to his own. Despite his efforts to avoid looking at anyone else out of respect, he couldn't help but notice the deep yellow and brown bruises on Khloe's back. If Maeve's version of why she was on trial was true, then it was likely she had been heavily beaten for refusing work at a Wellness Center. He looked away and tried to put the thought out of his mind but there was no escaping the cruelty and injustice of their situation, and Khloe's crime and subsequent sentence was the most unjust of them all. For refusing to be an indentured sex worker, she had been sentenced to die.

Finn was dressed first and he began the queue in front of the door. Owen arrived a few seconds after then steadily the rest lined up too. Soren and Maeve were last because the unlikely duo had wasted time chasing each other around the room and trying to whip each other with their old work vests, like a couple of drunk lovers on vacation. The door was then opened and they were marched into another space, which was clinical and spartan, besides a device in the center that resembled an X-ray security scanner. Captain Withers was also inside, along with six other offenders, each dressed in a jumpsuit like the one Finn was wearing but in the unique color of that individual's work sector. There were also a dozen more armed prefects, all of whom looked ready to pounce on the workers and beat them senseless at the drop of a hat.

"When your name is called, stand on the bioscanner and remain there until I say you can go," Captain Withers announced. Some unseen microphone was amplifying her voice, "then line up against the far wall and await further instructions." Withers referred to a sheet of paper on a clipboard in her hand then cleared her throat. "Worker Parker Davis, Volthaven. Crime: Negligent destruction of valuable resources."

A man wearing the red of the Power Production sector shuffled forward and stood on the bioscanner. He was missing his right-arm below the shoulder, and Finn figured it was likely the result of an accident related to the explosive rocket fuel that his sector produced.

"Worker Linden Hayes, Stonehaven. Crime: Liability to the state."

A haggard-looking man in an orange jumpsuit replaced Parker on the bioscanner. The worker was probably in his mid-forties, which was practically ancient for Stonehaven, but it was clear that the man was unfit to work because he could barely stand. This was what being a 'liability to the state' actually meant. Yet, even if you couldn't work, you could still prove useful by dying for the edification of the masses.

"Worker Skye Brooks, Stonehaven. Crime: Refusing a transfer order to the wellness center."

A short woman with extensive electrical burns to her hands, and fingernails that had been gnawed so short that they bled, replaced her Construction sector co-worker on the scanner. Her crime was the same as Khloe's – refusing to become a prostitute.

"Worker Grayson Wright, Makehaven. Crime: Grievous Violence against a Prefect."

A man in a purple jumpsuit approached the scanner, chattering to himself, though it was an incoherent babble of nonsense. The man was lanky and had bulging, wild eyes. As the bioscanner assessed him, Finn saw the number readout flash up zero twice. *A double-zero. Cannon fodder...* he thought.

"Worker Melody Fisher, Seedhaven. Crime: Homicide due to incompetence."

An attractive woman with curly, red hair stepped onto the scanning bed. She looked sad and resigned, and also familiar. Then Finn remembered an evening in the Recovery Center a few days earlier when several workers were talking about a woman from Seedhaven who had caused over a hundred deaths. She had apparently used contaminated water to produce a batch of algae that contained dangerous amounts of heavy metals. The product was quickly recalled but by then it was too late.

"Worker Cora Quinn, Spacehaven. Crime: Attempted desertion."

There were murmurs of interest from the others in the room, which were quickly silenced by the prefect supervisor, but everyone knew Worker Cora was a special case. Spacehaven workers were intelligent and educated, because they had to be in order to work on the Nimbus spacecraft. However, while they were afforded certain privileges and generally had a higher quality of life than the other workers, they were not golds, and they would never be permitted entry to the Nimbus Space Citadel. Cora, it seemed, had tried to get there under her own initiative, and it was going to cost the shrewd-looking woman her life.

Maeve was called next and her crimes of grievous violence and damage to a genetically-viable worker, matched what she'd already told them, as did Khloe's crime of refusing to work in a Wellness Center. There was considerable interest as Soren was called up and his crime was read out. "Contempt of the Authority by causing an affray in the presence of a Regent," was the most trumped-up nonsense charge out of everything they'd heard so far, and even Maeve looked shocked. Finn was called last, but in addition to the nothing charge that had gotten Owen and the others sent to trial, he had the added crime of "grievous violence against a prefect." It didn't take a genius to figure out that Finn had been the architect of the others' downfall, and the appalled and accusatory stares that he received as he walked from the scanner to the wall confirmed this.

The scanner device then descended into the floor and Captain Withers advanced, flanked by a dozen armed prefects. The woman handed her clipboard to her prefect supervisor then cleared her throat for a second time. Finn figured this was merely her pretentious way of preparing everyone to listen, rather than because she actually had an obstruction to clear.

"Your trial is scheduled for tomorrow at twenty-one hundred hours," Withers began.

There was a mixed reaction from the twelve assembled offenders, ranging from angry curses to frightened pleas until the crack of a gunshot shocked the room into silence. The supervisor had discharged his weapon into the wall above their heads, and as Finn glanced up, he could see many other similar bullet holes from earlier demonstrations of the prefect's authority. A chill then ran down his spine as he saw a hole at head height, close to where Corbin was standing. The wall had been scrubbed clean, but a faint spattering of blood was still visible.

"You have all watched trials before, so you know what to expect," Withers continued, content that her supervisor's demonstration of force had been effective. "Even so, it is our duty to explain what will happen tomorrow."

Withers took a step back and the prefect supervisor took her place, clipboard in hand.

"Your crucible is a one-mile by one-mile section of an under-construction Nimbus spacecraft launch facility," the supervisor began, in a plummy tone of voice. "Two prosecutors will enter the crucible with you. After a one-hundred-second head start, they will hunt you down and deliver swift justice."

Finn huffed a laugh under his breath. *Justice... What he means is death.*

"You are not permitted to escape the crucible. If you do so then you will be executed on the spot," the supervisor continued. "Your one chance of survival is to become the last man or woman standing. This means that all the other offenders are dead, and that both prosecutors have either been killed or incapacitated. If you achieve this then you will be granted clemency, and elevated to gold status, after which you will be transferred to the Authority sector and trained as a prosecutor."

Finn glanced at Maeve, and she was literally rubbing her knuckles in anticipation of getting started. Despite all her jokes, she was deadly serious about winning.

"Note that fewer than one in two-thousand offenders have ever achieved this feat, and that most that did, died shortly afterwards from injuries sustained in the crucible," the supervisor cautioned. "In order for you to become the next worker to win a trial, you must forsake all allegiances to your sectors and colleagues, and fight to become the sole survivor."

Parker, the man from Volthaven, raised his only arm. The supervisor scowled at the worker then glanced at Captain Withers, seeking her assent to take questions, and the officer nodded her approval.

"What is it, Worker Parker?"

"Sir, will we be given weapons?" Parker asked.

Soren snorted. "Haven't you ever seen a trial before, dumbass?"

The supervisor glowered at Soren and the man wisely backed down and looked at his shuffling feet.

"No, you will not be provided with anything beyond the uniforms you are wearing now, but any item that you find inside the crucible can be used as a weapon."

Finn glanced along the line but it didn't seem that anyone else was going to ask a question. However, since Parker had set a precedent, he decided to take a chance and ask one of his own.

"Sir, can you tell us who our prosecutors will be?"

The supervisor clearly didn't know the answer because the man looked embarrassed and had to again turned to his captain. Withers adopted a pouty expression and seemed angry, and Finn wished that he'd kept his mouth shut. Then, to his surprise, the officer actually responded.

"Very well, Worker Brasa," Captain Withers replied. "Normally, I would not countenance such a request, but in your case, I want you to know who will be hunting you inside the crucible." The woman then smiled, which implied that the choices were not beneficial to their chances of survival. "You will be facing Bloodletter and The Shadow."

"Fuck..."

It was Soren who had cursed and for good reason. Bloodletter had more confirmed kills than any other prosecutor in all of Zavetgrad. He was a sadistic torturer, who killed by dealing grievous wounds to offenders then letting them slowly bleed out and die. The man used a crossbow with special bolts that were designed to expand on impact and rip open flesh, rather than penetrate deeply. Then there was The Shadow, Elara Cage, the former Metalhaven worker who had famously survived her trial by being the last woman standing. Finn had already seen how deadly Elara Cage could be, and in combination with Bloodletter, it seemed that their deaths were mere formalities. This was, of course, the reason why Captain Withers had been more than happy to reveal their identities ahead of the trial.

Finn again glanced along the line and saw the sea of blank and terrified faces staring back. Even Soren couldn't manage to put on a front. Then he looked at Maeve and she was the exception. The powerful woman from Metalhaven had not been deterred by hearing the names of their soon-to-be assassins. If anything, she looked even more determined, and Finn was more certain than ever that she was as much a threat as the prosecutors.

"That is enough questions," Captain Withers said, shattering the icy silence. "You will now be separated into two groups according to your genetic viability and sent for processing."

Prefects advanced and rough-handled the twelve offenders into two sets, in opposite corners of the room. Finn found himself back with Owen, while Soren, Khloe and Maeve ended up in the opposite corner, among those unable to provide viable seed or eggs.

"Don't fight them this time, Finn," Owen whispered when the prefects weren't looking in their direction. "We need to save our strength so we can escape, remember?"

Finn nodded and smiled. "Don't worry, I won't cause a fuss. I have no desire to be stabbed in the balls without anesthetic this time."

His answer put Owen at ease, but not for long before other worries encroached upon the man's mind.

"Do you think we still have a chance to get out?" Owen added, so quietly that Finn struggled to hear him. "There must be a way, right, like you said?"

"I'm certain of it, Owen," Finn answered, hoping that his face hid the truth. "Just stick with me and stay alive. Can you do that?"

Owen smiled and nodded then held out his fist. "We're in this together, okay? You and me."

Finn bumped fists with his friend in solidarity of their pact but the truth was that he had told Owen a lie – the first lie he ever told his friend. With the crucible set inside Spacehaven, there was no possibility of escape. The only way that any of them would survive was by becoming the last man or woman standing. Finn had gotten his friend into this mess, and he was determined to ensure that Owen walked free, even if that meant sacrificing his own life in the process.

12

LAST MEAL

Finn opened his eyes then had to squint to dim the harsh glow from the overhead strip lights inside the treatment room. He felt groggy and his mouth was like cotton wool, but neither of those unpleasant sensations held a candle to the dull, throbbing ache in his groin.

"Just how much of my 'seed' did you take?" Finn asked, while delicately cradling his parts as if they were fragile eggs. It felt like someone had repeatedly punched him in the balls with brass knuckles.

"As much as we could reasonably get. After all, you are a double-five."

The bed was raised and Finn saw Captain Withers by the door, as usual guarded by a quartet of heavily-armed officers. The only other person in the room was the doctor who had just performed the T.E.S.A. procedure on him. He could still see the five-inch-long needle in a kidney tray by the side of the bed.

"I must confess, I considered petitioning the Regent of Metalhaven to commute your sentence, given the value of your genetic material," Withers continued, as Finn slid his legs off the side of the bed and sat upright. "It seems a shame to waste a double-five in a trial."

"Then why didn't you?" Finn asked, genuinely curious.

Withers smiled her well-practiced malicious smile. "Because Viktor and I are, shall we say, old friends," the officer replied, referring to Captain Viktor Roth, Head Prefect of Metalhaven. "Personally, I prefer a rugged-looking man, so the scar that you gave him does not bother me, but Viktor thinks otherwise."

Finn huffed a laugh. Though Withers had danced around the point, the fact she and Captain Roth were sexual partners explained a lot.

"I don't suppose that he'll accept an apology?" Finn asked.

"I'm afraid not," Withers replied, though there was no hint of remorse in her answer. "He's actually very much looking forward to you being ripped to shreds by Bloodletter, though my money is on The Shadow killing you. We're going to have a party, either way. It's not often that Viktor gets to visit Spacehaven, so we're going to make it a special night."

"I'm very happy for you both," Finn replied, sarcastically. "I'm sure you two will make wonderfully sadistic babies."

A prefect surged forward and smashed his nightstick across Finn's left thigh, dropping him to one knee. The weapon was raised again, but Captain Withers called for the officer to halt. Hissing with pain, Finn grasped his leg then saw the captain approach out of the corner of his eye.

"You don't know when to shut up, do you, Worker Brasa?" Withers grasped Finn's chin and forced him to look at her. "If the Regent wasn't adamant that his offenders be in tip-top condition for the trial, I would have you strapped to that bed and your mouth sewn shut. Nod if you understand me."

Finn nodded, then Withers shoved his chin, snapping his head back and almost causing him to fall over backwards. The officer backed away and nodded to the doctor, who stabbed him in the side of his neck with another needle. Cursing, he almost lashed out at the man for jumping on him without warning but managed to stop himself. The prefects in the room didn't need much of an excuse to employ their nightsticks in anger and Finn didn't want to give them one.

"That shot contained a serum that counteracts the effects of your anesthesia and will allow you to better enjoy what comes next," Withers explained.

Finn was afraid to ask what *did* come next but he didn't need to because Withers then opened the door of the treatment room and walked through it.

"Move!" one of the prefects barked.

Finn complied and hobbled through the door on account of the bruise that was rapidly developing on his thigh. He half-expected Withers to lead him to a cell but instead he entered a grand space that resembled a ballroom from a more civilized era in Earth's history. The other eleven offenders were already inside, and given their wonderstruck expressions, he guessed they had also only just entered.

"What is this?" Finn asked. A prefect delivered a stinging slap across the side of his face, and Finn again hissed with pain. "What is this, ma'am? ..." he corrected himself, while trying not to shoot dagger eyes at the man who had hit him.

Withers grinned, though this could have been due to the

enjoyment of watching her officer smack Finn around the face.

"Your last meal, Worker Brasa," Withers said, managing to make every word she spoke sound spiteful. "I suggest you enjoy it."

Captain Withers departed with her entourage, leaving Finn alone with the other offenders. He hobbled toward Owen, who was gawping, open-mouthed, at a table on the western wall that was stacked high with food, the likes of which he'd only ever seen in pictures. There was real fruit, meat and vegetables, some of which Finn recognized from his late-night studies, reading the data device that he had illegally concealed in his apartment. Another table contained dozens of bottles of dark red and amber liquids, along with a keg of beer that appeared to have come direct from a Recovery Center. A much smaller table beside that was laden with cigarettes and cigars, all containing the mood-soothing narcotic that his friend was practically hooked on.

"It's a fucking party!" Soren bellowed.

Soren slapped Corbin on the back then made a beeline for the table of drinks. He poured himself a pint of beer, downed it in one, then grabbed a bottle with an elegant swan neck that contained a ruby-red liquid.

"What the hell is this shit?" Soren said, sniffing the open bottle. He placed it to his lips and drank heartily, his eyes widening with each gulp. "Fuck me, this is amazing!" he added, before belching loudly. "It's a hundred times better than the filth they give us in the Recovery Centers."

"Be careful, big boy," Maeve said, snatching the bottle from Soren's grasp and taking a long swig from it. "This stuff will put you on your ass faster than a jolt from a prefect's nightstick."

Soren grabbed the bottle right back. "Then you'd better not drink any, thunder thighs," he hit back. "With an ass the size of yours, falling over could cause an earthquake."

Finn raised an eyebrow, curious to learn how Maeve was going to respond. He figured that she would either punch Soren on the nose and their last meal would descend into a brawl before anyone even managed to take a bite, or she'd join in with the fun. Thankfully, for all of their sakes, it was the latter, and Maeve burst into shrieks of laugher, before grabbing two more bottles from the table and carrying them to an alcove in the wall. Soren and Corbin followed, each of them picking up more booze enroute.

"We'd better get something before those greedy bastards take it all," Owen said.

Finn nodded but noticed that his friend was eyeing up the cigarettes on the table, rather than the spread of food.

"Stick to eating and drinking," Finn said, spotting the beads of sweat on his friend's brow, which were tell-tale signs of withdrawal. "The Authority hasn't put on this spread out of the goodness of their own hearts. They want us fattened, stoned and hung over when the trial starts, to make us easier prey. Don't fall for it."

Owen wiped the sweat from his skin but nodded his agreement, before turning toward the buffet. "We can still eat, though, right?"

Finn smiled. "You bet your ass we can…" He raced his friend to the table and grabbed the largest plates they could find, but faced with such a variety on unfamiliar foods, Owen was quickly stumped.

"What even *is* this stuff?" Owen asked, afraid to place anything on his plate in case it might be poison.

"That is meat, probably chicken," Finn said, pointing to a bowl of drumsticks. "Those red orbs are tomatoes, the yellow blocks look like cheese, and I think this is called a hamburger."

Finn picked up the hamburger, which was thick and dripping with grease.

"It smells good. What it is?"

"It's some kind of ground-up meat patty, fried and sandwiched between two bread buns," Finn replied, again drawing upon his secret knowledge. "The green stuff I think is called 'lettuce', and there's usually some cheese too."

"It looks weird," Owen complained. "I like what I'm used to."

It seemed that Owen was about to put the burger back on the table, but Finn stopped him.

"Hey, take a chance," Finn said, while continuing to load his own plate. "We'll never get to eat like this again, even after we escape, so I say we make the most of it."

Owen considered this then shrugged and took a massive bite out of the burger. At first his expression was confused, then surprised, then practically orgasmic. "Oh wow..." Owen said, mumbling the words because his mouth was full. He took another huge bite then threw his head back in an exalted manner. "This is *so good*..."

Finn laughed and continued to gather items onto his plate, though he was snacking on the hors d'oeuvres at the same time as serving himself. Owen was right, the food did taste incredible.

"Fucking hell, this is a real fish!" Soren boomed, a salmon

fillet flopping in his fat fingers. With a belly full of beer and wine, the man had seemingly lost the ability to moderate the volume of his gruff voice. "Only the gold bastards in the Authority Division get to eat real fish, while the rest of us get algae muck."

"Enjoy it, big boy, you won't get another chance..." Maeve said.

The woman snatched the fish out of Soren's hand and shoved it into her grinning mouth. Soren roared with laughter then grabbed another fish fillet and mashed it into his own mouth before piling more food onto an already overfull plate.

"Those two were about to kill each other only an hour ago, and now look at them," Owen muttered, shaking his head.

"Let them have their fun," Finn replied, trying to ignore the raucous shrieks from across the other side of the room. "Besides, if Soren's big mouth is full of food, then it means we don't have to listen to him yammer on."

Finn and Owen finished filling their plates then detoured past the drinks table, grabbing a couple of bottles of wine enroute. In addition to the alcoves there were also smaller tables and chairs set out in the middle of the room. Finn claimed one and dropped into the chair, immediately regretting it as his bruised testicles bounced off the metal seat, causing his body to seize up in agony. Once his breath had returned, he took a swig of wine, which was rich and sweet, like nothing he'd ever tasted, and immediately felt better.

Finn continued to eat while he surveyed the room. Soren, Corbin and Maeve had wasted no time availing themselves of the refreshments, and were squeezed into one of the dark alcoves, but the others had been far more subdued in their choices. Linden and Skye, the two oranges from Stonehaven, were sitting together near the east wall. Linden, the older man whom the Authority had deemed too physically debilitated to work, was hitting the drink hard, while Skye seemed content to watch and observe, like a vulture waiting for someone to keel over and die.

Parker, the one-armed man from Volthaven, and Melody, the red-headed green from Seedhaven, also sat together, and Finn wondered if they were bonding over their shared history of causing fatal accidents. It made him realize that, despite Captain Wither's attempts to turn everyone against each other, allegiances were still alive and well, at least for some. Grayson, the purple from Makehaven was an exception. The strung-out man sat alone in the corner, continuing to mutter incoherently to himself. Then there was Cora, who was also alone but seemingly by choice. The woman from Spacehaven sat as far away from everyone else as possible with a sensible portion of food and a glass of what appeared to be plain water in front of her.

"Where's Khloe?" Owen asked. His friend was already half-way through his massive plate.

Finn scowled and looked around the room before spotting their fellow Metalhaven worker in the same alcove as Maeve, Soren and Corbin. She was tucked into the corner, smoking a cigarette, which was the only item of comfort that she'd availed herself of. The woman looked weak and tired, and considering the ordeal they were about to face, Finn decided that she needed more than nicotine and narcotics to sustain her.

"Save my seat, I'll be back in a second," Finn said.

Owen mumbled a reply through a mouthful of pizza then Owen slid out of his chair and returned to the buffet table. He plated up a few items, including some Metalhaven staples like algae bread, then grabbed an ale and carried them over to the alcove. Soren and Corbin were too busy swilling liquor and joking amongst themselves to notice Finn approach, but Maeve hadn't taken her eyes off him from the moment he'd gotten out of his seat.

"Here, you need to eat something," Finn said, sliding the plate and pint of beer in front of Khloe. She looked at the food then looked at him before blowing a plume of smoke into the air.

"Thanks," she said, though she left the plate untouched.

"Aren't you the gentleman, sweet cheeks?" Maeve said, a grin expanding across her grease-stained mouth. "Are you going to serve something up for me too?" She waggled her eyebrows suggestively. "I know what you're packing inside that snug little outfit."

Finn looked at the carnage of empty plates and bottles on the table and laughed.

"I think you've already have enough," he replied, ignoring Maeve's innuendo.

"Then how about I give you something instead?" Maeve added. She looked him up and down then licked her lips. "One last fuck before the end of the world? What do you say?"

Soren swiveled his sizable frame and glared at Finn with jealous eyes. Maeve's proposal had secured the man's undivided attention.

"Don't bother with that pussy, he's probably still a virgin," Soren said, and Corbin laughed on cue. The bully then puffed out his chest and flashed his eyes at Maeve. "What you need is a real man. Someone who can satisfy you."

Maeve leaned into Soren and beckoned him closer. For one shocking and revolting moment, Finn thought they were going to kiss.

"If I see a real man, I'll let you know..."

Corbin burst out laughing and Soren slapped him across the chest with the back of his hand, causing the man to spit beer all across the table, including over Khloe's still untouched plate of food. The trio then returned to their boisterous ribbing of one another and Finn made a rapid retreat. He'd done his best to help Khloe but if she wasn't going to help herself then she was on her own. Turning back to his own table, he noticed that Owen was no longer there. His heart rate climbed for a moment, then he saw his friend sitting with Cora and he breathed a sigh of relief. Finn rejoined his worker buddy and sat down at the table, though while Cora seemed to have been charmed by Owen's affable nature, she was wary of him.

"I thought you'd run out on us," Finn said, also trying to turn on the charm. Cora remained steadfastly aloof toward him.

"Cora was just telling me how far she got," Owen said.

"How far she got to where?" Finn asked.

"To Nimbus, of course." Owen sparked up a match and lit a cigarette before handing it to Cora, then lighting another.

"When did you sneak those off the table?" Finn asked, scowling at his friend.

"When you were being propositioned by Maeve," Owen replied, plucking the cigarette out of his mouth and smirking at him. "I, for one, am very glad that you didn't accept her offer."

Finn snorted a laugh. "No shit. That's a trial that I don't think anyone would survive."

The two friends laughed and Finn figured that one last narcotic-laced cigarette wasn't likely to be the end of them, so he snatched the stick out of his friend's hands and took a long drag on it. The nicotine kick was instant, like having pure oxygen piped into his brain, then the mellowing effect of the drugs hit a few moments later.

"I got as far as the boarding tunnel leading into the spacecraft's passenger capsule," Cora said.

Finn recoiled from the woman, not even trying to hide the fact he was more than a little skeptical. "You really got that far?" he asked. "Ten more meters and we wouldn't be talking now, because you'd already be in orbit."

"Don't remind me," Cora replied.

In other circumstances, he might have probed Cora further to look for holes in her story but he figured there was no reason for her to lie, so took her at face value. Despite this, he still didn't understand why she had gambled her life – and lost – in order to reach the space citadel.

"Is it really so much better up there?" Finn asked, jabbing the half-smoked cigarette toward the ceiling. Owen snatched it back as he did so. "Is Nimbus worth risking your life for?"

Cora laughed and shook her head at him, genuinely flabbergasted at the question.

"You wouldn't ask that if you knew," the white-sector worker replied. "Nimbus is always seventy-five degrees with low humidity. There's no ice, no snow, and the people up there eat and drink like this every single day. The water is pure, the showers are hot, and no-one is worked to death, or forced to do something they don't want to do." Cora laughed again and tapped ash from her cigarette onto her empty plate. "Nimbus is paradise. If people knew what it was really like, they'd kill to get there."

Finn massaged his face and studied the woman. Nothing she'd said had surprised him, apart from the last sentence. "Did you?" he asked. "Kill someone, I mean?"

Cora glared at him and it was clear that the question and what it insinuated had angered and insulted her. "No," the woman replied, plainly. "I don't have it in me, which is a shame, considering what happens next." She sighed and took another long drag from the cigarette. "I guess that means I'll be one of the first to die tomorrow. The only question is whether the prosecutors kill me, or someone in this room does."

"Hey, you don't have to worry about that, at least not with us," Owen said, speaking with feeling. The man then hooked a thumb to the dark alcove on the other side of the room, where Soren and his cohort were partying. "I can't vouch for them, though."

"Don't worry, I'm going to stay well clear of Maeve and those morons," Cora replied.

Finn smiled, noticing how the Spacehaven worker had highlighted Maeve as the greatest threat, and not Soren or Corbin. It only emphasized how smart and observant the woman was.

"Hey, how do they get water up there?" Owen asked, suddenly veering off on a tangent. "You said the water is pure and the showers are hot, but where the hell does the water come from?"

"They mine ice from asteroids, mainly," Cora replied, shrugging. "You'd be surprised how much water there is just floating around in the void. And they recycle everything too, so they have vastly more than they need. The surplus actually gets used to generate oxygen for the air systems and hydrogen for fuel, using a process called photocatalysis, or water splitting."

Owen shook his head in amazement. "With smarts like yours, I'm surprised you're not up on Nimbus already."

Owen's question unintentionally struck a nerve and Cora began to scratch at the table with her fingernails to take out her frustrations. "I'm not up there because I'm sterile," she replied, bitterly. "You need more than brains to be on Nimbus, at least if you're a woman."

Finn sighed and massaged his face again, which was beginning to feel stiff and tired. He could understand why a low-bred worker like himself was never going to make the cut, despite being a double-five, but Cora was intelligent and clearly also resourceful, given how close she had gotten to escaping. The fact that being unable to bear children barred her entry to paradise seemed cruel, even for the Authority.

"I'm surprised those gold bastards don't ship up sterile men and women to use as sex workers," Owen commented. He had slouched down in his chair and was brooding like a dark cloud. "I suppose they have their own special class of hookers on Nimbus."

"I'm more surprised they didn't send some wellness workers to us, to make this a proper orgy," Finn added.

He was only half-joking but for some reason Owen laughed as if it were the funniest thing he'd heard in years.

"Looks like Soren already has that taken care of," his friend said, cocking his head toward the dark alcove.

Finn looked and wished he hadn't. Corbin and Khloe had both retreated from the alcove and for good reason, because the private space was now bring used for a private deed. Maeve was naked and sprawled out on the table and Soren's jumpsuit had been yanked down around his ankles. All Finn could see was Soren's hairy ass, thrusting back and forth like his life depended on it. The grunts and moans only added to Finn's torment.

"Kill me now and get this over with..." Finn said, pressing his eyes tight shut.

There was silence from the others, which Finn found hurtful, because he thought his comment had been genuinely funny. He opened his eyes to see Owen face down on the table, drool leaking from the corner of his mouth. Cora had also passed out in her chair. He went to grab his friend to shake him awake but suddenly he lost all feeling in his body and his eyes began to darken.

"What... the..." Finn began, but he was face down on the table, unconscious, before he could finish the sentence.

13

CANNON AND FLARE

Finn was jolted awake to the sound of a horn blaring and lights flashing on and off. He peeled his face off the table, massaged his aching jaw and tried to collect himself. The last thing he remembered was passing out in the room where the offenders had gathered for their last meal, and a quick look around him suggested he was still in the same place. Cora was stirring ahead of him, roused by the strobing lights, and Owen was already upright, groaning and rubbing his temples, like he was suffering from a heavy hangover. Another horn blared, then the lights finally stopped flashing and remained on.

"What the hell is going on?" Owen groaned.

Finn recalled that this was going to be his exact question before passing out, and he still didn't have the answer. Shuffling his chair back, he checked on the other offenders to see if they were in a similar state to himself, and if anything, they were worse. Soren and Maeve had collapsed, still naked and intertwined. Linden and Skye from Stonehaven were picking themselves off the floor, seemingly having fallen while making their way back from the buffet table, while the rest had been luckier and gone comatose while they were sitting down. At first, Finn thought Corbin was missing, until he spotted the man draped over a bistro table in the middle of the room, desperately clinging on to it like it was a life raft in stormy seas.

Suddenly, a door at the opposite end of the room to which they had originally entered was flung open and a dozen prefects marched inside, armed with pistols and nightsticks. Captain Withers strode in next, an amused smirk curling her lips, then sounded an air-horn into the room that was somehow even louder than the sirens that had instigated their rude awakening.

"Wakey, wakey, offenders!" Wither shouted before sounding the airhorn twice more. "Your trial begins in thirty minutes."

The captain's announcement did more to rouse Finn than any flashing light, alarm or airhorn could ever have managed. He jumped out of his chair and staggered into a table a few meters away, grabbing onto it for support, just as Corbin was doing. He looked at the clock on the wall and it read eight-thirty in the evening. Withers was not joking. Their trial was less than half an hour away.

"You drugged us?" Finn realized.

Withers approached him, watched closely by four of her prefect bodyguards, and drew up a chair at the table that Finn had clamped himself to.

"It's much easier this way," the captain said, rolling her nightstick back and forth across the tabletop. "Experience has taught us that allowing too much time between arrest and trial simply makes offenders become anxious and on edge. By the time they enter the crucible, fear has reduced them to gibbering wrecks, and the kills come too quickly and easily. Trials are an adversarial process, so the struggle to survive is a key part of delivering justice."

Finn laughed in the woman's face, which he knew was unwise, but he couldn't help himself. "You disgust me," he said, risking the captain's wrath. "This isn't justice. This is just a twisted game for the amusement of the golds."

Withers snatched her nightstick into her hand then hammered Finn's fingers, forcing him to release his hold on the table and crumple to the ground. He was still too groggy to stand unaided.

"Careful, Worker Brasa, or I will deliver your justice in this very room, and report to the Regent that you died suddenly of a heart attack." The woman stood up then slowly rounded the table before crouching beside him. "No-one will miss you, Worker Brasa. No-one cares if you die here or die in the crucible. You were born from nothing and you will die as nothing."

Finn dared to look the woman in the eyes but he clamped his jaw shut to make sure he didn't speak what was on his mind and get himself killed. He couldn't help Owen escape if he was already dead, and finding a way to keep his friend alive was the only motivation he had left to keep breathing.

"Fuck!"

All eyes turned to the dark alcove. Soren was finally awake, panicking and trying desperately to pull his skin-tight jumpsuit back up over his thick legs and bulbous gut.

"What the fuck is going on?!"

Withers marched over to Soren and the man realized his

mistake and snapped to attention like a first-year cadet at the prefect training academy.

"Your trial, Worker Driscoll, that is what's going on," Wither replied, at the same time as stroking her nightstick up and down the center of Soren's bare chest. She was briefly flicking the power on and off at a low setting, causing Soren to spasm like he was having a seizure. The captain then spotted Maeve, who was still collecting herself, and eyed the naked woman up and down like she was a steer at a market. "Though it seems that something else was going on until my drugs interrupted you." She laughed. "How tragic..."

Maeve staggered out the alcove, jumpsuit in one hand and bottle of wine in the other. Unlike Soren, she couldn't have cared less that she was naked, or that Captain Withers and a dozen armed prefects were gawping at her. The woman from Metalhaven briefly considered drinking from the bottle but thought better of it and tossed it over her head, before pulling on the jumpsuit and flopping into a chair, all without uttering a word.

"Wake him up," Withers said, pointing to Corbin with her nightstick. The man hadn't yet managed to unclamp himself from the bistro table. "Then all offenders will line up in front of the door."

Two prefects unfurled a fire hose from the wall and turned on the stream full blast. The ice-cold water smacked into Corbin's face and knocked him to the floor, but the prefects continued to drench him, despite his cries and protests, to the point where Corbin was half-drowned. The gleeful expressions on the faces of the officers would have turned Finn's stomach, were he not already feeling nauseous from the drugs. At the same time, Owen and Cora helped to pick Finn off the floor and together they formed up in a line, as ordered. The rest of the offenders quickly joined in behind them, with Corbin last. The man was shivering and coughing water up from his lungs like he'd just been pulled out of the freezing water of the Davis Strait.

"Drink this tonic," Withers said, pointing to a side table containing twelve paper cups that had been placed against the wall in the corridor leading out of the room.

Finn was at the head of the line and he approached the table first and picked up a cup. It was half-filled with a lime-green liquid that had the consistency of milk.

"It is not poison, Worker Brasa," Withers said, with a haughty air of exasperation, like a schoolmistress who was having to explain a concept to a student for the third time. "We want you fit for the trial, remember?"

"Then what is it?" Finn asked. Withers thumped him in the gut and he almost dropped the cup at his feet. "I mean, what is it, ma'am?" he said, this time with the expected deference.

"It is merely an isotonic drink with some additives that will help to flush the sedative we gave you from your system," Withers answered, perhaps hoping that humoring Finn would speed things along. "Drink it or don't drink it. I really do not care."

Finn nodded then held out the cup before slowly tipping its contents onto the floor. A prefect moved toward him and electrified his nightstick but Withers held up a hand and the officer obeyed and withdrew.

"Defiant to the very end, Worker Brasa," Withers said, now sounding more bored than exasperated. "I admire your consistency, if nothing else."

The captain nodded to the prefect who ushered Finn through the door and into an open courtyard. It was already dark outside and snow was falling lightly around him but the air was still. He looked up at the full moon, which was cutting through the clouds and causing the snow-covered roads and buildings to give off an ethereal glow, as if the ice was irradiated like the rest of their dead planet. A single armored ground car was waiting to take them to their crucible, and Finn was struck with the sudden, chilling reality that within minutes he could be dead.

At least it's a beautiful night, he thought, contemplating the prospect of his death for the first time. Up until that moment, it had all seemed like a dream. Turning back, he watched the other offenders file past the table of paper cups and smiled as not a single one of them drank, not even Soren. They were a varied group of wildly different people from different sectors but in that moment, they were united by a common hatred of the Authority.

Once all the offenders were assembled, they were marched into the armored ground car, which took off at speed. This time there were no windows to provide a view of the outside world, but the increasing rumble of the crowd that had gathered to watch the trial told Finn they were closing in on their crucible. Terror suddenly gripped him and he had to squeeze his fists so tightly that his fingernails bit into his flesh in order to stave off the fear. Others were coping less well, and in addition to frightened murmurs and the constant incoherent babble from Grayson, Finn could smell urine, and see it pooling on the deck around his boots. He had no idea who had lost control of their bladder, and he didn't care to know, for fear that the culprit might have been himself.

The ground car suddenly halted and the door was thrown open, letting in the full roar of the crowd. Prefects grabbed their arms and yanked them outside, before marching them to their starting positions in the dead center of the crucible. Finn looked at the hovering TV screens and the spectator stands, filled with whites from Spacehaven and oranges from Stonehaven. He remembered sitting in a stand just like it, little more than a day ago, though exactly how long it had been, he honestly wasn't sure. What he did remember was how the workers of Metalhaven had laughed and drank, and bet on who would die first and last, and which prosecutor would get the first kill. He despised that the golds had turned the deaths of honest men and women into a sport for the entertainment of the masses. Whilst being forced to endure the senseless slaughter of fellow workers in the trial in Reclamation Yard seven, he thought his hatred of the Authority had peaked. How wrong he had been.

The sound of the Regent's voice floated past Finn's ears, but he couldn't make out any of the words the aristocrat had spoken over the shrill, ringing sound in his ears. He lifted his chin and allowed the snow to caress his face then looked toward the two rocket launch towers inside the crucible. Once completed, the towers would house the next generation of spacecraft. The Nimbus Solaris Ignition V was reputed to have a five-hundred metric ton lift capacity, and the ability to ferry hundreds of precious, genetically-pure embryos and newborns to the space citadel in perfect safety. It seemed like a cruel irony for the arena of their deaths to be a location that was designed to deliver new life and hope to the human race.

Suddenly, there was a sound like a cannon firing and a flare raced into the sky above the crucible before exploding in a dazzling burst of orange sparks. The crowd cheered and Finn turned to Owen and Cora but both looked shellshocked, like soldiers that had somehow managed to survive storming the beaches at the Normandy landings. Then he heard the sound of boots crunching across fresh snow and he saw Khloe racing away from the group toward a cluster of shipping containers. The woman suddenly slid to a stop and stared at them like they were on fire.

"What are you all waiting for?" she cried out. "Run!"

Khloe vanished into the darkness but Finn was still in a daze. Then he saw a skycar race overhead and realized that had it taken off from somewhere inside the crucible. He scoured the arena, then he saw them. The Shadow and Bloodletter had been dropped off little more the fifty meters away, and both were slowly marching toward them.

"The cannon, the flare!" Finn said, grabbing Owen's shoulders and shaking the man out of his trance. "The trial has already started!"

A crossbow bolt shrieked through the air like a Stuka dive bomber and thudded into Grayson's neck. The dart exploded a moment later, tearing Grayson's throat open and splattering them all with blood, flesh and skin. A cheer erupted from the crowd and the first kill was announced over the PA system, but Finn had no intention of waiting around to learn who would be second. Grabbing Finn and Cora by their arms, he shoved them in the direction of the shipping containers that Khloe had fled toward, yelling at them both to run for their lives.

Parker and Melody were hot on his heels but the woman from Seedhaven tripped and fell. Acting on instinct, Finn slid to a stop and ran to her aid, dragging her out of the snow and shoving her forward. Another crossbow bolt shrieked past his face and he chanced a look at the prosecutors. Bloodletter was walking calmly toward them, but The Shadow was nowhere to be seen, her chameleonic armor already hiding her from view.

"Move, move, go!" Finn yelled, picking up the pace and racing Melody to the relative safety of the shipping containers.

Linden and Skye, the two oranges from Stonehaven, were also clustered behind the containers when he arrived, and Finn did a quick headcount. Grayson was dead, but with Owen and the others they numbered eight in total.

"Where's Soren?" Finn called out. "Has anyone seen Soren, Corbin and Maeve?"

A motor roared into life followed by the sound of tires screeching and slipping through the snow. A utility vehicle roared past, headed deeper into the crucible, and Finn saw Soren hanging out of the passenger side window.

"So long, fuckers!" the man yelled, waving a fist at them. Finn could see that Maeve was driving and that Corbin was also inside the cab. "I hope you die next, pussy!"

Linden and Skye then also made a run for it, darting out from behind the containers and heading toward the launch towers.

"Where are you going?" Finn called out. "We're safer together!"

"No-one is safe in here!" Skye called back. "It's everyone for themselves."

Finn considered going after them but another bolt whistled through the sky and thudded into the metal container wall. He pulled himself into cover and looked for the shooter but it couldn't have been Bloodletter, because they were still shielded from the man by the container.

"Watch out for The Shadow!" Finn said, withdrawing further. "She can blend in with the surroundings; she could be anywhere."

"Fuck this, I'm running!" Parker, the one-armed red from Volthaven, got up and made a dash for another cluster of containers, but he barely made it into the clearing before a crossbow bolt thudded into his remaining arm. The man screamed and tore the bolt from his flesh, but unlike the shot that had killed Grayson, the projectile didn't burst open.

"Get back here you fool!" Melody yelled.

The woman was about to run after Parker but Owen caught her and wrestled her to the snow as two more bolts shrieked past and exploded, kicking dirt into their faces. Finn cursed then spotted a flicker of movement, like a heat-haze, on the second floor of an under-construction building twenty metres to their right. He watched for a second longer and saw snow gathering upon the cloaked form of Elara Cage.

"She's up there, we have to move, now!"

Another bolt flew past but they now had no choice but to take a chance and run. Finn led the charge with Owen and Cora close behind, and the rush of air flowing past his ears deafened him to the sound of crossbow bolts chasing them. Reaching a cluster of pre-fab office blocks that were stacked three-high, he dove for cover into the thick snow then crawled to safety, lungs burning and heart pounding inside his bruised chest. More bodies arrived and again Finn did a count. *Owen, Cora, Melody, Parker...* they were all there. Somehow, they had run the gauntlet and survived.

"Why aren't they coming for us?" Owen said, ducking

and weaving like a boxer to check on the prosecutors without making himself an easy target.

"They know exactly where we are," Finn replied. He might have hated the Trials but he knew how they worked. "They both have tracking computers, like the C.O.N.F.I.R.M.E. devices the prefects use. It doesn't matter how far we run; they'll find us."

"Fuck, then what do we do?" Parker said.

The man was losing it faster than the others. In fact, Finn was astonished that more of them hadn't already crumbled under the pressure.

"These suits have built in tracer bands," Finn replied. Adrenaline was surging through his veins and his mind was fizzing like a nuclear chain reaction. "If we can find some tools in the crucible and cut the tracers out, it'll buy us some time."

"How do you know that?" Cora asked. "I've never heard about tracer bands, and we whites have more access to information in the Spacehaven sector than you get."

"Someone I used to know told me," Finn replied. "She was a Wellness Center worker who seemed to know a lot of things that people like us aren't supposed to know."

"Like what?" Cora replied, remaining skeptical.

"You must have heard of Haven?" Finn said.

"Of course I have, but it's a myth," the Spacehaven worker answered. "The only way out of Zavetgrad is up. Beyond the walls of this hellhole city, there's only death. Nimbus is all there is."

Finn signed and shrugged. "For all our sakes, you'd better wish you're wrong."

The group was silent for a few seconds before the perilous

nature of their situation refocused his mind on survival. Whether Cora was right or he was didn't matter in that moment. In the here and now, all that mattered was staying alive.

"This is your sector, Cora, so where do we go?" Owen asked. "We need tools and a place to hide out, somewhere that's safe from the prosecutors, at least for a while."

Cora pointed to one of the two launch towers. "The crew access tower on pad one is our best bet," the Spacehaven worker replied. "There's only one route up, and once we're that far above ground, it'll be impossible for those bastards to hit us with crossbow bolts."

Owen nodded again and the fact that they had the beginnings of a plan seemed to buoy his spirits and confidence.

"If there's only one way up then maybe we can find some weapons and defend it," Owen suggested. "I know that in this twisted game we either all die or one survives, but maybe we can change the rules? Maybe we can hold out long enough that they have to call it a draw?"

"That's a good idea," Finn replied, answering quickly to sustain the momentum. "I say we stick together and help one another. It's our best shot at surviving."

Finn maintained his poker face and the others seemed to also buy into the plan, but the truth was that he didn't believe for a second that Owen's idea could work. He knew that if a trial overran then all that happened was that the Authority changed the rules. One way or another, the prosecutors would find them and kill them, but it did no-one any good to voice that knowledge out loud. What everyone needed was hope, even if it was a false hope.

"I'll stay with you," Cora said, without hesitation. "We can't do this alone."

Finn turned to Melody and Parker. "What about you two? Will you stay and help us fight the prosecutors together?"

Melody shook her head. "I don't merit your help," the woman from Seedhaven said, backing away. "Unlike you, I actually deserve to be here. Don't risk your lives for me."

Before Finn had chance to reply, Melody turned and ran. Parker called out after her, but she ignored his pleas, and the red from Volthaven set off in pursuit. The man made it only a few paces before collapsing to his knees. Finn and Owen dragged him back, but Parker was foaming from the mouth and convulsing like a rabid animal. Then the man's body went rigid, like it had been frozen for years in the snow and ice of Zavetgrad's artic tundra.

"Poison..." Cora said, her voice desolate like the wasteland surrounding the city. "The Shadow uses poison darts and Parker was hit."

Finn lowered the man onto the snow-covered ground then checked for a pulse, but Parker from Volthaven was already dead. The Shadow had claimed her first victim and Finn knew in his bones that it would not be her last.

14

A BITTER MELODY

Finn drew his fingers across Parker's eyes to close them then backed away from the body, conscious that Bloodletter or The Shadow could still be close. The bolt that had poisoned Parker could just as easily have hit Owen or himself, and he shuddered at how close he'd come to being shot. They'd survived the opening few minutes of the trial on pure luck, but luck alone wasn't going to be enough to keep them alive.

"We have to keep moving and find the tools we need to remove the tracer bands," Finn said, scouring the crucible for places to lay low and find the equipment they needed. "Until we've removed the tracers, we should avoid the launch towers. We don't want to tip off the prosecutors to where we're going, while they can still track us."

"There's a smaller launch pad toward the left edge of the crucible, where the tank-farm is being built," Cora said. "There's a cluster of pre-fab units there and some are being used as storage areas. They might have what we need."

Finn nodded then took another look around, but the

crucible was eerily quiet. Cinematic TVs hummed overhead, carried by heavy-duty flying drones, but they clung to the edge of the arena and pointed out toward the residential areas, so that offenders couldn't use the broadcast to track the prosecutors. They didn't even have their work loggers, which could have at least told them the time, and where they were inside the crucible. The gut-wrenching truth was that they were alone with the odds heavily stacked against them, but they still had their wits, and they still had each other, for as long as their fragile alliance lasted.

"Follow me," Finn said, taking the lead only because someone had to. "We move fast and keep low, using the terrain for cover, and hope to God that the prosecutors stay focused on the others, not us."

As soon as he'd spoken the words, he regretted them, and what the Authority had already forced him to become. Wishing that trained killers would hunt and murder other innocent men and women rather than his group was exactly the sort of us-versus-them mentality that Captain Withers had tried to instill within them. Finn didn't want anyone to get hurt or killed but there was no escaping the fact they were in a fight for their lives. To survive, they would have to make difficult choices, Finn most of all.

He pushed those thoughts to the back of his mind and stalked into the night, wincing at the sound of snow and gravel crunching underfoot. As a construction site, there was no shortage of places to hide but moving from one place to another constantly forced them out into plain sight. They were only exposed for a few seconds at a time but the fear of being shot by a shrieking explosive bolt or poison dart was more unbearable even than the T.E.S.A procedure he'd endured without anesthetic.

Finally, they reached the small landing pad that Cora had highlighted, and Finn wasted no time yanking open the door to one of the pre-fab units and pulling himself inside. The others scrambled through moments later, then Owen closed to the door with a gentleness that Finn could not have managed in that moment. His heart was racing, and his hands were shaking, and he gripped the edge of a table to steady himself, in the hope of at least presenting the appearance of calm.

Suddenly, he was aware of a voice chattering in the darkness and he spun around, fearful that they had inadvertently stumbled upon another offender's hiding place. In his haste to get out of sight, he hadn't checked whether the unit was empty, which in hindsight was dangerous and foolish. For all he knew, Bloodletter could have been lurking in the gloom, machete in hand, ready to deal death by a thousand cuts.

"Who's there?" Finn said. Try as he might, he was unable to mask the fear in his voice. "Come out, so we can see you!"

There was no answer, beyond the same muttered phrases. He unfurled his fingers from the table edge and shuffled deeper inside until he made out the shadowy outline of a woman, cowering beneath a table. It was Khloe, and Finn let out the breath he'd been holding.

"The Metals are coming... The Metals are coming..." the woman was chanting, hugging her legs and rocking back and forth. "Just stay alive... Just stay alive... The Metals are coming..."

"Khloe..." The woman jerked back at the sound of his

voice and Finn realized that she hadn't noticed them enter. "Khloe, it's Finn. It's okay, I'm here with Owen and Cora. You're safe, we're not going to hurt you." He held out a hand to Khloe and smiled. "It's okay, we'll protect you. We'll protect each other."

Khloe shook her head. "You can't protect us, not in here. Not from them. But the Metals are coming. They promised they would. That's the only way out. I just have to stay alive."

Finn frowned at the woman. "What are you talking about? Who are the Metals?"

"Finn..."

It was Owen's voice, but he could barely see the man inside the pitch-black building. Reluctantly, he shuffled away from Khloe, keeping his head below the window line, and found Owen and Cora huddled around a toolkit.

"I think we can use these to cut out the tracer bands, but I don't know where they're hidden," Owen continued.

His friend had laid out a selection of tools on the floor, including a pair of snips, a hacksaw, an electrician's knife and more. He went straight for the snips, which were heavy and sharp.

"They're inside the left sleeve cuffs and right ankles of our jumpsuits," Finn said. He gripped his left cuff and pinched the material to highlight the thin metal band that had been inserted inside it. "We can use the snips to cut them so we can slide them out."

Finn got to work and within the space of a minute he'd already removed the tracer band from his sleeve. He slid the tracking device out of his cuff then dropped it onto the pile of tools.

"That's one down..." he said, starting work on the second

tracer band around his ankle, which was more difficult to get at.

Cora picked up the tracer and examined it, turning it over in her hands. She then picked up the knife from the toolkit and nibbled away the fabric coating, revealing a wafer-thin circuit board beneath.

"You were right..." Cora said, sounding surprised and a little embarrassed. "I know this circuit design. I used to make the labels that are fixed to cargo crates before they're loaded onto the Nimbus rockets, and each one contains a circuit like this to track and trace the cargo through the system."

Finn huffed a laugh. "In that case, it looks like we're the product being labelled. It's a shame they don't consider us as valuable as the freight they load onto the rockets."

Finn set to work on Owen's jumpsuit, starting with the trickier ankle band. After a couple of trial runs on himself, he was already becoming proficient at removing the tracers.

"If your friend from the Wellness Center was right about these then maybe she was right about Haven too," Cora added. She looked into Finn's eyes and hesitated before finally speaking the question that was on her lips. "What happened to her?"

"I don't know," Finn admitted, sliding the ankle band out from Owen's jumpsuit and starting on the cuff. "One day, she was just gone. I like to think she got out but the chances are she either killed herself or got sent to trial for refusing to work, just like Khloe."

"What was her name?"

It wasn't Cora who had asked this question but Khloe. The woman had crawled out from beneath the table while he'd been working and had been quietly listening in on their conversion. Finn handed the tool to Owen so that his friend could work on removing the tracer bands from Cora's jumpsuit, then gave Khloe his full attention.

"The wellness worker who told you about the tracers and about Haven… What was her name?" Khloe repeated.

"She was called Sienna," Finn replied. Just speaking her name out loud caused his gut to twist in knots. "She never told me her last name."

"What did she look like?"

Finn sighed then crossed his legs and massaged his stubbled chin. Now that Khloe had asked, he realized he could scarcely remember Sienna's face, even though it had only been a couple of years since she'd disappeared.

"She was sad, obviously," Finn replied, mentally reconstructing the wellness worker in his mind as he spoke. Then he smiled. "I remember her eyes most of all. They were large and hazel colored and had a brightness and life to them that most people in the center had already lost." He thought some more and the image in his mind began to crystalize. "Her hair was dark brown, like freshly-dug soil, and it fell almost to her waist. It was curly towards the ends but laser straight as it ran past her face." He laughed and shook his head, ruefully. "I could never figure out how that worked."

Finn closed his eyes and Sienna was there in his thoughts, staring right back at him with a Mona Lisa smile, but seeing her again only made him feel wretched.

"That's about all I can recall," he said, looking at Khloe and suddenly recognizing the same sadness within her. "I'm ashamed I don't remember more."

Khloe shuffled closer to him and held out her left wrist.

An hour earlier and Finn might have imagined that she wanted him to open her veins and end her misery, but the life he'd once seen in Sienna's eyes was now radiating from Khloe like a halo, and he realized that she was asking him to cut out the tracer.

"So, that was you," Khloe said, suddenly smiling. It was an alien expression that transformed her face and made her look years younger. "Sienna talked about you a lot."

Finn was struck dumb. He had a hundred questions on the tip of his tongue but he couldn't command his mouth to produce any of them. It was like his voice had been stolen out of his chest.

"Haven isn't a myth," Khloe continued, still smiling. "It's real, and it's where I'm going. I'm getting out tonight, and you can too."

Finn's head was all over the place and he could feel electricity surging through his body with enough current to power all of Metalhaven, but all he managed to say in reply was one word.

"How?"

"There's no time to explain, not here," Khloe answered. "But we have to reach the control center in the North of the crucible. That's where they'll be."

Finn was desperate to learn who would be waiting when a bloodcurdling scream gripped him like the horrifying wail of a banshee. Owen rushed to the window and a curse hissed from his fiend's lips.

"It's Bloodletter," Owen said, staying in the shadows so that he couldn't be seen through the glass. "He's hunting one of the others but I can't see who."

Finn jumped up and hurried to the window. He could see

Bloodletter and from his angle he could also see the prosecutor's quarry.

"It's Melody," Finn said. "And she's hurt."

Finn watched the woman from Seedhaven hobble toward a parked excavator, leaving a trail of blood in her wake. She was clutching a wound to her left arm and deep cuts had been sliced across both of her thighs. He felt rage burning inside him. Bloodletter was toying with her, carving her up piece by piece until she would no doubt eventually collapse and bleed out in the snow.

"Fuck this, I'm going out there," Finn said. He grabbed a shovel that was leaning up against the wall and ran to the door, but Owen blocked his path.

"Are you mad? He'll kill you too!"

"These bastards only win because we're too afraid to face them," Finn answered. "There are four of us and only one of him. We can take him."

"Owen is right, it's suicide," Cora said. "We need to stick together and listen to Khloe. If she has a way out then we've a better chance of making it as a group."

There was another scream followed by the distant roar of the crowd and Finn tightened his grip on the shovel, waiting for the announcement that Melody had been killed, but it didn't come. She was still alive yet he remained hidden away like a coward.

"You're right but I still have to try," Finn said, looking Owen in the eyes. "This is on me, and me alone. If I get hurt or killed then you go on without me."

"Finn…" Owen began, but he grabbed his friend's shoulder and shook his head.

"I can't leave her out there to die, Owen. Even if I did get out of this place, I couldn't live with it."

Owen's chin dropped and the man nodded solemnly, staring at the floor. He maneuvered his friend aside then grabbed the doorhandle and eased it open.

"Remember what I told you," Finn said, hovering on the threshold, ready to burst into a sprint. "You go on without me, come what may."

He didn't wait for an answer and pushed out into the snow, shovel in hand. The trail of blood led the way and he followed it without any care as to whether Bloodletter or The Shadow might be watching him. Then he heard laughter, thick and treacly, as if the sound had been formed inside the belly of a demon, and he charged around the side of the excavator to find Bloodletter standing over Melody, machete held high. He let out a roar like a war cry and accelerated, drawing the spade back at the same time. Bloodletter spun around and fired a snapshot with his crossbow but the bolt only nicked his side before vanishing harmlessly into the snow. He swung the spade with all his might and battered the prosecutor with the flat of the blade, sending the man tumbling into the pit that the earthmover had excavated. The momentum of his charge almost carried him down too but he dug in his heels and flattened his body to the ground, clawing into the gravel beneath the snow to arrest his fall. Breathless and shaking from adrenaline he then scrambled on his hands and knees toward Melody who was face down in the snow and not moving.

"Melody..." Finn whispered, scared that raising his voice might alert The Shadow, despite the fact the sound of him clobbering Bloodletter with a spade had rung out across the crucible like a church bell. "Melody, get up, we have to run!" The woman still didn't move and Finn shook her gently but she didn't stir. "Melody, come on!"

He flipped over the body and saw her eyes staring blankly up at him. The patch of snow where she lay was painted red and Finn saw more cuts across her arms and belly. Hands shaking, he felt for a pulse but there was none.

"Brasa!"

The sound of his name being shouted into the air chilled Finn's blood and he froze.

"Brasa! I'm going to kill you slow, fucker!"

Instinct compelled him to stand and run but despite the gnawing feeling that Bloodletter was chasing after him, he didn't look back, not even once. Reaching the pre-fab unit where the others were hiding, he threw open the door and was almost stabbed in the throat by Owen, who had been waiting behind it, electrician's knife in hand.

"We have to go, now!" Finn yelled, dragging his friend outside. "Now, come on!"

The others bolted after him without question and soon they were running again, though Finn had no idea where to. All he could think about was getting as far away from Bloodletter as he could.

"No, this way!" Cora called out.

Finn slid to a stop and saw the woman from Spacehaven detour down a sloping embankment that led to a concrete alley covered by a grated deck plating. The snow was so thick that it had clung to the metal and formed an opaque blanket that hid anyone inside from view.

"Khloe said we had to go north, and this gulley will take us close to the control center," Cora added, slipping and sliding down the embankment. "It doesn't stretch all the way, but it's our best chance."

Khloe follow Cora but Owen waited for Finn to catch up and together they slid down the embankment on their backsides, then hurried into the tunnel. Finn's mind was still racing at a million miles per hour, but Owen grabbed his shoulders and held firm.

"Take a breath, Finn, we're okay. You are okay..." Owen said, absorbing some of Finn's shivers into his own body. "But we have to stay calm and move quietly. Do you understand?"

Finn nodded then rested his hands on his knees and bent over, sucking in deep breaths in an effort to slow his heart rate and collect his jangling senses.

"What happened to Melody?" Owen asked in barely more than whisper. "Did you reach her in time?"

Finn blew out a sigh and straightened his back but the look in his eyes was enough for Owen to know the answer without him having to speak the words out loud.

"That's not on you," Owen said, his tone firm. "That was a brave thing you just did. Stupid, but brave."

Finn didn't feel brave, he just felt angry and afraid in equal measure. One of those emotions he knew would get him killed while the second might just save his life. Even so, he didn't want to let go of either.

"She didn't deserve to die, Owen," Finn had wrestled back enough control to speak without raising his voice. "No-one in here does, not even Soren, as much as it pains me to say it."

"Then keep your head and stay alive so we can all get out of here," Owen replied. "Then if Haven and these Metals really do exist, you can put that anger to use."

"How?" Finn asked.

"By fighting back," Owen said. "We've sat back and let this happen for too long. You were right, Finn. You were right all along, and I should have listened to you. We have to fight the Authority, and do you know why?" Finn shook his head and Owen's eyes burned brighter than lasers. "Because fuck them, that's why."

15

DROPPING IN

Cora switched on her flashlight and aimed it into the darkness ahead of them. The weather was on the turn, with rising winds and swirling black clouds gathering overhead, but inside the snow-cocooned alleyway, they were sheltered from the approaching storm.

"I don't remember getting issued with a flashlight before they dumped us in the crucible," Finn commented. He was following behind Cora and Khloe, who were leading the foray north, while Owen remained at his side.

"I found it inside the toolkit and figured it might come in handy," Cora replied, still focused ahead. "Looks like I was right."

Finn huffed a laugh. "Let's hope you're right about this alleyway too."

"Don't worry, I doubt the prosecutors even know it's here," Cora explained. "One advantage to being a Spacehaven native is that I know my way around."

They walked in silence for a time, accompanied by the musical whistling of the wind as it whipped through the tunnel, and Finn found that his mind began to wander. His thoughts initially dwelled on Sienna and his hope that the Wellness Center worker had escaped to the safety of Haven, rather than taken her own life, or had it taken from her. Then he thought about Soren, Corbin and Maeve, and the duo from Stonehaven; Skye and Linden. Their deaths had not been announced over the PA system, so he had to assume they were still alive somewhere inside the crucible. It went against his instincts to escape and leave them to their fates but Melody's death had been a painful reminder that he couldn't save everyone, no matter how hard he tried or how much he wanted to.

"Hey, Khloe, why are these guys from Haven called Metals, anyway?" Owen asked.

While his thoughts had been concerned with the moral Catch-22s of the crucible, it appeared that his friend had been pondering more lightweight topics. This wasn't surprising to Finn, since Owen rarely dwelled on the darker aspects of life in Zavetgrad.

"I don't know," Khloe replied, breezily. "I only know that there are dozens of them inside Zavetgrad, operating in secret, working the reclamation yards and farms, and even inside the Authority sector and Wellness Centers. That's how I was contacted. Inside a Wellness Center, I mean."

"Don't take this the wrong way, Khloe, but why you?" Finn asked, suddenly more intrigued by the machinations of Haven than their more immediate danger. He loved a mystery as much as the next man.

"I was friendly with the gold on the reception desk at my Wellness Center," Khloe explained. "She was called Gail and was the most un-gold-like gold I'd ever met."

"You mean she wasn't a total bitch to you, like other golds?" Finn asked.

Khloe laughed and just as when she'd smiled at him earlier, she looked years younger.

"I suppose so," the young woman replied. Then the joy and youthfulness vanished from her eyes and the weight of her ordeals pressed down on her. "When Gail heard that I'd refused to work, and learned what they did to me, she came to my room later that night and told me about Haven."

"Gail was a Metal?" Finn asked, and Khloe nodded.

"I know that when you look at me, all you see is a frightened girl, too weak to resist, but you're wrong," Khloe said with an unexpected fierceness. "The prefects interrogated me for days on end, trying to force me to comply with the Authority and return to work, but I refused, in spite of the humiliating abuses they subjected me to."

Khloe stopped and turned to face him. Illuminated only by the glaring beam from Cora's torch, she looked ghoulish and frightening, as if there had been a beast inhabiting her soul that the torchlight had suddenly revealed.

"That's why I was chosen," Khloe continued. "The Metals are attracted to strength, and strength comes in many forms. Haven is building an army and they need people with the will to resist and fight back."

"Hey, I'm sorry if I offended you," Finn said, feeling suddenly foolish. "I didn't mean to imply you were weak." He sighed and shrugged. "Though if I'm honest, I thought you were."

Khloe smiled again. "You're not the first to make that mistake, and you won't be the last."

They continued trudging through the tunnel for a time

and with each minute that passed without the threat of a crossbow bolt exploding inside their heads, Finn began to relax, and it seemed clear the others were too.

"How come these Metals take people from the Trials, instead of just grabbing them off the street, or something?" Owen asked, filling time by continuing to quiz Khloe about the secrets she held. "Surely it would be a lot easier?"

"You'd think so, but the problem is getting people out of the city, and that's actually easier during a trial," Khloe replied. "Regents don't leave their sub-oceanic villas lightly, and when they do, the prefecture has to deploy all of their resources to protect them and police the work sectors. That gives the Metals a window of opportunity to act, but it's a narrow window because trials almost never last more than a couple of hours."

Finn considered this, and figured that it was a reasonable explanation, but he still had questions.

"But if people get rescued from the Trials, why haven't we ever heard about it?" Finn asked. "The Trials are mandated viewing for all workers but not once have I ever seen an offender escape or go missing without explanation."

"I wondered the same thing," Khloe replied. "Gail told me that not everything we see on the giant TV screens is real. I don't know how they do it, but if someone gets out, the trial controllers simulate that offender getting killed instead, and we never know the truth."

Owen seemed skeptical. "How can they simulate something like that? Hell, I've watched a hundred trials, and every gory one of them was real enough to give me nightmares."

Khloe shrugged. "Beats me. My area of expertise was lying on my back, remember?"

The joke at her own expense was made with resentment and no-one laughed.

"You'd be surprised what the Authority can do with computers," Cora chipped in. As a Spacehaven worker, she had access to technology far more advanced than the lowly workers of Metalhaven ever saw. "Simulating someone getting killed is actually pretty easy. Unless people see it with their own eyes from the spectator stands instead of on a TV, you'd never be able to tell simulation from reality."

Finn frowned and ruminated on what Cora had said. He felt that she'd inadvertently hit upon something important, but he wasn't quite sure why or how to turn it to their advantage. He parked the thought for the time being, and continued listening to Khloe, who was turning out to be a fount of illicit knowledge, like the data device he'd kept hidden away inside his apartment.

"The Authority are experts at concealing the truth from us," Khloe said, seemingly lost in her own thoughts and thinking out loud. "It's how they've managed to keep Haven quiet for so long. The mere mention of its name is all that a prefect needs to..." she paused, searching for the right word, then added, "silence you..."

As fascinating as Khloe's revelations were, Finn was growing anxious that their window to escape was dwindling with each passing minute they spent underground.

"I'd love to hear more about the Metals and about Haven, but first we have to get out of this place," Finn said, steering the conversation back to urgent matters. "And if we're going to get out, we need to know how."

"There are tunnels built deep beneath Zavetgrad," Khloe said, pointing to the concrete surface of the alley under their feet. "They were once sewers until the Authority added waste recycling units to all the habitat blocks and they were no longer needed. Most were sealed off and filled with concrete but the Metals spent decades hollowing them out and making new tunnels too."

"And one of these tunnels leads past the control center?" Finn asked.

"Yes, but you're right that we have to hurry," Khloe replied. "Right now, a skycar is hidden somewhere outside the city, ready to take us across the Davis Straight to Haven, but it won't wait forever. The tunnel will be opened one hour into the trial, and the Metals will wait for ten minutes, and no more. If we miss the window, we're trapped here."

This timeline had come completely out of the blue and Finn was stunned. He jogged ahead and blocked Khloe's path, nerves jangling and mouth dry.

"Why didn't you say this before?" Finn said, fighting to keep his voice down. "We have no idea how long it's been since the trial started. What if the Metals have already come and gone?"

"The trial has been running for thirty-six minutes," Khloe said. Then she shrugged, nonchalantly. "Give or take a minute, either way."

Finn was so shocked he simply stood there with his mouth gaping wide open, but Cora asked the question that he hadn't put into words.

"How can you know that?" Cora asked. "Our watches and work loggers were taken from us during processing."

"Gail taught me how to count time in my head, so that I

wouldn't miss the rendezvous," Khloe explained. "After the prefects abused me, I spent a month in solitary mastering the technique. It's the only thing that kept me sane."

Owen laughed, which was not the reaction Finn was expecting, and judging by the bemused expression on their faces, the same was true of the others.

"I guess that's why you were quiet all the time," Owen said. "I can barely count to fifty in my head without losing count!"

"I'm quiet, because I like being quiet," Khloe replied, shooting the big man a gracious smile. "In my experience, talking only gets you into trouble."

Suddenly, there was a humming sound from beyond the snow-covered gratings above their heads that sounded like distant rotor blades. Finn clicked his fingers to get Cora's attention then pointed to the flashlight, and she killed the beam a heartbeat later, plunging them into an infinite black.

"What is it?" Owen whispered, his voice resonant inside the alleyway like a ghostly echo.

"Recon drones, maybe?" Finn suggested. "Without the tracer bands to locate us, the prosecutors are probably getting frustrated and turning to other means to hunt us down."

The rotor sound grew louder then suddenly vanished. They all waited in absolute silence and darkness, willing the drone to hum back into life and fly away, but it wasn't to be. Instead, sparks began to fly as a cutting tool shrieked into life and sliced through the metal grating above them.

"They've found us!" Owen called out. In the flickering light of the sparks, Finn could see that his friend was brandishing the electrician's knife.

Finn searched the tunnel floor for anything that might

work as a weapon and found a twisted offcut of metal about thirty centimeters long. He picked it up and decided it was weighty enough to do some damage.

"We smash this thing then run like hell," Finn said, as the sparks intensified, burning his face.

There were nods and calls of agreement, then a saucer-sized section of the metal grating dropped into the tunnel. Snow gushed inside, followed by a lump of metal the size and shape of an oil can. Owen roared and went to attack but Finn threw himself at his friend and pushed him back just in time to spare the little machine from a grizzly fate.

"It's okay, it's just Scraps!" Finn said, still struggling to restrain Owen, who was far stronger than he was. "It's my robot!"

The little robot righted itself then shook snow from its head. The machine quietly scrutinized Khloe and Cora, both of whom were petrified with fear, before turning to Finn and waving.

"Hi-hi!"

"Scraps!" Finn cried, tossing the bar and scooping the little robot into his arms. "Damn, it's good to see you, pal!"

"You know this robot?" Cora asked, switching the flashlight back on.

"Yes," Finn replied. "Scraps is a friend. I built him myself from parts salvaged from the reclamation yard, including an old Foreman Logic Processer."

"You re-programmed an FLP?" Cora said, aghast, though it was the impressed kind of shock, rather than the distressed kind.

"I did, though Scraps is pretty smart too, and he helped me a lot," Finn answered, still staring at the robot, dotingly.

Cora huffed a laugh. "I don't know how you managed that but color me impressed. Programming FLPs is something even us whites don't get to do. Only golds are allowed that knowledge." Then she frowned. "How the hell did you learn?"

Finn smiled. "You'll be surprised at what you can find inside the wreckage of old tanks and armored personnel carriers."

Scraps jumped out of Finn's arms and a rotor blade sprung from the top of his head, holding the robot in a hover at head height.

"Who thems?" Scraps asked, pointing at Cora and Khloe. "Friend-friend or bad-bad?"

"Definitely friend-friend, Scraps, so don't worry," Finn answered.

The little robot squealed with excitement then hovered next to Cora and perched himself on her shoulder, like a parrot.

"Scraps like-like," the robot said.

"I think you've made a friend," Finn said, smiling at Cora, who was regarding Scraps with doting eyes, just as he had done moments ago.

The robot's mechanical smile then stiffened and his eyes glowed wider. It jumped off Cora's shoulder and hovered close to the hole it had made in the grating.

"Danger-danger!" the robot said. "Bloodletter close. No lights..."

Cora switched off the flashlight then Scraps zoomed to the ground and picked up the section of metal grating he had cut away earlier, before wedging it back into place. His left arm extended though the grating and agitated the snow, causing it to fill the hole and conceal the robot's tracks. Scraps then dropped onto Finn's shoulder and pressed a metal finger to its mechanical mouth.

"Quiet-quiet…"

The robot's eyes dimmed, reducing the light level to a fraction above the pitch darkness that would have otherwise enveloped them. Then they heard the sound of boots crunching on fresh snow, growing louder by the second. A light dusting of icy powder rained onto their heads as Bloodletter drew near. Finn noticed that Scraps had sprung a little sensor dish from a compartment in his back and was angling it away from them.

"Trial Control, this is Bloodletter," a treacly voice said. It was difficult to be certain because of their location but Finn figured that the man was no more than ten meters away. "I've come to the area where you spotted the anomaly but there's nothing here but snow."

A radio crackled and voices answered but it was too faint for Finn to make out the words.

"You've got to do better, control!" Bloodletter roared. Clearly, the answer was not what he wanted. "These fucking criminals are making me look bad. I have a reputation to uphold!"

The radio crackled again and the voice on the end of the line replied. Everyone remained perfectly still. Finn was barely remembering to breathe.

"Due East of here? Are you sure?" Bloodletter said. The man cursed bitterly into the icy air. "Just find me Finn Brasa. I don't give a shit about the rest of them but that fucker is mine."

The radio crackled and Bloodletter cursed again. Then

they heard the sound of his footsteps moving away. After about thirty seconds, Scraps' eyes brightened and the bot leapt into a hover.

"Bad man gone. Scraps no like." The robot said.

"No, I don't like him either," Finn answered.

"Sent wrong signal," Scraps added, spinning around to show Finn the dish on his back. "Scraps mess with bad man's 'puter."

Cora laughed. "Clever little robot. You threw him off our scent?"

Scraps nodded and Cora patted the machine on his belly, causing the robot to giggle like a child. Finn also patted his robot then blew out a sigh. The close-call had focused his mind and made him remember that they were only ever seconds away from a grisly demise at the blade of Bloodletter or The Shadow. For now, they were still safe, but eventually the prosecutors would find them.

"How long do we have, Khloe?" Finn asked, hoping that all the excitement hadn't caused the woman to lose count in her head.

"Thirty-one minutes," Khloe replied, confidently. "We still have time, but what we don't have is time to waste."

16

JOY, HOWEVER BRIEF

Finn cautiously approached the exit to the snow-covered alleyway to check the coast was clear. Heavy cloud continued to blanket Zavetgrad, dulling what little illumination the low moon provided, and the near-blizzard conditions meant he could barely see a hundred meters in any direction. Willing his body on, he reached open ground and listened intently, but the howling wind masked everything, including the rumble of the crowds, who would still be watching, come hell or high water. He knew from past trials that inclement weather did little to dull the enthusiasm of spectating workers, who had hundreds of shift hours of beer chits invested in the outcome, though it had at least forced the hovering TV screens to ground.

"Scraps go check. Wait-wait…"

The little robot hovered off Finn's shoulder and sped outside before he could caution the machine to be careful. Though, considering Scraps had managed to escape his apartment, hitch a ride to Spacehaven and find them inside the crucible, all without being captured and torn down for parts, he figured that the bot knew what he was doing. Scraps zipped back to the alley a few moments later and dropped onto Cora's shoulder. There was a fresh dusting of snow on his head and body to show for his adventures.

"All okay!" the robot announced. "Follow Scraps!"

The robot leapt into the air and hovered outside, this time more slowly so that Finn and the others could follow. After a period of time sheltered from the snow and the biting wind, their sudden exposure to the elements was jarring and their jumpsuits did little to stave off the cold. Shivering and rubbing his arms, Finn followed Scraps into a building that was only part completed but at least had a roof and four walls, providing welcome respite from the storm.

"I recognize this place," said Cora, shaking snow out of her hair. "It's a viewing gallery and visitor center for the Regent and other high-ranking golds to watch the rocket launches. There's a skybridge at the other end of this structure that will lead us directly into the control center."

"Gail told me that the Metals will be in a sub-level storage area on the east side of the building, near to the backup power management facilities," Khloe cut in. "How quickly can this skybridge get us there?"

Cora considered the question, mentally addressing a map of the facility in her mind before answering. "Honestly, no more than ten minutes, I think," the woman finally replied, smiling with relief. "This will take us almost right where we need to be."

"We still have twenty-seven minutes until the Metals arrive," Khloe said, her tone betraying a rare flicker of optimism. "We can make it!"

The painfully tense expressions etched onto the faces of

Owen and Cora eased ever so slightly as they shared in Khloe's sense of relief, but Finn sensed they were far from safe. Bloodletter and The Shadow had demonstrated that they could appear in an instant and strike in a heartbeat, and ten minutes was ample time for them to be hunted down and slaughtered like animals.

"Let's keep going, there's a chance the Metals could be early," Finn said, keeping his fears from the others while offering motivation to keep them all moving.

Cora continued to lead the way, while Finn carried Scraps in his arms. The bot still had his little sensor dish extended and from the scowling vee-shape of his metal eyebrows, Finn figured he was hard at work scanning for the prosecutors. In only a few short minutes, they had climbed and descended several staircases and turned more corners than Finn could count, which made him extremely grateful for their knowledgeable guide. Then the skybridge came into view through the window and Finn allowed himself to feel a small measure of the optimism that had buoyed the spirits of his companions. Because of the storm, the other side of the overpass wasn't visible, instead dissolving into snowy darkness like a conduit to another dimension, but the mere sight of the passageway was enough to give him hope that their ordeal might soon end.

"I'd say the worker crews were forced to leave in a hurry," Owen said, crouching down beside a pile of bags that had been unceremoniously dumped in the corner of the room.

Finn joined his friend and began to rifle through the bags, looking for anything that might be useful as a tool or potential weapon. He found several algae-based protein bars, the staple snack-food of a twelve-hour shift worker, some flasks of cold coffee, a few bottles of water and not much else. Owen then plucked a fresh packet of cigarettes out of a pocket and held them up, triumphantly.

"See, there is a God!" he said, tearing open the packet and hastily shoving a stick into his mouth. Then he frowned and searched the bag some more before cursing. "Damn it, there are no matches."

"Looking for these?" Cora said. Owen spun around to see Cora strike a match. The sparkle and fizz of the matchhead igniting was followed by the steady burn of an orange flame. "I found them on a table, back there," she added.

Owen darted to Cora's side and bent down to shove the end of the cigarette into the flame, while Cora cradled the burning match in her hands to stop it blowing out. His friend then straightened his back and sucked a lungful of air through the cigarette, causing the end to burn as brightly as a rocket engine. Smoke billowed from Owen's mouth and nose, and for a moment, he was completely lost inside the cloud.

"You know, I think you might actually be an angel," Owen said, offering the cigarette to Cora.

"I think the angels all left this planet a long time ago," the woman replied, taking the cigarette from Owen and smiling at him. "But thanks, all the same."

Cora drew on the cigarette then handed it to Khloe, who smoked the stick down past the half-way mark before sidling up beside Finn and offering it to him.

"Smoke bad-bad," Scraps said, wagging a metal finger at the cigarette. "Make CPU crash."

Khloe laughed. "I'm sure you're right, Scraps, but my CPU is pretty corrupted already," the woman from

Metalhaven replied, while continuing to offer the cigarette to Finn.

"It's okay, Khloe, I'll stick to a different kind of fuel, thanks," Finn said, waving a protein bar at the woman before tearing open the packet. "I suggest you all have a bite to eat too. It might not seem like it, but thanks to Captain Withers and her drugged buffet, none of us have eaten a thing for about twelve hours."

"This will do me just fine," Owen said, sparking up another match and setting to work on a second cigarette. "Honestly, my stomach hasn't stopped doing somersaults ever since we were arrested; I couldn't eat even if I wanted to."

Finn couldn't blame his friend, and in truth he wasn't hungry either, but he nibbled at the protein bar all the same. At first, the cloying, sugary substance merely exacerbated his nausea but it wasn't long before the bar's energizing effects started to make him feel stronger.

"I don't know about the rest of you but I can smoke and walk," Owen said, lighting another cigarette and handing one each to Cora and Khloe, before taking a fresh one for himself. "Whatever drug they put into these things is helping but I'll still feel a whole hell of a lot better once we reach the rendezvous."

No-one argued with Owen's logic, and they left the treasure horde behind and continued toward the skybridge in a haze of narcotic-infused smoke. The drugs and the nicotine eased their tensions enough to allow a conversation to spark up, and for a time it seemed that their troubles were a thousand miles away.

"Hey, Cora, tell us something about yourself," Owen

said, walking with a renewed swagger, thanks to the induced high from the cigarette. "Something secret or illegal!"

Cora laughed, swayed by Owen's effortless charm and a headful of drugs. If Finn had tried asking the woman from Spacehaven the same question, she would have likely told him to mind his own goddamn business.

"You first," Cora replied, choosing to play the game but by her own rules.

Owen thought for a moment, cigarette bobbing up and down in his mouth as he strutted forward. "Okay, how about this..." he began, before clearing his throat. "I once got so mad at a foreman that I whacked it with the butt of my laser cutter and popped its head right off its shoulders," Owen said, smiling. "That's why I'm kind of a pacifist now, because anger gets you killed."

Rather than laughing, Cora looked horrified. "But willfully damaging a foreman is a trial offence," Cora replied. "How did you get away with it?"

Owen blew a puff of smoke into the air before nodding and smiling at Finn.

"Finn took the blame for me," Owen answered. "I was so worked up at the time that I couldn't think straight. I thought I was dead, for sure. But Finn spun some bullshit story, making out that it was an honest accident, and the prefects let him off with a beatdown. He saved my life that day, and not for the first time."

Cora turned to Finn, still with a traumatized look on her face, as if someone had doused her with a bucket of ice water.

"They didn't exactly let me off," Finn said, correcting his friend. "I got punched about twenty times in the face and punished with an extra eight-hours of shift duty for being 'clumsy'."

"Hey, I helped you work it off, didn't I?" Owen said, sounding oddly offended that he hadn't mentioned that part, but Finn conceded the point.

"That's still a pretty lenient sentence," Cora said, still in shock. "You must have a magical way with words to talk a prefect out of sending you to trial."

Finn and Owen both laughed, though the joke was obviously lost on Cora, who wasn't aware of his special ability to walk on a razor's edge without getting sliced in half.

"I'm a double-five, so that gets me a pass in a lot of situations," Finn explained. He laughed again and gestured to the crucible surrounding them. "Though not always, as you can see."

"But surely the prefects would have interrogated the foreman's logic processor and seen what really happened, through the robot's own eyes?" Cora asked, still not convinced by Finn's explanations.

"They couldn't because he swiped the processor out of the machine's head, before any other foremen or prefects got there," Owen answered, though even this wasn't enough to placate the woman from Spacehaven.

"Come on, possession of an FLP is an even more serious offence than damaging a foreman!" Cora said. "If you were caught with that chip, they'd have probably shot you on the spot, double-five or not."

"But they didn't catch me with it," Finn answered, allowing himself a proud smile. He then hooked a thumb at Scraps, who was now sitting on his shoulder. "In fact, I still have it."

Scraps waved at Cora and the woman from Spacehaven laughed and finally accepted their story, as unbelievable as it sounded, because evidence of its truth was literally staring her in the face.

"Now it's your turn," Owen said, nudging Cora with his powerful shoulder. "Tell us a secret. Something juicy…"

Cora thought for a moment but the smile had left her face and she appeared suddenly sad and contemplative. She blew out a heavy sigh and looked Owen in the eyes.

"What the hell, it's not like admitting it now can get me in any worse trouble," Cora said. "I was in relationship with a gold. A prefect, actually."

"Bullshit!" Owen said, though it was a good-natured rebuttal.

"It's the truth!" Cora protested, shoving Owen and causing him to stagger off course.

Finn and Khloe laughed too, partly at Owen's outrageous response, but also because they knew that Cora was most likely telling a white-lie. The lower colors were forbidden from having relationships of any kind, which was why the Authority provided Wellness Centers, so that workers could get their rocks off whenever they liked. Finn had also long suspected that the drugs in the cigarettes and even in the beer they served in the Recovery Centers were designed to chemically suppress the need for companionship, beyond simple sexual desire. Even so, he knew that people did hook up, and that it happened more often than the Authority would ever admit, but it was a very dangerous game. At best, workers who were suspected of being in a relationship would be sent to different zones within a work sector, or different sectors entirely. At worst, they would be sent to trial or reassigned to a Wellness Center to ensure the seeds of romance died before they could take root.

"So, who was this mythical gold that swept you off your feet?" Owen asked, continuing to tease Cora. "Tell us everything..."

"I will tell you, whether you believe me or not!" Cora replied, taking it all in good spirits. "He was actually the person who helped me to get the fake ID and gear I needed to board the Nimbus rocket." The woman sighed again. "And he did love me, truly. But he also knew we could never be together because golds and other colors don't mix. That's why he tried to get me away from this godforsaken place." She shrugged. "The rest is history."

Owen was now looking at Cora with more circumspection. "Are you being serious?"

Cora nodded. "It's the truth. God's honest..."

Finn tried to read the woman's expression and body language for any clues she was lying, but if she was making up the story then she had the best poker face in all of Zavetgrad.

"What happened to him?" Finn asked, taking a leap of faith and assuming Cora's secret was genuine.

"I never saw or heard from him again after I was arrested, but we all know that they don't send golds to trial," Cora answered.

Finn nodded but didn't enquire further because, reading between the lines, they all knew what had most likely happened to the prefect. In the eyes of the public, golds were supposed to be flawless, and any imperfections were eradicated with ruthless efficiency. Even Owen's cigarette had gone out as if to symbolize how the fire and energy contained within their brief moment of joyful companionship had fizzled to nothing.

"What was his name?" Khloe asked. As usual, she had remained quiet, partly because it was her way, but also to keep the stopwatch ticking in her mind.

"Tucker," Cora answered, solemnly. "His name was Tucker."

Owen struck a match then held it up like a beacon. "Here's to Tucker," he said, relighting his cigarette. "He sounds like he was one of the good guys."

Everyone nodded and repeated the salute, then they continued in silence onto the skybridge that led inside the Control Center and to what they hoped was their salvation. Bringing up the rear, Finn stepped onto the overland walkway last, and at the same time as his boot struck the metal, a cry of unadulterated terror shattered the silence.

"Everyone, down!" Finn called out in a hushed but urgent tone, and the others ducked below the window line and pushed their bodies tightly to the wall of the skybridge.

Another panicked yell cut through the wail of the wind and Finn chanced a look outside. Linden, one of the two offenders from Stonehaven, was hobbling out into open ground, almost directly beneath the skybridge. The man was limping away from a parked crane-lift, and the door was left open, suggesting that the frail-looking older man had been using the vehicle as a bolt hole. Bloodletter then appeared, stepping inside the footprints in the snow that Linden had left behind, and perfectly masking his trail. The prosecutor's crossbow was in the man's left hand, while the machete was in his right, blood dripping from the tip of the blade.

"What is it?" Owen whispered. "What do you see?"

"Bloodletter..." Finn replied, the words leaking from his lips like the blood from the prosecutor's machete. "He's going after Linden."

"Damn it, why did he have to lead the prosecutors here, of all places?" Cora hissed.

It was a harsh statement given that Linden's life was hanging by the thinnest of threads but Finn understood the sentiment. The prosecutors could just as easily have been a mile away on the other side of the crucible, but instead they were practically breathing down their necks.

"Where's Skye?" Owen asked. "Those two were thick as thieves."

Finn shook his head. He couldn't see the woman. "Skye was adamant that the trial was everyone for themselves. Maybe, she saw Linden as dead weight and dumped him."

As he was speaking, Linden collapsed whilst trying to scale a low wall, then slumped down next to it and pressed his back to the slabs. Blood was pooling around his waist and Finn could just about make out the savage gash that Bloodletter had sliced into the worker's gut. Panicking, Linden scrambled around in the snow looking for a weapon. Chance favored the Stonehaven worker and the man pulled a chisel out of the snow. It was no match for the machete but at least it would give the man a fighting chance.

Come on, Linden! Owen urged as the Stonehaven worker pushed himself up, driven by adrenaline and a biological urge to survive. *Stab that thing into his rotten neck! Kill the bastard!*

Linden's sudden forceful vigor appeared to give Bloodletter pause, and the prosecutor became more cautious, holding the machete in a defensive grip. Finn allowed himself the hope that, despite the odds, Linden would prevail. Then an indistinct blur of movement shimmered toward the man from Stonehaven, and a blade appeared out of nowhere and was plunged into the man's throat. Linden froze as if gripped by invisible forces, then a black roundel dagger was removed from the man' flesh, and blood gushed into the snow like water from a broken fire hydrant. Linden collapsed, face first, and suddenly the shimmer resolved into the shape of a woman: The Shadow, Elara Cage.

The Shadow had claimed her next victim, but mourning Linden would have to wait, because the prosecutors had arrived in the one place in all of Zavetgrad that Finn desperately wished them not to be.

17

METAL... BLOOD...

Watching Elara Kage slaughter Linden like an animal could have tipped them all over the edge into panic, but the death of the Stonehaven worker focused Finn's mind like a whetstone sharpening a blade. Not all of them had reacted the same way. Owen and Khloe had also kept their heads and kept sight of their goal of fleeing Zavetgrad, but the arrival of the prosecutors had struck terror into Cora's heart and she was close to breaking point.

"How long until the Metals arrival?" Finn asked, coming to a stop at the far end of the skybridge and hurrying the others through into the control center.

"Fourteen minutes," Khloe replied, breathless from the sprint across the overground passageway.

Finn turned to Cora and held her shoulders. The woman from Spacehaven was shivering like a rocket engine during blast off, and it took several seconds for her tearful eyes to meet his own.

"You're up, Cora," Finn said, once he felt sure he had the woman's full attention. "We need to reach the sub-level storage room on the east side, close to the backup power management facilities, right?" Finn looked to Khloe for her confirmation and she nodded.

"I know the way but what if they're out there?" Cora said, her voice shaky like her trembling body. "What if we're walking into a trap?"

"It doesn't matter either way," Finn said. "We either get out or we die. There are no other options, so we have to take the chance."

"Scraps scans!" the robot said, leaping from Finn's shoulder to Cora's. "Scraps warn if bad men near."

"You hear that?" Finn said, smiling at his robot, who was proving to be the most fearless of them all. "Scraps will raise the alarm if the prosecutors are close, so all we need you to do is guide us to that room. Can you do that?"

Cora nodded and blew out a heavy breath through chattering teeth. Feeling Scraps clamped down on her shoulder had smoothed over her frayed edges. "Okay…" she said, nodding and attempting a smile. "I can do this. Follow me."

Cora led them inside the control center and Scraps remained on her shoulder, acting as an emotional support robot and early-warning detection system in one. Unlike much of the rest of the construction site, the control center was in a mostly-finished state, ready for furnishing. It was a long, narrow building on four floors that was curved like the arch of a foot. Tall ceilings and full-length glass walls meant there was enough light to navigate the corridors without needing to risk Cora's torch, but it also felt dangerously exposed, as if the prosecutors could spot them at any moment.

"It's not much further, maybe two more minutes," Cora said, becoming more relaxed and confident with each step closer to their objective.

Suddenly, Scraps became agitated. The robot flew off Cora's shoulder and hovered directly in her path, petite metal hands outstretched.

"Wait-wait!" Scraps called out, and everyone stopped on a dime. "Truck coming. Look-look!"

Scraps flew to the window and pointed outside. Finn darted to the robot's side and scoured the horizon but the worsening weather meant that visibility had dropped to barely more than fifty meters.

"I don't see a truck..." Finn began, then he caught movement in his peripheral vision and his eyes snapped to it like a magnet pointing north. "Wait, I do see it..." he corrected himself.

"Is it the prosecutors?" Owen asked. His friend was just behind his right shoulder, electrician's knife in hand.

Finn squinted his eyes and concentrated on the vehicle but it wasn't armored like the sort of ground car he would have expected the prosecutors to use. It was more like a utility vehicle. Then the answer came to him and his blood ran cold.

"Shit, it's Soren!" Finn said. "That's the same truck we saw Maeve drive away at the start of the trial."

"Is it all three of them?" Owen asked. "I can't make out shit in this blizzard."

Finn saw the door of the vehicle fly open but the weather was too bad to make out how many people had been inside the truck, or how many had gotten out.

"As much as I'd like to believe Maeve and Corbin killed

each other, we have to assume they're both still with him," Finn replied.

He backed away from the window, fearing that a crossbow bolt might punch through the glass at any moment and end his hopes of escape in a fit of poison-fueled anguish. Owen backed away too, and Finn saw that his friend's knuckles were white from gripping the handle of the blade so tightly.

"First Linden, and now Soren and the others," Cora said. She had pressed her back to the wall and looked like a rabbit in headlights. "Why is everyone coming here?"

"Golds did it," Scraps said. The bot flew back onto Cora's shoulder and the tautness in the woman's back and neck relaxed. "Golds used foremen. Push people here."

"Damn it, they're doing it on purpose," Owen said. "If we're all in one place they can kill us more easily, and in full view of the crowd."

Finn recognized the tactic from other trials and knew that it meant the end phase was near. Whenever a trial went on too long or needed to be cut short for whatever reason, the golds controlling the crucible would release flying drones and modified foremen into the arena to force offenders into a kill zone. He guessed that the worsening weather was the reason for expediting the end phase, though he worried that perhaps the Regent had gotten wind of their escape attempt and was trying to thwart it.

"None of us are going to die today," Finn said, desperate to recapture their lost optimism. "All we have to do is make the rendezvous with the Metals, then we can leave all this behind. We have to keep moving."

Cora nodded and pushed away from the wall. Her legs

were like jello and Finn thought she was going to crumple to her knees, but Khloe hooked an arm through hers and together they compelled one foot to step in front of the other, through sheer force of will. Progress was slow and each precious second that elapsed felt like the tick of a doomsday clock counting to the end of days.

"Wait-wait!" Scraps said, this time remaining on Cora's shoulder.

"What's wrong, pal?" Finn whispered. He dare not speak any louder. "We don't have a lot of time."

"Person close..." Scraps said, now also whispering. "But not bad men..."

Finn scowled at the robot. "If it's not the prosecutors then who?"

He heard footsteps approaching and fear gripped him, but Finn held his ground, fighting his primal instinct to run. Owen was there a heartbeat later, ready to fight with him side-by-side, but it wasn't the prosecutors who stepped into view, but Skye.

"For fuck's sake, Skye, I could have killed you!" Finn said, relieved but furious. "What the hell are doing, creeping around like that?"

"Where's Linden?" Skye asked, seemingly oblivious to his outburst. The woman was scratching at her knuckles and Finn could see that they were bloody and raw. "I heard a scream. Is he... safe?"

Finn didn't know whether to be honest or lie and he had only a fraction of second to decide. Any delay, not matter how slight, risked them missing the rendezvous.

"He's dead, Skye," Finn said, making his choice for better

or worse. "The prosecutors got him, and they'll get us too if we don't keep moving."

"Dead?" Skye replied, shaking her head, and digging another lump of skin out of her hand. "No, he can't be dead. He went to find somewhere safe to hide. He said he'd be back."

"Skye, he's dead, but there's still a way you can survive this," Finn said, trying to reach the woman. "But you have to come with us, now."

He took a step closer but Skye backed away, suddenly wary of him. Then the woman spotted Scraps perched on Cora's shoulder and her anger flared like a match being struck.

"You have a robot?" Skye said, pointing a bloodied finger at Scraps. "Only golds have personal robots." Her eyes widened and her mouth fell open. "You're working for them! You're working for the golds!"

"Damn it, keep your voice down!" Finn hissed, holding up his hands and trying to appear non-threatening, but Skye was hysterical and incapable of listening to reason.

"No, you're lying!" Skye pulled a knife from inside her boot, similar to the electrician's blade that Owen was wielding. "You're with them and you're going to kill me too!"

Skye slashed at Finn with the knife, cutting his shoulder and forcing him to dodge back, before lunging and scraping the blade across his thigh, drawing more blood. He grabbed her forearms and tried to wrestle her away but Skye continued to claw at him with blood-stained fingers, like a zombie feasting on his flesh.

"Get off him!"

Owen shoved Skye back and she collided with the glass

wall, causing it to flex dangerously from the impact, but the Stonehaven woman showed no signs of backing down. She was in a frenzy, fueled by blind terror, and there was no way to reason with her. Skye then screamed and charged at Owen but the man sidestepped her lunge and the Stonehaven woman careened into Khloe, knocking her to the floor.

"Bitch!" Skye roared, climbing onto the woman's slender frame and raising the knife above her head. "Fucking traitor!"

With no care as to his own safety, Finn launched himself at Skye and dragged her away from Khloe just as the knife began its thrust toward her heart. By chance, Skye wound up on top of him, blade still in hand. Owen raced to his aid, but Skye slashed his friend across the midsection and he staggered back, grimacing and clutching the wound. Taking advantage of the distraction, Finn grabbed Skye's wrists and tried to force the knife from her grasp, but her grip was unbreakable like the weapon was a part of her. They tumbled across the floor, interlocked in a desperate struggle for survival, before toppling down a flight of stairs. They hit the bottom hard with Finn on top, and he felt the blade slide through Skye's flesh with sickening ease. The woman's eyes went wide, though this time it was from shock rather than madness. Finn pushed himself off her and scrambled away, shaking uncontrollably as blood gushed freely from a scalpel-like cut across Skye's abdomen.

"Finn..."

He heard someone call his name but he didn't know who. His universe was now only Skye and the rapidly expanding pool of blood collecting around her dying body.

"Finn, come on!"

He felt a sharp sting of pain and pressed his hand the side

of his face, which was hot like a laser burn. Then he felt hands grappling his arms and body, dragging him to his feet, but still all he could see was the woman he had just killed.

"Finn, snap out of it," Owen yelled. "We only have six minutes. Six minutes!"

Suddenly, the rest of the world resolved around him, and he saw Owen, Khloe and Cora looking into his eyes, faces drawn and panicked. His friend had a piece of orange jumpsuit fabric wrapped around the cut to his stomach as a makeshift tourniquet. It was stained red in places but had succeeded in stemming any bleeding.

"Shit, are you okay?" Finn said, suddenly only concerned with his friend. "Is it bad?"

"I'll live," Owen replied. The man then grunted a weary laugh. "At least for the next five minutes. After that, who knows?"

Finn felt angry with himself for wasting what little time they had left. Then he saw Skye again and had to turn away.

"Which way, Cora?" Finn said, his voice cracking as he spoke.

"It's just along here," Cora answered, taking his arm to guide him. Khloe already had hold of his other arm and he realized that she had been holding him up. "We're so close, Finn. I'll help you, we both will. Just come with us..."

Finn allowed himself to be led but whether he was going east or west, or up a flight of stairs or down one, he had no idea. He just walked, and everywhere he went, Skye's dead eyes followed him.

"We're here!" Cora said. "This is the door into the storage area!"

The announcement was like a shot of adrenaline to his

heart. He shook his head and looked at the door, but the handle was missing.

"On three, we kick it down together," Owen said, gripping Finn's shoulder so hard that pain coursed through his body, but it was a welcome tonic. It reminded him that he was still alive.

Finn took a step back, then his friend began the count and together they hammered the heels of their boots into the door and smashed it clean of its hinges. It clattered into the space below a moment later and a cold wind howled through the opening.

"There aren't any stairs!" Cora yelled, hands gripping the back of her head and pulling her hair tight. "How do we get down?"

Finn felt like he'd just died and been resuscitated. He rushed to the door but Cora was right. It was an unfinished space with no way down.

"That's why there wasn't a handle, so no-one opened the door and accidentally fell inside," Owen said, peering into the chasm. "Are you sure we're in the right place?"

Cora nodded. "I'm certain of it. This is the room."

Finn was about to ask Scraps to fly down and check it out when the robot zoomed further along the corridor, electronic eyes focused on the junction at the end.

"Danger!" the robot warned, its little scanner dish angled sharply ahead.

"It's too late!" Cora said, moving behind Owen and shielding herself behind the man's broad shoulders. "They've found us..."

Finn ran to Scraps and turned the robot's oil-can body to face him. The machine looked afraid but no less determined.

"Find somewhere to hide, pal, and stay there till I say it's safe to come out!"

Scraps nodded and zoomed away into the darkness. At the same time, Finn ran to the open door and grabbed one of the metal bars that had been placed in preparation for the concrete staircase to be built. He yanked and pulled at the bar until it broke free in his hand, then raced to Owen's side.

"We rush them, together," Finn said, gripping the bar so tightly that it bruised his flesh. "There's only two of them. We can do it!"

Owen nodded, knife held in a reverse grip, then both steeled themselves ready to charge. Shadows crept around the corner and Finn was about to run, but rather than two shapes, there were three, and he hesitated. Soren then appeared, breathless and caked in mud, followed soon after by Corbin and finally Maeve, who hung back in the shadows.

"What the fuck are you doing here?" Soren yelled, stopping dead in his tracks. He had a metal pipe in his hand, sharpened at the end like a quill pen, while Corbin was wielding a clawhammer. "You'll lead them straight to us, if you haven't already!"

Finn's head was spinning. "You know about the Metals too?"

Soren's face scrunched up in anger and confusion. "Metal what? What the fuck are you talking about?"

"You don't know?" Finn asked.

"Don't know what?" Soren yelled. "So help, me Finn, you'd better start talking sense, or I'm gonna fucking kill you myself!"

Finn had never much believed in luck but it seemed that fate had seen fit to curse him. Soren had no idea what lay below them in the empty storage room and had simply stumbled upon them by chance.

"We were here first, so you leave!" Owen yelled, aiming the knife at Soren.

"Enough! Maeve roared. The woman pushed between her companions, and Finn saw that she had a fire-axe in her right hand. "There's only four of them, and those scrawny-ass women won't put up much of a fight. Let's just kill them and be done with it!"

Khloe marched beside Owen, radiating aggression like a rabid wolverine. "Why don't you come over here and find out how much fight I have in me?"

Maeve smiled and the woman took a step forward, then a voice sliced through the tension like a laser beam.

"Metal!"

Maeve froze and no-one else moved a muscle.

"Who said that?" Soren hissed, his head suddenly on a swivel. "Is there someone else here?"

"Metal!" the call came again, this time louder.

"Blood!" Khloe called back.

Again they waited and still no-one moved. Then the top of a ladder thudded against the open doorway to the sub-level and the sound of someone climbing resonated through the corridor. Seconds later, a man with messy yellow hair and a black bandana mask poked his head above the floor line.

"What the hell is this?" the Metal said. "There was only supposed to be one of you."

18

CHROMES OF METALHAVEN

The Haven operative, known as a Metal, climbed the final section of the ladder then pulled himself inside the corridor and stood by the door. Soren barged past Maeve and thrust his improvised weapon at the man, who didn't flinch and didn't take his eyes off the bully even for a second.

"Who the fuck are you?" Soren demanded, continuing to brandish the weapon with hostile intent. "Don't give me any bullshit or I'll cut you open from ear to ear."

The yellow-haired man coolly slid a pistol out of a shoulder holster that was concealed inside his jacket then aimed the weapon at Soren with his finger pressed along the frame.

"Don't even think about it," the Metal said. He spoke in an even tone while showing no fear. "One more step toward this ladder, and I will kill you without a second thought."

"He's come for Khloe, not you," Finn said, fearful that Soren was stupid enough to test the Metal's resolve. "She's getting out of here, to Haven."

"Bullshit," Soren snapped. "Haven is a myth. Anyone with half a brain knows that."

Finn could have gone for the easy win and poked fun at Soren's lack of intelligence but the last thing anyone needed was for him and his old rival to break into a fight. That was how their troubles had started.

"If Haven is just a myth, then you'll have no problem letting her leave, right?" Finn answered.

He nodded to Khloe and the woman took a step toward the exit but Soren shifted position and jabbed his makeshift spear at her instead.

"How come she gets out?" Soren asked, doubt already creeping into the bully's mind. "What's special about her?"

Finn knew Soren all too well. The man's beliefs were like shifting sands, without solid foundations and ever changing from one moment to the next. He knew that Soren wouldn't risk being wrong, not when the stakes were so high.

"We don't have time for this," the Metal cut in. His tone and manner were forceful and intimidating, like a prefect, and Finn wondered if the man had once been part of Zavetgrad's authorization police force. "My orders were to rescue Khloe Symons and no-one else." The man pointed to Khloe. "That's her, right there. She comes with me and everyone else stays."

While the Metal was clearly angry, the man had kept his composure and stayed focused on his mission. Finn figured that the operative's skillset made him adept at coping with high-stress, rapidly-evolving situations like the one he'd found himself in.

"No fucking way is she leaving without us," Soren said. As expected, he'd already changed his mind and was now fully on-board with Haven's existence. "If she's getting out then so am I, and no fucker in this room is going to stop me."

"I'll stop you..." The Metal clicked back the hammer on the weapon to emphasize his point and Soren wisely stayed put. "No-one leaves without my say so, and you'd better believe that I will shoot every last one of you before I let you compromise my operation."

"You shoot that thing and the prosecutors will be all over us in a heartbeat," Maeve countered. She moved beside Soren in solidarity, despite the Metal's threat to shoot them. "The way I see it, you don't have a choice, blondie. You either take us with you, or you die here too."

The chatter of a distant voice crackled through a communications device that was inserted in the Metal's ear, and the man was briefly distracted while he listened. He tapped the device twice then cursed under his breath before looking at each of the faces staring back at him.

"I can take a maximum of four, but only if we leave now," the Metal growled, and Soren smiled, knowing that they'd called the operative's bluff. "Any more than four and my aircar will be too heavy to make it back across the Davis Strait on the fuel I have left. And trust me, ditching in the water is as much of a death sentence as this trial."

Finn counted the number of bodies but the simple fact was that the math didn't add up. Finn, Owen, Khloe and Cora, plus Soren, Corbin and Maeve made seven – three more than the Metal could take.

"Since it's Finn's fault that Corbin and I are here, I say that he stays!" Soren said, aiming the makeshift spear at him. "Owen too, since they're both as much to blame as each other." Then the man pointed to Cora and smiled. "And the

Spacehaven bitch can stay too." Soren licked his lips and leered at Khloe. "But the scrawny one can sit on my lap. It looks like she could use a little meat in her..."

Finn saw a spark of anger behind Maeve's eyes and the woman inched away from Soren, but the bully was oblivious to this, because an argument had broken out over who should get to escape. Insults and accusations were being hurled from all quarters. Cora stood by Khloe arguing that Soren should stay because his zero genetic rating mean that he couldn't contribute to Haven's gene pool, while Corbin predictably stood by his master, like a loyal dog snapping at the heels of an intruder. Finn stayed quiet throughout and watched the Metal closely. The situation was spiraling, and he fully believed that the Haven operative would rather risk shooting them dead and alerting the prosecutors, than being overrun and forced to take them all. Finn already knew what to do, and in some ways his decision came as a relief.

"I'll stay..." Finn said, but his words were lost in the melee of insults and cusses crisscrossing the corridor. "I'll stay!" he said again, this time shouting so that no-one could mistake him.

A stunned silence followed and Finn noticed that the Haven operative was looking at him with a mixture of curiosity and surprise. Owen, however, was struck dumb with shock, though Finn knew it would only delay his friend's protests, not prevent them entirely.

"Great, so Finn stays!" Soren said, predictably viewing his sacrificial act as a cause for celebration. "That means we just need two more to stay!"

Finn clenched his jaw and looked at Owen, hoping that his friend wasn't going to be noble and choose to stay too, but that was as futile as expecting the sun not to rise in the morning.

"If you're staying then so am I," Owen said, moving to his side and rooting himself to the spot. "We're in this together, remember?"

"Great, then that's two!" said a jubilant Soren. He took a step toward the Metal but the barrel of the pistol was thrust into his face.

"You still need one more to remain," the operative said, holding fast. "You have to agree on all three to stay before I let anyone down this ladder. And you have to be certain, because once we leave, there's no turning back."

More squabbles and arguments broke out but Finn left them to it and turned to his friend. He appreciated what Owen was doing but he couldn't let him sacrifice himself too.

"I want you on that aircar to Haven, Owen," Finn said, shutting out everything else to focus solely on convincing his friend. "Soren was right, it's my fault that you're here and I can't let you die because of my mistake."

Owen shook his head. "No way, Finn, we agreed that we'd do this together…"

"Damn it, Owen, we don't have time to argue!" Finn snapped. "I need you on that aircar, do you understand me?"

Owen again shook his head, even more firmly.

"What do you take me for, Finn?" Owen said, sounding wounded and angry. "It wouldn't matter if I did get to Haven, I'd never forgive myself for leaving you here to die." The man stood tall, like a soldier addressing his officer in command. "I'd rather go out fighting the prosecutors and the Authority than be a coward and run out on my best friend."

"They'll kill us either way, Owen," Finn said, trying to

barter despite knowing in his bones that it was hopeless. "Even if we kill the prosecutors, only one person gets to walk out alive. You know the rules."

"So we change the rules, like you said…" Owen hit back, parroting the line that Finn had fed him after their arrest. "We take out Bloodletter and The Shadow and we make the Authority recognize us both as winners." The man shrugged. "And if they still kill us then fuck them. We'll have shown all of Zavetgrad that the Authority couldn't turn us against one another. We'll show them that chromes from Metalhaven can't be broken. That has to mean something, right?"

Finn wanted to tell Owen that the Authority didn't bend their rules for anyone, and dying side-by-side as a show of defiance wouldn't make a damned bit of difference, but he didn't. If Owen was staying then it meant there was only one way to keep him alive. They would kill the prosecutors and stand alone in the crucible. Then he would take his own life to save a life more worthy of existing.

"Okay, Owen," Finn said, smiling and clasping his hands around his friend's broad shoulders. "We stay and fight them, together."

With the decision made, he turned to the Haven operative, who seemed not to have taken his eyes off them for a moment. "Owen and I will both stay," Finn announced.

"Yeah, we already knew that," Soren said, dismissing him with a flourish of his chubby hand. "But this selfish bitch from Spacehaven won't do the right thing!"

"Sixty seconds and I'm gone," the Haven operative cut in. The man was losing his cool, which didn't bode well for any of them. "Either four come with me or none of you do, so make your goddamn choice!"

Maeve suddenly grabbed Soren from behind and pressed the blade of her axe to his throat.

"Then I'll make the choice for us," the woman snarled, pressing harder and drawing blood. "I'd like to say I'm sorry, lover boy, but I'm not..."

Soren screamed as the blade cut deeper but before his throat was cut, Corbin had swung his clawhammer and crushed Maeve's skull, splattering blood across the wall and over the side of Soren's face. Maeve crumpled to the ground and the axe fell, clattering and scraping against the tiled floor with ear-splitting harshness.

"Now there are four of us," Corbin said, tossing the hammer then grabbing Soren's arms to ensure the shellshocked man stayed standing.

Finally, the Haven operative stepped away from the door and allowed Corbin to guide Soren onto the ladder. Cora and Khloe had been closer but both women looked as traumatized as Soren, though not because of the violence they'd witnessed. Their group was being split up and it wasn't a temporary parting. Once they stepped onto the ladder and descended into the tunnel network beneath Zavetgrad, they would never see Owen or Finn again. Realizing this had hit them harder than the hammer strike to Maeve's head.

"It should be you two on that ladder with me," the Haven operative said, addressing Finn and Owen while Soren descended out of view. "Haven needs people like you, not people like them," he added, nodding toward Corbin and Soren.

"Then why didn't you choose?" Finn asked.

"We Metals don't decide who is saved and who isn't," the

operative answered, solemnly. "It's only our job to get people out."

Khloe and Cora then stepped forward and the Metal backed away. "Thirty seconds..." the man said, recognizing the need for the two women to say their goodbyes. "But then we really must go."

"He's right, you should be on the aircar to Haven, not Soren and Corbin," Cora said. She was upset but anger was her dominant emotion.

"Neither of those assholes would give up their place without a fight and we don't have time for that," Finn replied. He forced himself to smile. "Don't worry about us. We're not finished yet."

"Not you, not yet," the Metal said. Soren was already on his way down the ladder but the Haven operative had pushed Corbin back at gunpoint. "You go last, once the other two are safely down the ladder."

Corbin gritted his teeth and Finn could see that the man was contemplating doing something rash, but the pistol pointed at the man's black heart kept him in check.

"Fine, then hurry it up, for fuck's sake," Corbin said, impatiently. "Your tearful goodbyes are going to get us all killed!"

"Spacehaven lady, you're up," the operative said, waving Cora over.

The woman nodded then looked at Finn and he could see that she still had so much to say, but no time in which to say it. Instead, she leaned in and kissed him softly on the cheek then smiled at Owen and hurried away. Finn blew out a sigh and watched Cora step onto the ladder and begin her descent. Then Khloe took his hands into hers and her grip was surprisingly strong. She looked young again, as if the weight of an enormous burden had finally been lifted, but it was tinged with sadness too.

"Thank you," she said.

Finn frowned at her. "For what?"

"For restoring my faith in humanity," Khloe answered. "I'd forgotten that there were still good people in Zavetgrad."

Finn huffed a laugh but he accepted the compliment graciously, albeit with a flush of embarrassment. He was no good at taking praise, especially when he felt it unwarranted.

"Once you step on that ladder, there will be one less good person in Zavetgrad," Finn replied. Then he looked toward the door but Cora was already out of sight. "Two less, actually. But I'm glad you'll both be safe."

Khloe smiled again then a sharp hiss split the air and the woman's face twisted with pain. A second later, a crossbow bolt exploded inside Khloe's back, ripping her apart from the inside out.

19

STRANGE SHADOWS

Khloe's blood splattered across his face and painted his chrome jumpsuit red but Finn kept hold of her hands, even as her legs gave way and her dead body collapsed under its own weight, pulling him down with her. Another bolt flashed past and he felt the projectile scratch his face but still he didn't let go of Khloe's hands, because as soon as he did, he'd have to accept that she was gone.

"Get down!" the Haven operative yelled.

The deafening report of gunfire rang out, jolting Finn's senses and snapping him back to the moment. He released Khloe then held his trembling hands in front of his face. They were covered in blood.

But is it hers, or mine?

"Brasa!"

Bloodletter was pinned down by gunfire from the Haven operative, but still the prosecutor was yelling Finn's name into the air like he'd wronged the man in some unforgivable manner.

"Get out here, Brasa!" the prosecutor roared, risking a

bullet in order to shout his challenge. "Get out here and fight me!"

Rage filled Finn up, consuming his fear and sorrow so that only hatred remained. Hatred for the Authority. Hatred for the golds. And, most of all, hatred for Bloodletter, who had claimed yet another innocent soul. He rose to his feet and stepped over Khloe's mutilated body, intent on tearing out Bloodletter's heart with his bare hands. The prosecutor saw him coming and aimed his crossbow but Owen tackled Finn to the ground and the bolt whistled over their heads, ripping a wall panel to shreds behind them.

"What the hell are you doing?" Owen said, using his brute strength to muscle Finn into an empty side room. "You won't get close to Bloodletter before he blows yours head off!"

"I don't care!" Finn cried, shrugging Owen off him. "If I'm going to die then let me die with my hands around that bastard's throat!"

Finn tried again to rush outside but Owen held him back, and like the tug of gravity, his pull was inescapable.

"Damn it Owen, let me go!" Finn roared but he was unable to free himself.

"Not a chance in hell," his friend replied, tightening his hold. "And don't think for a second that I'm letting that murdering piece of shit off the hook. But if we're going to take him out, we have to be smart."

More gunshots rang out then the Haven operative was forced to reload. Bloodletter seized his chance and darted into the open, firing his crossbow and sinking the bolt into the Metal's hand. It exploded a moment later, ripping open bone, flesh and tendon. The man screamed in agony and dropped the pistol, which spun across the polished tile floor and came to rest tantalizingly close to Corbin.

"Take it!" Finn yelled at Corbin, but the man was cowering inside another room on the opposite side of the corridor. "Take the gun and shoot him!" he added, practically screaming at the man, but Corbin was petrified with fear, and Finn doubted that his words had even registered.

"Hi-hi!" Scraps called out.

The sound of his robot's voice appeared to come out of nowhere and Finn searched the room, finally spotting Scraps at the far end of the space, next to another door. He'd forgotten that he'd asked the robot to lay low and stay hidden and was overjoyed to see his little machine helper again.

"Scraps helps. Lead you away!" the robot added, waving them over.

Finn glanced outside and saw Bloodletter making his way toward them. The Haven operative was gone, climbing down the ladder one-handed, while the man's weapon remained in the middle of the corridor, just out of reach. He looked to where Corbin had been hiding, intending to warn him about Bloodletter's advance, but the Metalhaven worker had gone, abandoning not only the gun but his chance of getting out.

"Quick-quick!" Scraps yelled. "Bad man near!"

Finn heard his robot but he wasn't yet ready to abandon their only hope of escape, not when the door to salvation was literally across the other side of the corridor.

"You can still make it out of here," Finn said, turning to his friend, who had eased his limpet-like grip on him. "I can distract Bloodletter, while you make a run for the ladder and climb down. With Corbin gone and Khloe dead, there's enough room on the aircar to take you to Haven."

"There's enough room for us both," Owen corrected him.

"Come out, Brasa!" Bloodletter roared. "Come out, and I'll make it quick!"

The man was punctuating his slow advance by clashing his machete against walls and doors, as if trying to startle him out of hiding. Finn sensed that the prosecutor was close, perhaps no more than ten meters away.

"We won't both make it, you know that," Finn said, angry at his friend for making what should have been a simple decision complicated. "I deserve to be on trial but you don't, so take the chance and go!"

Owen refused. "Nothing's changed, Finn. We either both get out or neither of us do."

"Finn come!" Scraps screeched, ramping up his volume circuit to maximum. "Bad man outside!"

There was a sound like an empty oil can rolling down a road, then a canister the size of a drinking flask trundled inside the room and exploded. Finn and Owen were thrown clear by the blast and sent barreling across the room, coming to rest in a heap by the far wall. Dust and smoke stung his eyes but through it Finn could see the outline of a man in armor. A musical note sang and the glint of a razor-sharp machete gleamed through the smog.

"You're mine, Brasa!" Bloodletter called out, though the man was still little more than a blur.

Owen pulled him up and together they ran for the other doorway where they'd last seen Scraps. A crossbow bolt flashed through the air and sunk into Finn's shoulder, and for a brief, terrifying moment, he thought he was about to lose his arm, but the missile didn't explode. He tore it out and saw that it was a regular bolt, then he heard Bloodletter laughing like a maniac clown.

"Oh no, that would be too easy!" the prosecutor yelled, laughing to himself. "You made me look like a fool, Brasa, and for that I'm gonna bleed you, nice and slow. I'm gonna make you beg for death, Brasa! Do you hear me, fucker?!"

The man's words trailed off as Finn and Owen raced back into the corridor. He chanced a look back but the grenade blast had collapsed the roof over the door into the basement, and to the tunnels that led beyond Zavetgrad, sealing off their only avenue of escape.

"Here-here!" Scraps called out, waving at them from a junction at the end of the passageway. "Quick-quick!"

They ran then Owen cried out and stumbled but Finn managed to grab his friend's arm and stop him from falling. They reached the end of the corridor and pulled themselves around the corner, just as another bolt thudded into the wall and exploded, spitting wood and plaster at them like an improvised frag grenade. Finn felt splinters dig into his back and neck but he blocked out the pain and focused on his friend. Owen was bleeding from a bad cut to his thigh where one of Bloodletter's bolts had shorn through his flesh, like a drill.

"It looks like the dart burst open when it hit me, but I got lucky," Owen said, tearing off a section of his jumpsuit to bandage the wound. "An inch to the right and it would have blown my leg clean off."

Bloodletter's maniacal yells drowned out the sound of fabric being torn and tied around Owen's leg. The prosecutor continued to call out Finn's name, taunting him with threats of a slow, agonizing death. He glanced around the corner and saw the hunter unhurriedly pacing toward them, while sliding fresh bolts into his crossbow. The man's machete was still in his right hand, the edge wiped clean of its last victim's blood, but if the prosecutor had his way, it would soon be stained with Finn's.

"This way!" Scraps called out, his electronic voice sounding desperate. "Finn and Owen on wrong side!"

The machine sounded distant and it took a few seconds for Finn to spot the robot on the opposite side of the intersection. He cursed and threw his head back, hands clasped around the base of his neck. In their haste, he and Owen had turned the corner in the wrong direction and backed themselves into a dead end. An elevator shaft was ahead of them but it had yet to be finished, and there wasn't even a cable dangling down from above that could offer them a means of escape.

"We'll have to make a run for it," Owen said. "Maybe we can make it across before Bloodletter gets a shot off?"

It was a half-hearted suggestion and it was obvious that his friend doubted his own plan. Bloodletter was now so close that if they so much as poked their heads around the corner, the marksman would put a bolt through their eye without even blinking. Even so, Finn knew that they had no choice but to try.

"Let me go first," he said, readying himself for the charge. "That crossbow can only fire one bolt at a time, so if he misses me then you can get across without any danger."

Owen shook his head at him, which was becoming an annoyingly common occurrence.

"Stop trying to be a martyr," Owen growled, seeing through Finn and his motives like he was made of glass. "We go together so he has to choose a target. If that bastard hesitates even for a fraction of a second, we have a chance."

Finn disagreed but there was no time to argue, and the only other option was to stay put and wait for Bloodletter to round the corner and kill them.

"That's a dead end, Brasa!" the prosecutor laughed and it sickened Finn how much the sadist enjoyed tormenting them.

The man sounded so close that Finn feared Bloodletter might reach out and grab him. He searched again for a way out but the prosecutor was right. They were trapped and at the hunter's mercy.

"Tell you what, Brasa, I'll do you a deal," Bloodletter added, sounding suddenly earnest, which was bizarrely more unsettling than the man's maddened cackles. "Face me, one-on-one, in full view of the cameras, and I'll grant your worker buddy clemency." The prosecutor now had Finn's undivided attention. "I'll radio the trial controllers and have him picked up and set free. I have that power. So how about it, Brasa? Save your friend, or die together... Your choice!"

"Don't even think about it," Owen said, grabbing Finn's shoulder to make sure he didn't try to slip away. "He's only telling you what you want to hear. Nothing's changed, Finn. We either both get out, or neither of us do."

Finn desperately wanted to believe that Bloodletter's offer was genuine, but his instincts were screaming at him to see sense. In the end, Owen was right. There was only one choice – the same choice they'd always had – to stand and fight together.

"Okay, Owen," Finn replied, thumping the man on the arm. "Together, or not at all."

"Ten seconds, Brasa!" Bloodletter called out. The click of

the crossbow being loaded echoed off the walls. "Ten seconds or I'm comin' to kill you both!"

Finn steeled himself, ready to charge the prosecutor, when Scraps screeched an alarm, and the robot suddenly zoomed into the darkness. A door was flung open across the other side of the junction and a shimmering blur in female form stepped through. The sight of The Shadow left him petrified, as if Elara Cage had a Medusa-like ability to turn men to stone. Then a grenade slid from the woman's hand and hurtled toward them. Finn grabbed Owen and pulled him down, but instead of being aimed at them, the trajectory of the explosive took it toward the corridor where Bloodletter was waiting. It bounced off the wall like a pool ball striking a cushion, then they heard the prosecutor curse their names before an explosion rocked the building. The blast drove them hard against the wall and Finn came to inside a cloud of smoke and dust, his ears ringing as if someone had clashed a cymbal next to his head. He found Owen beneath a pile of brick a plaster and dug the man out, but remarkably he hadn't sustained any further injuries.

"What the hell just happened?" Owen said, coughing and hacking black mucus from his lungs.

Finn looked to the other side of the junction but all he could see was settling dust. The door that The Shadow had entered through remained open and the shimmering form of the prosecutor herself was gone.

"I don't know but let's get the hell out of here before Bloodletter recovers," Finn said, hauling himself and his friend to their feet.

"Surely, he couldn't have survived that explosion?"

Finn staggered to the junction and peered around the

corner. The ceiling had collapsed like a cave-in, blocking the corridor, but through gaps in the rubble he could still make out the muscular, armored torso of the cruel hunter.

"He's still alive," Finn said, though if he hadn't seen it with his own eyes, he wouldn't have believed it possible. "That fucker is even more stubborn than you are."

"Very funny," Owen said, ironically unamused. "But let's not wait around for him to recover. We have to get out while we still can."

The smoke and dust were beginning to clear and Finn clambered across the loose brick and mortar and made his way to the open door. Scraps was on the other side, waiting for them. The little robot was shaking with fear but his eyes brightened at the sight of them both, and he zoomed towards him, grabbing his jumpsuit with his metal fingers and hugging Finn tightly.

"Scraps scared!" the robot said, clinging to him like a barnacle on a ship's hull. "Scraps worry bad man gets you!"

"Not yet, pal," Finn said, patting the robot on the back. "Are you okay?"

"Scraps okay!" the robot said, leaping off his chest and settling into a hover. It was like the trauma of only a few seconds ago was gone, and Finn envied his robot's ability to recover so rapidly. "Upstairs is safe," Scraps added, pointing the way.

Finn looked around the room they'd entered and realized that it was an emergency exit staircase, and that the only direction they could go was up.

"Upstairs it is then," Finn said. He was about to step onto the bottom rung when Owen grabbed his shoulder and held him back.

"Woah, what about The Shadow?" Owen said.

Finn cursed. In the confusion, he'd completely forgotten that it was Bloodletter's co-hunter who'd thrown the grenade that had allowed them to escape.

"Scraps, is the other bad man upstairs?" Finn asked.

The robot shook his head. "Lady-bad-man went away."

Finn felt some of the tension in his battered and bruised muscles relax, but while Scraps had given them some much needed good news, there were still many unanswered questions.

"Why did she help us?" Owen said, thinking along the same lines. "She could have killed us both, but instead she lobbed that grenade at Bloodletter."

Finn wished he had answers but all he had were assumptions, none of which made any sense. "Maybe it was an accident?" he said, picking the one idea that had a faint chance of being true. "Maybe she was trying to throw the grenade at us, and just messed up?"

Owen considered this while they both raced up the stairs but his friend didn't seem any more convinced than Finn was.

"She doesn't seem to me like the type who misses," Owen eventually replied, breathless from the sprint. "Certainly not from that range."

Finn reached the top of the stairs first and stood by the door, waiting for his friend to catch up. Thanks to the cut to his thigh and the earlier wound to his gut, Owen was moving sluggishly and Finn could see that sweat was beading around his brow. The tourniquets were also saturated with blood and barely having any effect.

"How are you doing?" Finn asked, trying not to sound

too worried, knowing that his friend would brush off any suggestion he was badly hurt.

"Don't worry about me," Owen replied, putting on a predictably brave front. "Once we kill those two hunters and they make us golds, I'll have the pleasure of using Zavetgrad's top medical facilities."

Finn grunted but let it slide, since even if his friend was hurt more badly than the man was admitting, there was nothing he could do about it.

"Maybe we can find some weapons on this floor, though I wish we'd gotten hold of the Metal's pistol before we ran," Finn said, grasping the handle. "A gun would certainly make things a lot easier." He was about to pull open the door when he felt a shiver of doubt race down his spine, and he turned to Scraps for reassurance. "You're certain that bad-man or lady bad-man are not on the other side of this door?"

Scraps nodded. "Scraps sure."

Finn blew out a sigh then turned the handle and pulled. The door swung freely and he found himself staring directly into the eyes of a feverish Corbin Radcliffe.

20

TRUST ME...

Finn wrapped his hands around Corbin's thick neck and drove the man into the wall so hard the plasterboard buckled. Corbin broke the hold and swung a wild haymaker that Finn ducked under, leaving the man open to attack. Corbin soaked up four blows before coming to his senses and fighting back, muscling Finn off him then throwing a fast right that left him reeling. The bigger man followed up with another ferocious haymaker but Finn dodged it then and elbowed Corbin in the kidneys before sweeping his legs and sending the man crashing to the ground like a bulldozed wall.

"Stop, I don't want to fight you!" Corbin cried, throwing out his hands and cowering from Finn, just as the man had done from Bloodletter one floor below them. "I got left behind too, remember? I'm on my own!"

"You should have thought about that before throwing in your lot with Soren and Maeve!" Finn yelled, barely managing to hold himself back. "Don't come crying to us now your gang is gone." He snorted and shook his head. "You can shove it, Corbin. Like you said, you're on your own."

Owen stepped between them and from the look on his friend's face Finn knew that he was about to play peacemaker.

"Hold up, Finn, we could use his help," Owen said, proving him right. "He might be an asshole, but three on two sounds like better odds to me."

"No way, Owen, he'll knife us in the back at the first opportunity," Finn replied, sticking to his guns. "We can't trust him."

"You can trust me!" Corbin cut in. He was now on his knees, hands outstretched, imploring Finn to take him in, like the prodigal son returned. "Owen is right, three against two means we have a chance!"

"You already had a chance and you blew it!" Finn snapped, causing Corbin to shrink away from him. "The Metal's gun was on the floor right in front of you. All you had to do was take it and shoot Bloodletter and we'd only have one prosecutor left!"

"Look, I panicked, okay?" Corbin said, with a sudden flare of anger. "You'd have done the same in my place!"

Finn snorted at the man again. He was already sick of Corbin's bullshit excuses and pathetic attempts to bargain with him.

"You didn't have any problem caving in Maeve's head when she had an axe to Soren's throat," Finn pointed out. Then it dawned on him why Corbin hadn't struggled to kill Maeve, and why the man had always been skulking in the background whenever Soren caused trouble. "But I guess it's easy to sucker-punch someone, right? It's different when your own ass is on the line too."

Scraps let out a muted screech of alarm then landed on Owen's shoulder, giving his friend a double-dose of fright.

"Bad-man coming!" Scraps said, pointing to the emergency exit stairwell. "Must go! Quick-quick!"

Finn turned to the robot but he was more cautious to accept the warning, given Scraps' earlier error.

"Are you sure, pal?" Finn asked. "You said there was no 'bad-man' behind this door, but Corbin was right there!"

Scraps frowned his little metal eyebrows. "That not bad-man," he replied, pointing to Corbin. "That dumb-man."

Finn gave the robot an exasperated eye-roll but he could hardly blame Scraps for the mix-up, since the bot hadn't technically been wrong.

"What the hell is that thing?" Corbin yelled, jumping to his feet and pulling back a fist, as if he were preparing to box the robot.

"Scraps is why we're still alive, and he's our best chance of staying that way," Finn answered, drawing Corbin's fist down. "Now do us all a favor and shut up."

To his surprise, Corbin complied, then noises filtered up from the stairwell and Finn remembered that the worker was the least of their worries. He inched through the door and peered down to the level below. Bloodletter had just staggered onto the landing, caked in dust and dried blood, but the prosecutor's machete and crossbow were still firmly in the man's grasp.

"Brasa!" the hunter called out, and Finn ducked out of sight, but not before the prosecutor had glimpsed him. "I'm tired of this, Brasa. I offered to let your scumbag buddy go free and you threw it back in my face! Now, I'll make you watch as he dies screaming!"

Finn heard boots striking metal and he chanced another look over the railings. Bloodletter was moving slowly and with a limp, which gave him some time to think, though not much.

"We need to get to the roof," Finn said, backing away from the door with the sound of the prosecutor's footsteps striking a regular beat like a metronome.

"What good will that do us?" Corbin said. "We need to get out of this place, not trap ourselves even higher up!"

"There's no *we*, Corbin, there's just me and Owen," Finn answered, whirling on the man and jabbing a finger into Corbin's chest. "You can do whatever the hell you like."

He turned to Owen to back him up but his friend looked contrite, just as he always did when Owen's opinion differed from his own, but was too polite to admit it. Finn cursed under his breath and looked back to Corbin, who remained cowed into silence.

"Fine, we stick together," Finn said, barking at Corbin like an angry dog. "But if you're with us then you do things our way, and that means we go to the roof."

Corbin gritted his teeth, desperate to object, but another cry of "Brasa!" from the prosecutor put paid to any further protest.

"Whatever, but can we just get moving, before that fucker reaches the top of the stairs and shoots us?"

"That's the first sensible thing I've heard you say," Finn said. He then slapped his friend on the shoulder and together they headed away from the door with Corbin bringing up the rear.

"What's your plan when we get to the roof, anyway?" Corbin asked, as Finn navigated the corridors without any knowledge of where they were leading. He did, however, know what he was looking for. "You do have a plan, right?"

"Yes, I have a plan," Finn snapped. "If we go outside then we're easy targets, not just for Bloodletter, but The Shadow too." The mention of the second hunter made Corbin go quiet, and it seemed clear that the man had forgotten about the stealthy assassin. "But there's only one way to reach the roof, which means that if Bloodletter wants us, we know exactly where he'll be."

"That might actually work," Corbin said. "We can hide out then rush that bastard as soon as he pokes his head out!"

"Thanks for the vote of confidence," Finn replied, heaping on the sarcasm. He then stopped at a door and tried the handle but it was locked.

"What are you looking for?" asked Owen.

"A way up," Finn answered, trying another door, which simply led into an empty storeroom. "There must be another staircase or a ceiling hatch that leads to the roof."

"Scraps knows!" the robot said. He'd been hovering behind them as quiet as a mouse, and Finn felt foolish for not thinking to ask his robot sooner. "Follow Scraps!"

The robot zoomed ahead so fast that it was a struggle for their injured, weary bodies to keep up. Scraps zipped left and right, navigating the maze of corridors like a drone racer, before eventually stopping in front of a door. Finn caught up a few seconds later but had to rest against the wall to catch his breath. Corbin was similarly winded but Owen looked more than merely tired. His friend's clammy skin had lost all its vibrancy and Finn could see that fresh blood had oozed into the tourniquet, adding to the darker dried blood that was already there. He wanted to ask if his friend was okay but as before he knew there was no point, and he also didn't want to tip-off Corbin that Owen might be weak and vulnerable.

Despite his assurances, Finn didn't trust the hefty man as far as he could throw him.

"This go roof!" Scraps said, tapping his metal hand on the door.

Finn nodded them blew out an exhausted sigh and tried the handle but it was locked. "Corbin, introduce the door to your size twelves," Finn said, stepping back, hands on hips.

"Why don't you kick it down yourself?" Corbin complained.

"You're not here for your brains, numb nuts, so just do as you're told," Finn hit back.

Corbin muttered curses and insults under his breath but without Soren by his side, the man was meek and pliable. Corbin Radcliffe was a follower not a leader, and Finn could understand how Soren had so easily wrought the man to his will.

Corbin took a couple of paces back then launched a kick just to the left of the handle but instead of smashing open the door, the heavy-set worker's boot went straight through the wood. Cursing some more, Corbin yanked his foot clear, then he threw his shoulder and his substantial mass into the effort of breaking it down. Finally the door collapsed. The momentum of his charge carried Corbin through too and the man found himself tumbling into a dark abyss. He cried out in terror and spun around, managing to catch the lip of the floor with one hand.

"Help!" Corbin yelled, dangling above a sheer drop. As with the entrance to the basement, the stairwell to the roof had yet to be completed, and Corbin had just thrown himself into a vacant space.

Finn dove and managed to catch the man's wrist just as

Corbin's grip gave way, and suddenly, the worker's full weight was dragging him into the chasm too. He clawed at the floor with his other hand and tried to use the rubbery soles of his boots as brakes but he was still sliding. Then he felt hands tightening around his ankles and saw Owen behind him, hauling him back.

"Give me your other hand!" Finn called out, as Corbin peered up at him, white with fear. He reached out, safe in the knowledge that Owen was a secure anchor, but Corbin continued to kick and flail like a fish on a hook. "Give me your other hand, damn it!" Finn yelled, and finally they clasped wrists.

Owen heaved them up and slowly Corbin was pulled out of the void and onto the cold tile floor. For a time, they each just lay on their backs, gasping for air like shipwreck survivors that had almost drowned. Finn's hands were throbbing from the effort of holding Corbin, and friction burns stung his wrists and forearms where the pressure of the man's weakening hold had chafed and scraped his skin raw.

"Bad man!"

Scraps' warning cry was so shrill it could have woken the dead, and it made Finn move faster than he'd ever moved in life. A crossbow bolt fizzed through the air and exploded in the wall inches from his head, then a second bolt hit the floor and shattered the tiles, splintering him and the others with razor sharp fragments of polished stone.

"Follow!"

Scraps was hovering in the middle of an intersecting corridor, waving his arms at them so fast they were a blur of motion. Finn ran, dragging Owen with him, and Corbin wasn't far behind. The cry of "Brasa!" chased them with even more vigor than the crossbow bolts had done, but the injured prosecutor was too lame to keep pace and soon Bloodletter was out of sight.

"Scraps, we need a way out!" Finn yelled, struggling to keep himself and his wounded friend upright.

"No way out!" Scraps replied, and Finn was suddenly consumed with despair.

"There has to be something!" Corbin yelled, as they bundled through a door and into an empty room, with floor-to-ceiling glass windows on two sides. "Another staircase or an elevator? Anything!"

Scraps shook his little head. "Nope-nope. We trapped!"

"Then we stand and fight," Finn said, propping Owen up against the wall. His friend nodded and gave him the thumbs up, but it seemed clear that he was fading with each passing minute. "Search the room for anything we can use as a weapon! It's still three on one."

Finn and Corbin threw open doors and cupboards, looking for anything that might defeat Bloodletter's armor and stop the man for good, but there was nothing. With desperation creeping into his bones like a rot, he flung open the final closet doors and struck gold, finding a toolchest inside.

"Over here!" Finn yelled, calling the others to him.

He dragged the toolchest out of the closet then tipped it onto its side, spilling its contents onto the coarse carpet tiles. Sifting through the tools, he separated out a hefty crowbar and a club hammer. Then saw something else pushed into the corner of the closet, behind where the toolchest had been sat. He picked it up and allowed himself to smile.

"Let's see how Bloodletter likes a taste of his own

medicine," Finn said, stepping out of the closet with a twenty-three-gauge nail gun in his hand.

"That ain't a pistol, dumbass," Corbin said, returning to his old ways disappointing quickly. "You can't shoot that across the room, not that it would do much damage even if you did."

Finn shoved Corbin against the wall then pressed the nailer to a torn patch of the man's jumpsuit and squeezed the trigger. A nail thudded into the wall and Corbin growled and cursed and he wrestled to free his uniform, ripping it further in the process.

"I'm not going to shoot it like a gun, numb nuts," Finn hit back. "But if I can get close enough to that bastard, I guarantee this will do the trick."

"Brasa!"

Owen cursed and shook his head. "Man, I'd give up an entire week's worth of cigarette chits if that asshole would just shut the hell up…"

"Here, I think you know how to use one of these," Finn said, handing Corbin the club hammer. "Just remember who you're supposed to be hitting."

"Yeah, very funny," Corbin replied, snatching the tool from his hand.

Finn then pressed the crowbar into Owen's clammy fingers but didn't immediately let go so that his friend was forced to stop and look him in the eyes.

"Are you up to this?" Finn asked. "I know you're hurt worse than you are letting on, Owen. Let me and Corbin do the grunt work this time."

"I'm fine," Owen snapped, yanking the crowbar out of

Finn's hand, and demonstrating that he was still strong. "But if it makes you feel better, then I have a plan."

Finn scowled. "What do you mean?"

"Just wait beside the door, and be ready with that nailer," Owen answered. "And no matter what you see, trust me, okay?"

"Trust you? What the hell are you going to do?"

Another of Bloodletter's bellowed taunts filled the room and the prosecutor's loping footsteps grew louder. The man's gait was marred by injury, and he was dragging one foot behind the other, each step more of a struggle than the last. Bloodletter was like a wounded predator, relentless in his pursuit despite his evident pain. Finn wondered if the man was even human, or a robot foreman who had been programmed to hound them to the ends of the Earth.

"Finn, trust me," Owen said again, more forcefully. "Go, before it's too late."

Doubt continued to swirl in his mind but he trusted his friend and ran to the side of the door. Through the tinted glass of the floor-to-ceiling windows, he could just about make out the lights of Spacehaven and the glow from the hovering TV screens, which told him that that the weather had eased and the worker population was still watching.

If they want a show then I'll give it to them... Finn thought tightening his hold on the nail gun. *I'll give them something they've never seen before...*

He glanced back at Owen and his breath was caught in his lungs. Owen was on his knees with Corbin stood behind him, hammer held high like an executioner's axe. His friend was looking right at him but he didn't see fear in Owen's eyes. Instead, his friend was imploring him not to act, and it took everything Finn had to stay where he was instead of charging at Corbin and driving a nail between the bastard's eyes.

"It must kill you that you almost got out," the prosecutor bellowed. Finn pressed himself flat to the wall. Bloodletter was just outside the door. "But now you'll never know what Haven really is. You'll never taste freedom, like your traitorous, scumbag friends. But don't worry, little workers, because Haven won't be there much longer. We know all about your secret operatives and your tunnels. It won't be long before Haven is a scorched pile of blackened rubble, just like the rest of this fucked up planet!"

Bloodletter's shadow crept through the open door but the man suddenly froze as he saw Corbin and Owen.

"What the fuck is this?" the prosecutor called out.

"If you want Brasa, then I want a deal!" Corbin yelled. "I want out of here!"

Bloodletter's shadow crept nearer but still the man wasn't inside the room.

"I could kill you two now and find Brasa myself," the prosecutor answered. "Why the fuck do I need your help?"

"You'll never find him," Corbin said. The man sounded so confident that Finn almost believed the ruse himself. "Another group from Haven is coming to get him. Maybe they already have."

"Bullshit..." Bloodletter hissed.

Corbin shrugged. "Don't believe me then, but the longer you wait, the further away he gets, laughing all the way to Haven. Is that what you want? You think he made a fool of you before, but wait until he tells everyone how he humiliated and beat the great Bloodletter..."

"No-one beats me!" Bloodletter roared.

The prosecutor took the bait and as the man stepped through the door, Finn pounced on him like a striking viper, except his fangs were inch-long galvanized nails. Bloodletter reacted with freakish agility, twisting his body away from Finn and blocking the nail gun with the palm of his hand just as he squeezed the trigger. The nail punched clean through Bloodletter's armored glove and scraped across the hunter's face from the corner of his eye to the top of his ear, but it wasn't enough to put him down. A left hook from Bloodletter's armored fist stunned Finn and left him tottering, then the man's crossbow was thrust at his head. Finn threw out his hands in a reflex action and deflected the weapon, causing the bolt to whistle past his face and shatter one of the three-meter glass windows. Freezing-cold air billowed through the opening and the gusting winds blew sleet into his face, forcing his eyes shut. Then Bloodletter's fingers were around his throat, squeezing hard.

Still fighting on pure instinct, Finn drove his hands between Bloodletter's wrists to break the hold then fractured his opponent's nose like an egg with a brutal headbutt. The prosecutor staggered back, on the brink of tumbling through the smashed window, but his desperate flailing hands managed to grasp the frame, sparing the man from a crippling fall. Bloodletter's puffy, bloodshot eyes met Finn's and for the first time he saw that the hunter was afraid. Summoning all the strength left in him, he hurled the nail gun at Bloodletter like an Olympic hammer throw and struck the man cleanly on the chest plate, propelling the prosecutor through the window and out into the freezing darkness.

21

THE FIRING ROOM

BATTLING the icy winds that were still howling through the broken window, Finn rushed to the opening and peered outside. He was expecting to see Bloodletter's broken body sprawled out in the snow but the man wasn't there.

"You got him!" Owen cried, hurrying to his side and wrapping his muscular arm around his neck. The other arm cradled the wound to his gut. "I can't believe that actually worked!"

"I'm not sure it did," Finn replied, though the wind carried his words away and Owen was still too caught up in celebration to hear him.

"Where is he?" Corbin said, leaning out of the window. "I don't see a body."

Owen did hear this time and his arm was rapidly unslung from around Finn's neck.

"He has to be there!" Owen said, willing it to be so. "Finn beat the shit out of him then the asshole fell a full two storeys to the ground. No man could have survived that!"

"Well, he ain't there," Corbin snapped.

The man hammered his fist on the window frame and stormed away from the opening, cursing and muttering under his breath. Owen took Corbin's place and grabbed the window frame, leaning out even further than Corbin had done, but Finn already knew that his friend wouldn't find anything. He'd spotted a man-sized depression in a tarpaulin that was covering some insulation material leftover from the building's construction. There were traces of blood leading away from the Control Centre, where the prosecutor had dragged his bleeding body off the polyethylene sheet.

"He might have survived the fall but he has to be badly hurt," Finn said, trying to focus on the positives. "We won this round."

Corbin snorted a laugh. "*This round*? This ain't a boxing match, Finn. And Bloodletter ain't the only prosecutor out there."

"A few minutes ago we were as good as dead, but we're still alive, all three of us." Finn was determined not to let Corbin's pessimism drag them down. "That plan you two cooked up to lure Bloodletter inside worked, which only proves that if we stick together, and work together as a team, we can beat them."

Corbin was still brooding but there was no denying what Finn had said, and the man didn't try to refute him. Finn figured that Corbin was just as scared and angry as he was, but when they had needed him to step up, he'd delivered.

"Anyone know what this is?" Owen asked. His friend had found an object lying on the floor close to the door and was turning it over in his hands. "It looks a bit like one of the C.O.N.F.I.R.M.E computers that prefects use."

Owen gave him the device before wrapping his arm back

around the worst of his wounds. Blood was trickling over his hip and down his thigh.

"It's Bloodletter's tracking computer," Finn said, recognizing the object right away. A rush of excitement tingled through his body. "With this, we might actually be able to track the prosecutors and know where they are."

The unexpected find piqued Corbin's interest and the man stopped moping for long enough to join them. "That's gold-level tech," Corbin said, scowling at the wrist-mounted computer. "Do you even know how it works?"

"Finn knows!" Scraps said. The bot suddenly dropped onto Finn's shoulder like a hawk diving to attack a shrew.

Corbin jumped back and pressed his hand to his heart. "For fuck's sake, does it have to do that?" Corbin yelled. The man looked like he was one more jump-scare away from a nervous breakdown.

"Finn built Scraps!" the robot continued, undeterred. "Now Scraps help Finn fix this 'puter."

"Do you really think you can get it working?" Owen asked, cautiously optimistic.

Finn continued to examine the device but it was sealed and the interface was locked using a biometric key. He'd never actually had his hands on a C.O.N.F.I.R.M.E device before but he was fairly sure he could figure it out, especially with Scraps' help. He was then suddenly aware of drones hovering in the darkness outside, visible only by the reflections off their camera lenses. The machines had gathered to film them, so that the inhabitants of Spacehaven and beyond could continue with their evening's entertainment. Finn felt some measure of satisfaction from the hope that Zavetgrad's workers might have witnessed Bloodletter's literal fall from grace, but he remained cautious. The drone feed would also inform Trial Control of exactly where they were, and that information was almost certainly being passed to the prosecutors.

"I think there's a chance I can make this work, but not here," Finn said, moving away from the window and beckoning the others to follow. "We need to find somewhere inside the Control Center where we can lay low while I crack it open to get at its circuitry. Somewhere that we can defend, if need be."

Owen and Corbin set their minds to the task but the truth was that without Cora to guide them, the Spacehaven construction site might as well have been another planet.

"Scraps has idea!" the robot said, his enthusiasm as persistent as the stars. "Firing room is safe-safe. Follow Scraps!"

The robot leapt off Finn's shoulder and hovered out of the door. Finn tried to follow but the wear and tear on his body had taken a toll and he was unable to keep pace with the sprightly machine.

"Slow down, Scraps!" Finn called out. "We're not exactly at our best."

The robot stopped abruptly as if it had been ensnared in a net then hovered back to Finn's side. His little eyes probed the injuries on his body and he looked sad.

"Finn hurt?"

"I'll be okay," Finn replied, offering the robot a comforting smile. "Just don't go so fast, okay?"

Scraps nodded and returned the smile. Then the machine's metal eyebrows rose in surprise, as if he'd just remembered something important.

"Finn needs tools!"

The robot zipped back into the room and began searching through the contents of the tipped-over tool chest. Screwdrivers and wrenches went flying as the machine tossed the unwanted items over his shoulder, while occasionally attaching others to his body via magnetism.

"Without that little robot, we'd be dead," Owen commented, reclined against the wall and taking full advantage of the delay. His friend then became more melancholy. "Hey, do you think Cora got out?"

Finn glanced through the windows and could just about make out a skycar creeping through the snow-dense sky. He knew that the chances of it being the Haven skycar were almost zero but he chose to believe otherwise.

"Sure, I think she go out," Finn replied, and Owen smiled. "She's probably sat in some bar in Haven right now, drinking an ice-cold beer."

Owen laughed and Finn allowed the illusion of the Spacehaven worker enjoying her first drink liberated from the Authority's iron grip to fill him up, before the bitter memory that Soren Driscoll had also escaped spoiled the pleasant fiction.

"Ready-ready!" Scraps said, zooming in front of them. "Follow Scraps!"

The bot raced away before remembering what Finn had told him, and slowing down so that the war-weary trio could follow at a pace their bodies could sustain. Finn picked up the nail gun that had landed just inside the room after bouncing off Bloodletter's armor, and they cautiously circumnavigated the Control Centre, remaining vigilant. Owen and Corbin had both also kept hold of their weapons, a crowbar and a hammer, and Finn expected it wouldn't be long before they'd need to again use them in anger.

"Here-here!" Scraps said, stopping in front of a large double-door. They had travelled to the opposite side of the building, which faced inward, toward the launch platforms. "This firing room!"

Finn tried the handle and was relieved to discover that it turned freely. Inching open the door, he cautiously peered inside before Scraps zoomed past his face, so fast and so close that it blew his hair back.

"Safe-safe!" the robot announced, waving them inside. "No bad-men."

Finn pushed the door open fully and stepped inside, though despite Scraps' assertions, he still felt like he was being watched. He looked around the room for the tell-tale shimmer that The Shadow's chameleonic armor produced but everything was calm and still, as if the building had been left abandoned for a century.

"It looks like there are only two ways in or out of this room," Owen said. His friend had already scouted their new hideout, seemingly more comforted by the robot's assurances than Finn had been. "We could push a few of these heavier desks up against the doors, then at least no-one can barge in and surprise us."

"Good idea," Finn said, setting the nail gun down on a side table. The weight of it had begun to make his wrist ache. "Corbin can you give you a hand."

To his surprise, Corbin agreed without protest and the two men put their muscular bodies, which had been fashioned through years of hard toil in the reclamation yards, to good use dragging heavy furniture across the carpet-tiled floor. While they worked, Finn checked inside cupboards and drawers but found nothing besides the occasional loose screw and empty protein-bar wrapper. Giving up on the search, he moved to the bank of floor-to-ceiling glass windows that looked out on the launch platforms. The firing room was where the golds from Spacehaven, dutifully assisted by whites such as Cora, would manage the rocket launch missions to Nimbus. He pressed his face to the cool glass and looked up but for once the space citadel wasn't visible, instead being hidden behind a thick blanket of dark clouds.

"Alright, check this out!" Owen said.

His friend's euphoric cheer spun Finn around like a turnstile, his heart racing with anticipation. He'd hoped to see Owen holding a loaded pistol or perhaps a medical kit, or even an uneaten lunch box. Instead the burly worker was clutching a half-smoked packet of cigarettes, as if the narcotic-laced smokes were more valuable than the air in the room.

"Shit, Owen, for a second I thought you'd found something *actually* useful..." Finn said, making his disappointment abundantly clear through a judicial use of sarcasm.

"My wrecked nerves think these are pretty damned useful," Owen countered, sliding a cigarette out of the pack and popping it into his mouth. He peered into the open packet then cursed. "Shit, there are no matches!"

Owen began vigorously patting himself down, becoming more agitated with each failed attempt to turn up a method of lighting his cigarette from inside his jumpsuit's non-existent pockets.

"Looking for these?" Corbin said, holding up a dog-eared book of matches. There were two left. Owen breathed a sigh of relief and reached for the matches but Corbin snatched them away at the last second. "I have one condition..."

Owen's cheerful mood evaporated like snow on the barrel of a laser cutter, and the two men squared off.

"What do you want, Corbin?" Owen said, with menace.

Corbin came nose to nose with his Owen and Finn was about to step in when the man suddenly smiled and pointed to the pack of cigarettes.

"Can I bum a smoke off you?" Corbin said, deadpan, though still smiling.

Owen laughed and shook his head before holding out the packet. "You're one crazy bastard, do you know that?"

Corbin shrugged then placed a cigarette into his mouth and lit it with one of the two precious matches, before shielding the flame with his hand and lighting Owen's smoke as well. The two men drew deeply from the drug-infused tobacco and the effect was instantaneous, causing the tautness in their faces and necks to disappear.

"Don't you smoke?" Corbin said while jumping onto a table and sliding himself back.

"I try to avoid it," Finn replied, honestly.

Corbin snorted. "You don't like playing by the rules, do you?" he said, taking another long drag from the cigarette. "The Authority wants us to smoke, so you don't smoke. The Authority bans us from having tech, so you build your own fucking robot. The Authority wants us to screw ourselves silly in the Wellness Centers, so you keep your pecker in your pants. I could go on..."

"Please, don't bother on my account," Finn replied.

Corbin laughed, though it wasn't meant cruelly. The

drugs were doing their job well, and both Corbin and Owen had mellowed like evening sunlight through hazy cloud.

"Soren may be a bastard, but he was right about you," Corbin continued, with a more acidic bite. "You refuse anything that's good in this fucked up world. What gets me is why?"

"Nothing the Authority wants for us is good," Finn answered, taking a few steps toward Corbin, which made the man nervous. "Everything they do is to keep us compliant and happy. Even this stupid trial is just an extension of their control. They bribe us with extra beer and the chance to win time off work to make us like them, but in the end, twelve workers lie dead in the mud, and that's what people remember. We remember that if we step out of line, we'll be next to be murdered for other people's entertainment."

Corbin didn't seem convinced. "I never thought of the Trials like that. If you ask me, you read too much into everything."

"I didn't ask, but since we're in an inquisitive mood, let me ask you a question," Finn replied.

"Shoot," Corbin said, shrugging again.

"If the Trials are just a bit of harmless fun to you, then why did you practically piss your pants when we got arrested by Captain Roth?"

Corbin bristled and sat more upright, puffing out his chest. "I didn't piss my pants. I was worried, is all. Everyone knows you're as good as dead if you get sent to trial."

Finn raised an eyebrow and smiled. Corbin had just made his point for him, and from the flush of color on the man's cheeks, it was clear the worker was embarrassed by that fact.

"Besides, I don't always deny myself the simple pleasures,"

Finn added, surprising both Corbin and Owen by sliding a cigarette out of the packet and placing it into his mouth. He then looked at Corbin, expectantly. "Got a light?".

For a second or two, the big man was lost for words, then Corbin laughed boisterously and struck the final match.

"Maybe you're not such a massive asshole, after all," Corbin said, lighting Finn's cigarette.

Finn sucked in the smoke while Owen and Corbin made use of the dwindling flame by lighting two more cigarettes, even though they'd yet to finish their first. As someone who didn't smoke, the nicotine hit was far more potent than the narcotic impact, which crept up more slowly, like an assassin. He felt lightheaded but at the same time his mind was fizzing, and he had to grab hold of a chair back to stop himself falling over. Mercifully, neither of the other two men appeared to notice.

"So, what's your story then?" Owen said, leaning against the edge of a desk and studying Corbin through a cloud of smoke. "How come you ended up hanging out with a loser like Soren Driscoll?"

"You don't know anything about him," Corbin said, jumping to the defense of his friend and sidekick. "Sure, he has his faults, but who doesn't, Mr. Perfect aside?" he added, jabbing his cigarette at Finn in the process. Ash fell from the tip and scorched a pea-sized section of carpet tile black.

"I know everything I need to know about Soren Driscoll," Finn said, annoyed that Corbin was still defending the man, despite the fact Soren had ditched him to save his own ass, without giving it a second thought. "He's a bully, pure and simple. It's not complicated."

"Takes one to know one," Corbin snapped.

Finn recoiled and accidently knocked ash onto a bare patch of skin that was showing through his torn jumpsuit. The shock of Corbin's comment was more painful than the burn.

"You think I'm a bully?" Finn said. "That's insane!"

"Yeah, you are," Corbin replied, undiscouraged. "Maybe not in the same way, but if you ask me, folk were more scared of you than they were of Soren."

"That's crazy talk!" Finn snapped. "I helped people, I never mocked them like your buddy."

Corbin laughed and this time it was meant cruelly. "You really have no clue!" Corbin snapped. "How do you think folk felt when you lorded yourself over them, making them feel bad for smoking or drinking or screwing?" The man tutted and shook his head bitterly. "All anyone wanted was a quiet life, without the prefects bashing-in their skulls, but Finn Brasa, the famous double-five, had to go poking the bear and making trouble."

Finn looked to Owen to defend him, just as Corbin had defended Soren, but his friend was curiously quiet.

"Really? You think the same?" Finn asked. He felt like he'd stepped through a door to another dimension.

"You can be pretty intense," Owen said, apologetically. "But most people know that you meant well."

Finn felt like throwing open the door and storming out but since that would only get him killed, he focused on smoking the rest of the cigarette as rapidly as possible, in the hope that the drugs would make him forget Owen's well-meaning treachery and everything he'd just heard.

"And as for why I stuck by Soren, it's because he stuck by me," Corbin continued, buoyed by the fact Owen had remained annoyingly – but predictably – neutral in the argument. "Before Soren I had no-one. I'm not like you, Finn. I'm a zero-three worker, which means I'm only ever one fuck-up away from a trial or being sent to a Wellness Center. Folk used to tease me about that, but Soren stuck up for me. If it wasn't for him, I'd have been thrown into a crucible like this a long time ago. He treated me like I was someone worth listening to. Like I mattered. Would you have done the same?"

Finn took a moment to digest what Corbin had said. The first number in the man's zero-three rating meant that his seed was damaged and certain to cause serious genetic defects in any offspring. Corbin would have been sterilized as a result. Then there was the worker of rating of three, which was borderline for skilled roles, such as using a laser cutter. Foremen evaluated and updated everyone's worker ratings on a monthly basis, which meant that Corbin lived in perpetual fear of being downgraded to a two rating or lower and taken off to the reclamation yards. With a high genetic rating, he would have simply been reassigned to an unskilled role, perhaps in another sector, but as a zero he was useless to the Authority and its plans of repopulating the species on Nimbus. If Corbin was lucky, he might get assigned to a Wellness Center, but because of his size and strength, it was more likely that the prefects would send him to trial, where he would put on a decent show for the masses.

"I didn't know any of that, I'm sorry," Finn said, sincerely.

His apology was genuine but Corbin was in no mood to be placated.

"Fuck you, Finn, I don't need your pity," Corbin snapped. "Soren is worth ten of you."

"Hey, take it easy, Corbin," Owen cut in. The man had sat back and stayed out of it but Owen had a line like everyone else, and Corbin had just stepped over it. "Finn has always looked out for the workers of Metalhaven, from giving them food chits to working extra hours to make sure they met their quotas. And he took heat for people too, exactly because he *is* a double-five, and he can get away with it. If it wasn't for Finn then I'd already be dead, and I'm not the only one." Owen sighed and tapped the long line of ash off his cigarette. "Soren might have been your friend, but he only ever looked out for himself. You know that better than anyone."

Returning the conversation to the undeniable fact that Soren had bailed on his supposed best friend shut Corbin up like turning off a tap. Then a series of excited squawks and cheers alerted them to Scraps, who had been quietly sitting on a table a few meters away. Finn had thought that the robot was just minding his own business, but instead Scraps had been busy working on Bloodletter's tracking device. Loose screws and metal panels lay strewn across the desk and for a second Finn feared that the robot had damaged the device beyond repair, when in fact the opposite was true.

"Scraps fix!" the robot shouted, waving his hands in the air triumphally. "Tracker work!"

Finn scurried over to the table and picked up the device. The screen was active and showing a map view of the crucible, plus a number of markers, none of which had any obvious meaning. Then Scraps tapped the screen in two places where red chevrons were slowly moving across the terrain. One had the letter "S" inside it and the other showed "B".

"Bad-man and lady-bad-man," Scraps said, before growling like an angry shih-tzu.

"Scraps, are you saying that you've reprogrammed this to track the prosecutors instead of us?" Finn asked.

Scraps smiled and nodded. "Scraps clever." The robot tapped his head. "Computation chip good. Finn gave to Scraps!"

Finn laughed, remembering the components that he'd fed to his little friend, shortly before the fateful evening that had led them all this this moment. He patted the robot on the head, like a doting father.

"Scraps, you're a genius!" Finn said, and the robot quivered with pride. "Now, let's see how much the prosecutors like being hunted."

22

RED CHEVRONS

"There ain't no way that talking oil-can just hacked a prosecutor's tracker," Corbin said, bustling over and barging Finn out of the way to get a better look at the device's screen. "Prove it to me. Show me where they are."

Finn shoved Corbin back and for a second he thought that they might come to blows, until Owen's shadow crept across them both and their Metalhaven compatriot bit his tongue and stood down.

"This talking oil can has a name, Scraps, and he's smarter than you'll ever be," Finn said. Scraps growled at Corbin as he said this, which only made the man angrier. "But since you asked me so nicely, I'll show you exactly where Bloodletter and The Shadow are."

Finn picked up the device and held it out so that both Owen and Corbin could see the screen, then scrolled the display to a chevron marked 'B'.

"That's Bloodletter," Finn explained. "He's still close to the Control Center, maybe a couple of hundred meters away, but he's not currently on the move."

Owen huffed a laugh. "Maybe the asshole collapsed and is bleeding to death, just like he does to his victims."

"We can only hope…" Finn replied, wistfully. He then highlighted the chevron labeled 'S' and the map focused on the area surrounding the marker, which was slowly creeping toward them across the digital representation of the crucible. "This is The Shadow, and she's definitely alive and on the move." He pointed to a marker, labelled 'O' for offenders. "And this is where we are, inside the building."

Corbin scowled at the screen. His eyes flicked left and right as he read the various labels, his lips moving like he was reciting a silent prayer.

"But if that map is right then The Shadow is coming right at us?" Corbin said, redirecting his consternated frown at Finn.

"She is, though since we removed our tracer bands, I don't understand how she knows where we are."

As soon as Finn had said the words, he and Owen exchanged knowing looks, and they both cursed at the same time.

"We removed our tracers, but you still have yours," Owen said, looking accusingly at Corbin.

"I don't know what the hell you're talking about," Corbin snapped, jumping on the defensive. "Ain't no-one tracking me!"

"They're sewn into your jumpsuit, numb nuts," Owen added. He grabbed Corbin's arm and muscled the bewildered worker into a chair before Corbin could protest. "Just sit tight. We need to cut them out."

"Cut them out!" Corbin said, bizarrely covering his

genitals, which he clearly considered to be his most important organ. "You're not cutting on me!"

"Not you, your jumpsuit," Finn said, showing him the part of his own jumpsuit's cuff where one of the tracer bands had resided. He then picked up a sharp-looking screwdriver from the small collection of tools that Scraps had brought with him and handed it to Owen. "Just sit tight, this won't take long."

Corbin continued to protect his vital assets while Owen roughly tore open the ankle of the worker's jumpsuit, using the screwdriver to scratch open the seams. Within a minute, he'd removed the tracer and tossed it into Corbin's lap. The man finally stopped covering his groin and picked up the band.

"Is this it?" Corbin said, scrunching up his nose at the object. "This is how they track us?"

"This is how they were tracking you, since Finn and I got rid of them already," Finn corrected him. Owen was now working on the tracer in Corbin's cuff. "But once we remove your bands and sling them down an elevator shaft, The Shadow won't know where any of us are."

"But we'll still know where she is," Owen pointed out, wrenching the second band out of Corbin's uniform, with far less care than he'd displayed when performing the same task on Cora. "And that gives us an advantage."

Owen collected both tracer bands in his hand then looked for some way to get rid of them, but the windows in the firing room didn't open and there wasn't a trash chute.

"We'll have to ditch these here and head out," Finn said, taking the bands off his friend and tossing them into a trash can. "The longer we stay, the nearer Elara Cage gets."

"But even if we do manage to kill that crazy bitch and Bloodletter, what then?" Corbin asked. "You know the rules of this game. Only one man walks out alive, which means that, one way or another, two of us have to die."

Finn knew the rules and he'd avoided tackling the question with Corbin because of the awkward problem it posed. He and Owen had a pact to go down fighting if there was no other option, even though Finn secretly intended his friend to live, but Corbin hadn't been party to that contract, and would never agree to it.

"One problem at a time, Corbin," Finn said, trying to deflect the question. "First, let's actually kill the prosecutors."

Corbin shook his head. "Nah, that ain't good enough," he said, pushing himself out of the chair. "You two are worker buddies and friends, and it ain't no secret that you hate my guts. If I help you to kill the hunters then you'll just turn around and slit my throat next."

"Come on, Corbin, just this once use your head for something other than knocking people out," Finn hit back. "If it comes down to me and Owen then one of us has to kill the other, and can you really see us fighting to the death?"

Corbin scowled at Finn, partly because he was smarting from the insult, but also because the cogs inside the man's head were whirring.

"If you don't fight each other then the golds will kill you both," Corbin pointed out.

"Maybe…" Finn shrugged. He needed a way to placate Corbin and fell back on the same fiction that he'd once told Owen to give him hope. "But I've watched at least a hundred trials and only once have I ever seen the prosecutors get taken out or killed."

"The Shadow..." Corbin said. He knew the story of Metalhaven's most infamous worker just as well as they did.

"Right, so if we do beat the odds and kill the prosecutors, who's to say that the golds won't let two people walk free, or even three?" Finn continued. "It would be a once in a lifetime event, and you know how the Regents love to put on a spectacular show."

Corbin rubbed his chin and considered what Finn had said but despite his worker rating of three, Corbin wasn't stupid or gullible.

"I don't believe that," Corbin grunted. He then snorted mucus from his nose into his mouth and spat a globule of green snot beside Finn's boot. "And I don't think you believe it either."

Corbin started to walk away, and Finn felt suddenly panicky, assuming that the worker was planning to head out of the door and go it alone. In some ways, he'd have preferred that, given the man's temperamental nature, but he couldn't overlook the fact they still needed him.

"We still have a better chance of killing the prosecutors together," Finn said. "If you leave now then The Shadow will pick you off before you knew what hit you."

"I ain't leaving," Corbin replied. He stood in the corner and slid down the zipper in his jumpsuit. "I'm just taking a leak..."

Finn and Owen both pulled the same disgusted face at the same time and backed away from where Corbin had decided to relieve himself. At the same time, Finn strapped the tracking computer around his wrist, and updated the location of the two prosecutors. Bloodletter hadn't moved, but it seemed clear that The Shadow was still on the prowl and hunting them.

"He's going to be a problem, you know that, right?" Owen said, speaking quietly so that the third member of their party couldn't overhear. "Corbin's only interested in saving himself. Despite what you said, he's convinced we'll try to kill him at the earliest opportunity. Once we've dealt with the prosecutors, he'll move quickly to take out at least one of us, and even the odds."

"I know," Finn replied, watching Corbin out of the corner of his eye. The man was cursing and shaking his left boot, where the stream of urine had hit the wall and flowed back at him. "But one problem at a time, okay? Right now, The Shadow is our biggest concern."

Owen nodded then pointed to the tracker. "Speaking of which, where is she now?"

Finn raised his wrist and accidently brushed the bulky tracker against the side of a table. The device bleeped and the screen changed. He cursed and his pulse quickened, fearing that he'd just messed up the data, but the chevrons showing Bloodletter and The Shadow were still there, along with a dozen new icons.

"Were those green boxes there before?" Owen asked.

"No, I must have added them when I knocked the tracker," Finn replied. The boxes were scattered all across the crucible but in unusual and hard-to-reach places.

"Look, Bloodletter's right next to one," Owen pointed out. "And it looks like The Shadow is heading toward us from the direction of another box."

Finn tried to think but his mind was frazzled, partly from exhaustion and injury, but also from the lingering effects of the cigarette he'd smoked. Giving up, he turned to Scraps, who had been occupying his time using the tools he'd collected to adjust his rotor system.

"Hey, pal, do you have any idea what these green boxes might be?" Finn asked, showing the screen to Scraps.

"Yes-yes!" Scraps replied, without even looking at the screen. "Them supply drops. Make bad-men better."

"Supply drops as in crates of equipment, and maybe weapons?" Finn asked, heart racing again.

"Yes-yes!" Scraps replied, cheerfully. The robot then suddenly growled, running hot and cold like a faulty faucet. "Scraps think bad-men cheaters!"

"I think so too," Finn replied, laughing. He scooped up his robot and placed Scraps onto his shoulder. "But if we both cheat then all's fair, right?"

Scraps shrugged. "Bad-men no play fair. Scraps no like bad-men."

"Leaving without me?" Corbin said. He'd returned about halfway into the room and was standing with his arms folded across his barrel chest.

"Considering how long it was taking you to have a piss, I wasn't sure we'd have much choice," Finn replied, snarkily. "But if you can stand to be around us two worker buddies for a little longer, we might have a way to take out the prosecutors, without losing our own heads in the process."

Corbin was suspicious but intrigued enough to stop sulking. He sidled over to them but Finn noticed that the man was keeping his distance more than he had before. The battle lines were being drawn.

"Scraps says that these are supply drops," Finn explained, angling the screen of the tracker toward Corbin, who had to squint his eyes to see it. "If you think about it, the Authority wouldn't just leave the prosecutors in here with only the gear they brought with them. They'd need extra weapons, medical supplies, that sort of thing, and this is where they get them from."

Corbin rubbed his chin again but the simple fact that he hadn't shot back an aggressive retort meant that he was interested.

"So, we find one of these crates and tool up," Corbin said. "Then we really do have a chance."

Finn nodded. He highlighted one of the supply drops on the map and adjusted the display so that the green box and the chevron marking their location were both visible.

"The closest crate that isn't also near to Bloodletter or The Shadow is inside the flame trench on Launch Pad two," Finn explained. "It's not far from here, and since we know where the prosecutors are, we can head outside without running into them, or a crossbow bolt."

Corbin continued to rub his face for a few seconds while thinking, then he picked up his club hammer and stood tall.

"Okay, so let's do it," Corbin said. "But you should know that if it comes down to us three, or me and either one of you, I ain't gonna be the one doing the dying." He snorted more snot into his mouth and spat it onto the floor in front of Finn and Owen. "This deal we got going ends as soon as those gold fuckers out there are dead. Then all bets are off, agreed?"

Finn narrowed his eyes at Corbin then glanced at Owen, who was equally resolute.

"Okay, Corbin," Finn answered. "Then we all know where we stand."

23

I DON'T WANT TO DIE

Finn carefully opened a side door that led out of the control center and was buffeted back by icy winds and snow. He shielded his face with his hands and scanned the horizon but if The Shadow was out there, as the tracking device had indicated, then he couldn't see her.

"We're going to have to make a run for it," Finn said, drawing back into the shelter of the building. "The tracker says that Cage is somewhere between us and launch platform two but even without her chameleonic armor, the weather out there will make it hard to see her."

"But that cuts both ways," Owen pointed out. "If we can't see her then she can't see us either."

Finn puffed out his cheeks and nodded. "Let's hope so..."

He held up the tracker so that Owen and Corbin could see the screen then pointed to an object marked on the map. "This is a small vehicle park, with a few trucks and some lighter plant equipment, like excavators," Finn explained. He then pointed outside. "If you look, you can just about see it, about two-thirds of the way between this building and the launch platform. It's an eighty-meter sprint, give or take."

"And where exactly is The Shadow now?" Corbin asked. Finn's suggestion that they make a daredevil run for cover hadn't won him over.

"She's about twenty meters from the vehicle park," Finn admitted, realizing that this probably wasn't the answer Corbin was hoping for. "But my guess is that she's just watching the exits and trying to work out why her tracker says we've stopped moving. She can't know that we have access to Bloodletter's device."

Corbin snorted and shook his head. "Those are some pretty big assumptions. If you ask me, it's too much of a risk. One person should run out and get the supplies, while the other two stay here."

"I didn't ask you," Finn said, flatly. "But you're welcome to stay here by yourself, while Owen and I raid the drop and get the weapons and supplies."

The worker snorted again, even more scathingly. "And let you two chumps take all the best gear for yourself, and leave me the dregs? Not a chance."

"Then how about you just shut up and do as I ask?" Finn said, snapping back the retort in short order and shocking Corbin into silence.

Finn was growing more exasperated with Corbin by the minute and he began to wonder whether they would be better off without his help, despite the success of their collaboration against Bloodletter proving otherwise. Corbin continued to scowl at him, making a face like he was chewing tobacco, but whatever comeback or insult the man was brewing in his thoughts, he didn't speak it out loud.

"Whatever you say, fearless leader," Corbin eventually grumbled, acquiescing, though in typically pugnacious style.

Finn sighed then checked the tracker to update The Shadow's position, but her marker wasn't shown and his heart skipped a beat.

"Shit, she's gone!" Finn said, shaking the tracker, as if that might suddenly make the chevron labelled with an "S" reappear.

"What do you mean she's gone?!" Corbin barked. "She was right there. We all saw her!"

Finn shook the device some more and slapped it with the palm of his hand, but the symbol denoting the position of Elara Gage was gone.

"It could be the weather interfering with the scanners," Owen suggested, managing to remain optimistic. "Either way, we can't stay here. Corbin's tracer bands are still in the firing room so it's a good bet that The Shadow is heading for this building."

Owen's words of reason had a sobering effect on Corbin and the man swallowed any further objections. Without the argumentative worker distracting him, Finn picked up Scraps and anchored the robot to his shoulder, then got ready to run. He chanced one last glance at the tracker, hoping that the 'S' chevron had miraculously reappeared, but Elara Cage was still indistinguishable from the white noise of wind and snow outside.

"Go..." Owen said, slapping him on the back like a rancher trying to gee-up cattle, and Finn sprinted out into the night.

Without the protection of the control center's solid walls, the storm buffeted him like a kite, and he struggled to run in a straight line, stumbling and tripping like he was drunk. Glancing over his shoulder, he saw Owen hot on his heels, making better headway due to his greater mass and momentum, while Corbin was not far behind. Focusing ahead, he locked his eyes onto the vehicle park and a three-ton dumpster whose tarpaulin cover had been blown off by the wind. He was close to reaching his waypoint when he saw something move in his peripheral vision and swiveled his head to look, but the blizzard was consuming everything. He was about to discount it as a mirage when the air seemed to shimmer and distort. Sliding to a stop just before the vehicle park, he watched the shimmer resolve into the shape of a woman, with a crossbow held outstretched.

"Owen, get down!"

Finn's warning cry was accelerated by the howling winds and Owen threw his body to the ground just as the bolt was loosed. The projectile soared directly over Owen's head and nicked Corbin's thigh instead. The man pressed his hand to the wound as if he'd been stung then tripped and tumbled heavily across the gravel and snow.

"Where did she go?!" Owen cried, crouched low and shielding his eyes in the hope of spotting The Shadow. "I don't see her!"

Finn tried again to discern the telltale shimmer of the hunter's chameleonic armor, but all he saw was a blinding whiteout of swirling ice and snow. Focusing on his other senses, he listened for footsteps or the click and whir of a crossbow being armed, but the chaotic symphony of the storm consumed any other sounds.

"I don't see her either," Finn yelled back, fighting the wind to reach his friend. Corbin was still face down in the dirt a few meters away. "Help me with Corbin, he looks dazed."

They each grabbed one of Corbin's heavy arms and dragged him toward the vehicle park. Finn could see blood trickling from the wound to the man's thigh, and while it wasn't deep, a dark bruise-like patch was forming around it.

"We're almost there," Owen said, propping Corbin up against the side of the dumpster. "Another twenty meters and we'll be at the launch pad, where there's shelter."

Finn tucked himself into cover then checked the tracker. The letter 'S' was flickering like candlelight in a breeze and its location was shifting, as if there were a dozen Elara Cages surrounding them, all encased in stealth armor.

"She's close, but the tracker is next to useless in this storm," Finn said. He cursed and shook his head. "We're just going to have to risk it again."

Owen nodded then looked at Corbin. The man was rousing but the fall had taken more out of him than Finn had expected.

"It'll slow us down too much if we have to carry him," Finn said.

"We're not leaving him here, so don't get any funny ideas," Owen said, quick to dispel any notion of abandoning Corbin to his fate.

"I wasn't suggesting that," Finn replied, though if he was being brutally honest, he had thought about it. "But the three of us bunched up together are a big target. Even with winds like these, Cage wouldn't struggle to tag at least one of us with a crossbow bolt."

Suddenly, Scraps leapt off Finn's shoulder and flew into the air, screeching an alarm that was so shrill even the storm couldn't drown it out. A beam of torchlight shone from the robot's eyes and swept across the terrain like a lighthouse beacon. Light was reflected back toward them and Scraps focused his eyes on the twinkling outline of a woman, part-camouflaged by the blizzard and partly by her covert armor. Finn and Owen were both too stunned to react, then The Shadow deactivated her chameleonic shield and revealed herself to them for the first time since the trial had begun.

Instinct took over, and Finn pushed himself up, intending to charge the hunter and kill her with his bare fists if he had too, but the sight of a crossbow aimed at his chest made him freeze like the icicles dangling from the dump truck. He peered into the woman's eyes, vivid and green like emeralds in a jewelers display case, then she adjusted her aim and fired. Finn flinched but the bolt raced over his head and struck Scraps in his center of mass. The robot screeched and wailed and flew out of control, sparks erupting from his tin-can body. Finn ran after him, paying no regard to his own safety, and was forced to watch his robot friend crash out of sight into a deep ravine beside the vehicle park.

Enraged, Finn turned back to The Shadow, fists clenched and teeth bared. The hunter had reloaded her crossbow and it was now aimed at Owen, despite the fact he was the closer and easier target. In his grief and fury, Finn lost all sense and reason, and the threat of being shot by Elara Cage meant nothing to him. He kicked off and charged at the woman, putting his own body between The Shadow and his friend. Her finger was already on the trigger and there was no question that she had him dead to rights but the weapon was not fired, and instead Finn ploughed into Elara Cage like a tiger bringing down prey at a full sprint. They tumbled through the snow, loose stones and rubble biting into Finn's shoulders and back with each painful revolution. Then he was on top of her, raining punches into her head and body, but the blows hurt him more than they did the prosecutor. The Shadow protected her head with the skill of a professional fighter, while her armor was simply too strong for bare fists to damage.

Suddenly, Elara Cage grabbed Finn around the neck and twisted her hips, flipping them over in an instant so that he was now on his back, defenseless. A black-bladed roundel dagger was slid from its sheath and pressed to his neck, but the hunter hesitated.

"I don't want you!" Cage yelled, spitting with rage. Her green eyes burned him like lasers but they were not the eyes of a cruel woman, or a maniac. "Stay out of my way!"

Finn couldn't speak because of the weight of the woman's armored body pressing down on his chest, then she was knocked off him like she'd been run over by a ground car. Struggling to his knees Finn saw Owen picking himself out of the snow, while Elara Cage barreled down the side of the same steep ravine where Scraps had crashed moments earlier.

"Quickly, while she's down!" Owen said, hobbling toward him with The Shadow's crossbow in his hand.

Finn climbed to his feet, suddenly aware of the stinging pain in his knuckles, which had been scraped raw from his frenzied attack on Elara Cage. Pushing on, he reached the dump truck and found Corbin slumped in the same position they'd left him in.

"Sleep when you're dead!" Owen said, grabbing the man's shoulder and shaking him, but Corbin was like a marionette who'd had his strings cut. "Wake up, damn you!" Owen yelled, shaking the man again but with the same result.

Finn considered slapping Corbin around the face when his eyes were drawn to the wound on the man's leg. The dark bruise had grown and looked angrier, and he suddenly realized why.

"She shoots poison darts," Finn said, tearing open Corbin's jumpsuit to see the full extent of the spread. The spider-like bruise had reached his hip and was climbing up his gut. "He only got clipped by the bolt but some poison will have still gotten into his bloodstream."

"Then we'll have to carry him," Owen said, hoisting one half of the man up. He looked at Finn, who had not rushed in to take up the slack. "Come on, Finn, we're not leaving a man here to die. That would make us no better than him and Soren."

Finn cursed then slung Corbin's other arm over his shoulder. The man was a dead weight and even with the combined strength of himself and Owen, it was a struggle to move the stocky Metalhaven worker. The twenty meters they needed to cover to reach the launch platform felt like twenty miles, and Finn spent the time alternating his gaze between the tracking device and the ravine where Elara Cage had tumbled out of sight. The winds had abated and the 'S' chevron was now stable on the screen and it wasn't moving.

"He's dying," Owen said, dumping Corbin in the corner of the flame trench at launch pad two. "Maybe the supply drop has some medicines that might help him?"

Finn noticed that Owen's machete wound had opened up again and was oozing fresh blood. His friend looked half-dead, like Corbin, though he hoped that this was just due to the debilitating effect of exposure to Zavetgrad's bitter nighttime temperatures.

"If the crate has any medicines then use them on yourself first," Finn said, employing the tracker to find the hidden supply drop. He glanced at his friend and knew instinctively that Owen's first consideration would have been to help others. Not on this occasion. "I mean it, Owen. Treat yourself before that sack of shit."

"How about you find us some meds first, then I'll think about it," Owen said, slumping down beside his Metalhaven co-worker.

Finn upped the speed of his search but he was painfully aware that he didn't have the first clue how the supply drops were hidden. For all he knew, they were buried in secret compartments and used biometric locks that made them inaccessible to the offenders on trial. He was about to give up hope when he spotted what looked like a metal door built into the wall. It was covered over with ice and snow and protected only by a simple padlock.

"I might have found something," Finn said.

Owen didn't answer and Finn saw that the man's eyes were closed and that his head was resting against the wall. He convinced himself that his friend had simply not heard him, rather than anything more ominous, and pressed on, searching the ground for a tool to prise open the lock. He kicked around in the snow and found a bent metal bar. He tested it and the implement slid into the loop of the padlock as if it were made for the task. Yanking back hard, he forced the lock then pulled open the door to the hidden compartment and searched inside, finding a black canvas holdall. He allowed himself to feel some of the excitement of the find before sliding the bag out of its stow and rushing back to his friend.

Owen opened his eyes and smiled. "Thought I was dead, didn't you?"

Finn snorted. "Of course not," he lied. "You're too stubborn to die."

Owen laughed then winced and clutched his gut. Finn opened the bag and began emptying the contents onto the concrete floor. First, there were weapons, including a loaded pistol and two spare magazines, plus knives and a machete that was a carbon copy of the one that Bloodletter used. He set the weapons aside and dug deeper, finding some tools then finally a selection of medical equipment and drugs. Focusing on these, he picked up a skin stapler and held it out to Owen.

"Here, use this before your innards fall out," Finn said.

Owen took the tool though he wasn't happy about it. Accidents were commonplace in the reclamation yards and every Metalhaven worker was tediously familiar with skin staplers, along with a dozen other unpleasant but necessary medical devices.

"Thanks..." Owen replied, sarcastically.

"And this too," Finn said, tossing an antibiotic wound spray at him.

This was a less commonly-seen item, at least amongst the worker class, but anyone with a genetic rating of four or higher, like Finn, merited additional medical care. This wasn't for their benefit, of course, and was simply to make sure they didn't die and were no longer able to supply their precious seed to populate the Nimbus Space Citadel.

Suddenly, Corbin slumped over and fell onto his side, and Finn temporarily abandoned his search of the canvas holdall to check on the man. Resting Corbin on his back, he checked for a pulse, which was present but weak, then inspected the wound. The spidery pattern caused by the poison was creeping toward his heart.

"There must be an antidote in that bag," Owen said, the click of the skin stapler punctuating each pained word he spoke. "You know, in case they accidently poison themselves."

"Maybe," Finn conceded, returning to the bag and searching through the remaining items but most of it was unfamiliar to him. "But how the hell do we know what it is?"

"Don't let me die…"

Corbin's eyes flickered and his hand was outstretched like a dying man reaching out to an apparition of Christ or another deity. "I'm sorry…" the man whispered. "I don't want to die…"

No matter what Finn thought of him, Corbin's harrowing pleas were difficult to hear. The man was beyond terrified, and despite the sub-zero temperature inside the crucible, a chill ran down his spine.

"What about this?" Owen said.

His friend was holding a bag of auto-injector pens, each with a label of a different color. Finn had seen a similar pen used to administer a tetanus dose to a worker who had been cut by a badly-rusted chunk of tank armor.

"They could be antidotes, but how do we know which one to use?" Finn replied. "If we get it wrong, we might kill him rather than cure him."

Owen shrugged. "He's dead anyway, so we have to try."

His friend tore open the bag and set out the devices on his lap but choosing which one to administer was a pure guessing game. Owen picked out a pen with yellow label then popped off the cap and shuffled toward Corbin. He was about to stab it into the man's neck when Finn had a thought.

"Wait, didn't you pick up The Shadow's crossbow?" Finn asked.

"Yeah, it's just there, beside the bag," Owen pointed out.

Finn grabbed the crossbow and inspected the bolts. It was loaded with darts that had a blue-colored tip. Setting the weapon down, he sifted through the remaining auto-injectors and found one with a label in a matching color, called NeuroGuard.

"Use this one," Finn said, thrusting the implement at his friend. "It says it counteracts Batrachotoxin Poison, whatever that is."

"Deadly, is my guess," Owen replied.

His friend swapped the yellow pen for the blue one and was about to press the device to Corbin's neck when Finn caught his wrist.

"Wait, we should think about this…" Finn said, suddenly wracked with doubt, and guilt.

"About what?" Owen snapped. "The choice is to save a man's life or let him die. What's there to think about?"

Finn felt dirty for even contemplating letting Corbin slip away but in his mind they had to face reality. Only one person got out alive, and Corbin desperately wanted to be that person. Saving the man's life was not in their interest.

"Think about it Owen, The Shadow may be out, which means we only need to take down Bloodletter, and we already know he's hurt," Finn explained, trying to reason with his friend. "Me and you together is already two versus one. We don't need Corbin, and we already know that he'll try to kill us once the prosecutors are dead. He told us as much."

Owen sighed but didn't loosen his grip, forcing Finn to keep the auto-injector pulled away from Corbin's neck.

"You're right, Finn," Owen said, and some of the tension in his powerful arm was relaxed. "You always did know the right thing to do, even when it wasn't easy. Truth is, there's as much gold in you as there is chrome, but the difference between you and them is that you have a good heart." His friend smiled at him. "I know the smart thing is to let him die but I can't do it, Finn. I'd rather die myself."

In his weakened state, Finn could have overpowered his friend, but despite the hard truth that saving Corbin put them at more risk, he couldn't betray his friend's wishes. Owen had said there was as much gold in him as chrome, and maybe he was right, but callously betraying his friend's wishes would tip the scales in a direction Finn didn't want them to go. He was a chrome from Metalhaven, and live or die, that's who he wanted to be.

"I hope we live to regret this choice," Finn said, removing his hand from Owen's arm and allowing his friend to administer the antidote.

"So do I," came the solemn reply.

Corbin began to toss and turn, moaning incoherently, but the effect of the medicine was immediate and the dark patterns on the man's body had already begun to recede. Conscious that a rejuvenated Corbin would try to claim the best weapons and gear for himself, Finn shuffled away from the man and seized the loaded pistol first.

Suddenly, the thrum of an aircar's rotor shook the sky above them, replacing the wind and thunder of the storm that had finally passed over the city of Zavetgrad. Finn hurried to the ladder leading out of the flame pit and climbed it until he was able to see the aircar hovering over the ravine where the The Shadow and his robot had fallen. Two medics in gold uniforms rappelled down a rope then the body of Elara Cage was reclaimed and hauled out of the crucible.

The Shadow had been defeated and now only Bloodletter remained.

24

THE COLOR GOLD

Corbin used the coarse concrete wall of the flame trench to claw himself upright then managed to stand without any help from Finn or Owen. Considering that the man had been at death's door only minutes earlier, it was remarkable that he could stand at all, and only highlighted that the man was a fighter, for better or worse.

"What happened?" Corbin grunted, wedging himself into a corner and staring at his trembling hands.

"You were poisoned by one of The Shadow's darts but we found an antidote in the supply drop," Finn explained.

Corbin frowned at him. "You brought me here and cured me?"

Finn huffed a laugh. "Are you surprised that we didn't leave you to die?"

Corbin's frown deepened to a scowl and it was clear that in his debilitated condition the big man was struggling to take everything in.

"Yes..." Corbin eventually replied. "That's what I'd have done."

Finn laughed out loud this time. "A simple thank you would be enough."

Corbin's addled brain couldn't process sarcasm and Finn decided that there was no point in continuing the conversation, such as it was.

"Here, this is for you..."

He tossed an auto injector pen at the man and it bounced off his broad chest and landed in the snow at his feet. He could have handed the device to him, since Corbin's reactions were shot and there was no way he could have caught it, but Finn didn't feel like doing the ungrateful bastard any more favors.

"What is it?" Corbin grunted.

"Owen worked out that they're stims," Finn replied. "Just inject it into your neck and it'll wake you up faster than a pint of algae beer poured over your head."

Corbin turned his scowl onto the device at his feet then slowly crouched down to pick it up, grimacing and groaning like an old man as he did so. The marks on his body were rapidly fading and it seemed that the worker was growing stronger with each passing second.

"How do I know you're not trying to poison me?" Corbin said, holding the injector gingerly between thumb and forefinger.

"You're really asking me that, after we just cured you?"

Finn felt like taking the pen and poking it into the man's eye. He was willing to make some allowances for Corbin's condition but the question was beyond insulting, and the man's reddening cheeks suggested that Corbin understood how foolish he'd sounded too. It also reinforced how quickly he was healing. Only minutes earlier, Corbin's skin was indistinguishable in color from Metalhaven chrome, but now it was flush with life.

"You can't blame me for asking," Corbin mumbled. He popped the lid off the injector pen then raised it, as if offering a toast. "Anyway, thanks," the man added before applying the device to his neck.

The thank you sounded insincere but Finn didn't want or need the man's gratitude – if it had been his choice alone, Corbin would be dead. But since the oaf still drew breath, he needed Corbin Radcliffe strong enough to fight Bloodletter.

"I've laid out all the weapons that were in the canvas bag," Owen said. His friend had been beyond earshot of his conversation with Corbin and was now walking over with two glass bottles in his hands. "And I found these too. I don't know what they are but they taste a million times better than the algae-based probiotic goop they gave us in Metalhaven."

"You already drank one?" Finn asked, taking a bottle from Owen.

"I figured that the prosecutors wouldn't include anything in the supply drop that would kill them, weapons aside," Owen explained.

Finn judged that to be one almighty assumption but since his friend had already imbibed and wasn't dead, he figured that the drink was safe. He twisted off the metal cap and was met with a thick, fragrant aroma unlike anything he'd experienced before. At first, he sampled only a thimble-sized amount, but the sweet, clean taste of the drink quickly had him finishing the bottle. Apart from the enjoyment of something so delicious, he found that he was invigorated, like he'd just woken from an uninterrupted night's sleep.

"Wow, I could drink about another ten of those," Finn said, setting the empty bottle down by the wall.

Corbin had waited until Finn had finished his drink before taking the final bottle from Owen's waiting hand. Like Finn, Corbin was cautious at first, but as soon as the first drop of the ambrosia-like liquid had touched the man's tongue, he finished the rest as if he'd inhaled it.

"Fuck me, that was good!" Corbin said, carelessly tossing the bottle into the snow. Miraculously, it didn't smash. "I don't suppose there are any more?"

Owen shook his head. "Believe me, if there were, I'd have already drunk them."

Corbin managed a strained smile and it was clear that the restorative drink, combined with the stimulant, had given the man a powerful second wind. Corbin's gaze then shifted toward the pile of weapons and he was about to stake his claim when a guttural voice boomed somewhere above them.

"Brasa!"

The call sent a shiver rushing down Finn's spine. Should he beat the odds and survive the trial, he knew he'd hear that voice echoing in his nightmares for the rest of his life.

"Let's finish this, Brasa!" Bloodletter roared. It was as if the man's voice was being amplified through every brick and stone in the crucible. "Get up here, and bring whoever is left with you, or I'll send in an army of foremen to flush you out!"

Finn checked the tracking device and Bloodletter's chevron was displayed clearly. The storm had blown over and the night had become perfectly still and clear, like they were in the eye of hurricane. There was no longer any place to hide but Finn was done hiding. Bloodletter was on his own, and it was three versus one. He had no right to believe they had a chance, but he'd already faced the hunter once before and won. He believed in his bones that he could win again. In the end, he had no choice.

"Hurry, take whatever weapons you can carry," Owen said, rushing back to the stockpile.

Corbin tried to muscle his way in to get first pick, but Owen shoved the man aside and claimed a hunting knife and a crossbow pistol before he could get to them. Finn was already content with his choice and didn't need anything else. Drawing upon the secret knowledge he'd gained from his illicit data device at home, he double-checked that the pistol was loaded, while Corbin eyed the weapon greedily.

"There has to be more than this," Corbin said, adding a machete to his arsenal. "One gun and a bunch of knives won't be enough to kill him."

"Finn almost killed him with a headbutt," Owen pointed out. "We'll make it work."

Corbin growled his discontent then headed to the cubby in the wall where Finn had found the canvas holdall. While the man searched inside, Finn spotted a lone glove in the pile of weapons that looked to be missing its companion. He picked it up and saw that it was lined with wires and covered in tiny spikes. There was a plug on the wrist section, which was thick like insulating tape. Another object caught his eye and he recognized it as a battery. The two objects clicked together and the glove briefly crackled with electrical energy, which could be cycled on and off via a switch close to the thumb.

"Trust you to figure out how that thing works," Owen said, proud of his friend for making the discovery but also jealous that he'd not cracked the problem himself. "It looks more useful than most of this junk."

Suddenly, Corbin laughed. It was unsettling, like the cackle of a lunatic, and Finn found himself raising his pistol a fraction in readiness to shoot.

"You dumb fucks didn't check the compartment walls, did you?" Corbin said. The man removed a rifle from the cubby and Finn's heart sank. "This was attached to the roof lining. Such a shame you didn't look more closely."

"We were too busy saving your worthless life," Owen answered, arms folded across his chest and with a face like thunder.

"It's a laser weapon," Corbin said, excited by his new toy. "I reckon it uses the same tech that's in our cutting tools."

Finn moved closer to check out the weapon and Corbin clutched it to his body like a mother with a newborn, fearful that he might try to steal it.

"Relax, I just want to see how it works," Finn said, though Corbin remained wary. "The power cell is a fraction the size of our cutters, which means it's probably only good for a few shots; maybe three or four at the most."

"I only need one," Corbin answered, before shooting Finn a devilish smile. "One for Bloodletter, anyways…"

Owen went to the cubby and picked up the search from where Corbin had left off. A few seconds later his friend smiled and pulled a sawn-off shotgun out of the hole.

"Now we're talking!" Owen said, sizing up the weapon, though it was clear he didn't know how to use it.

Finn was careful to deflect the barrel away from his face, then he plucked a cartridge from the stow on the weapon's frame and showed Owen how to load it.

"For this to work, you need to get close," Finn explained, again drawing upon his secret knowledge. "At any kind of range, it'll just make a loud bang and piss Bloodletter off."

Owen nodded then another roar from Bloodletter got their attention. Finn checked his tracker and the man was almost on top of them. He looked into the calm, starlit sky and the drones were now clearly visible, relaying their position to Bloodletter via the Trial Controllers.

"Last chance, Brasa!" Bloodletter yelled. "I know you're down there. Come out and let's give everyone a finale to this trial that they'll never forget!"

Finn shook his head. Even now, all Bloodletter cared about was his precious image and reputation. Finn had embarrassed the man twice, and almost killed him once, and he realized that the threat of unleashing foremen into the arena was a bluff. Bloodletter needed to kill him, and he needed everyone in Zavetgrad to see him do it, or his name would be mud.

"We take him down together," Finn said, grabbing a rung on the ladder. "But we have to kill him in full view of the spectators, out in the open. That way, the golds can't create a lie using simulated footage, like Cora told us they've done in the past. If the workers see us kill Bloodletter with their own eyes, no-one can deny it."

"Whatever," Corbin grunted, barging Finn off the ladder and beginning his climb. "But if you ask me, it don't matter how we kill him, so long as he's dead."

Finn waited for Corbin to climb ahead then looked to Owen. "Are you still glad we saved him?"

Owen managed a weary laugh. "Ask me again in ten minutes."

Finn climbed the ladder next with Owen never more than a rung or two behind, and before long they were standing in the virgin snow of the crucible, facing-off against Bloodletter, like Old West gunmen. Even from a distance, it was clear that the prosecutor had also availed himself of a supply drop. The man had a robotic exoskeleton fixed to his arms, legs and back, and was holding a small shield, no larger than a trash-can lid. The familiar crossbow was stowed on his hip, and instead Bloodletter favored his machete, which was the clearest signal yet that the hunter intended to make his kills personal.

"No-one has found a supply drop before," Bloodletter called out, while slowly pacing toward them. "At least you three will all die famous…"

Suddenly, the drones that had been hovering above them descended and flooded their battleground with a clinical white light. A cheer rumbled across the arena, and Finn found himself wondering whether the spectators from Spacehaven and Stonehaven were rooting for them or for the sadistic killer facing them down.

"This is the endgame, you worker scum," Bloodletter continued. "The whole of Zavetgrad is going to see me dice you like carrots. And when I'm done, I'll be hailed as the greatest prosecutor in trial history."

Finn walked out to meet their adversary, flanked by his Metalhaven compatriots. He flexed his fingers, which were sweaty on the grip of the gun, despite the freezing cold.

"Just think how famous you'll be as the prosecutor who lost the greatest trial in history."

His defiant statement was met by a roar from the crowd louder than any Finn had heard in his life, and he was left in no doubt as to who the workers of Zavetgrad favored. All that remained was to be worthy of their applause.

The shield on Bloodletter's left arm suddenly expanded to almost the man's full height, leaving only a narrow slit for the prosecutor to peer through. At the same time, the hunter charged at them, not even bothering to dodge or weave. Owen panicked and opened fire with the shotgun but the range was too long and the lead pellets dissipated harmlessly around their target. Corbin also panicked and shot the laser rifle but the beam of red energy merely scorched a groove into the shield, leaving Bloodletter unharmed.

"Wait till he's close!" Finn cried out, taking pot shots with his pistol in the hope of squeezing a bullet through the viewing slit in the shield, but the slugs just ricocheted off the barrier and vanished into the darkness.

Ten meters from them, Bloodletter ground to a halt and dug his shield into the snow. Metal struts expanded from its base, creating a free-standing barrier that provided the prosecutor with ample cover. Corbin fired a second laser beam to no effect then Owen blasted the barrier with buckshot but it held firm. Moments later, the hunter ducked out of cover and shot Owen in the neck using a weapon mounted on the man's wrist. Electricity coursed through his friend's body and Owen spasmed and contorted in agony before collapsing into a heap where he stood.

Fully in the grip of fear and unable to help his friend, Finn roared like a madman and emptied his pistol at Bloodletter, but the prosecutor was already safely behind his shield, which repelled the onslaught of bullets. Corbin charged at Bloodletter, screaming a frenzied, petrified war cry, fueled by a desperate will to survive, but the man met his advance and swatted him aside like he was nothing. Bloodletter's powered exoskeleton whirred and hissed as the hunter flexed the mechanized arm he'd used to batter Corbin to the ground. The prosecutor smiled, clearly enjoying his work, then fixed his gaze onto his next and most valuable target. Finn.

"I said I'd make you watch as I cut on your friends, and I'm a man of my word," Bloodletter said, pacing toward Finn as he desperately tried to reload the pistol, but his hands were shaking from fear and cold. "You fucked with the wrong guy, Brasa. Golds don't lose to chrome scum like you. Gold is the brightest of all colors."

Unable to reload the forearm, Finn ran to Owen, who was still out cold in the snow, and grabbed his friend's machete, but at the same time Bloodletter put on a burst of augmented speed and thumped a kick into his gut. He felt ribs crack as he barreled across the frozen ground, before finally coming to rest face-down in the snow. Spitting blood, he pushed himself up and found that the machete was still grasped between his fingers. The shadow of Bloodletter crept over him, and in his arrogance the man had discarded his shield. Finn swung hard, striking the hunter's leg, and the blade sang like a hammer striking an anvil, but it didn't penetrate the man's exoskeleton, let alone his armor.

"You've got spirit, Brasa," Bloodletter said, kicking him across the ground for a second time. "I admire that. But it won't save you."

Willing his muscles to comply, Finn forced himself to stand and squared off against the prosecutor. This time he didn't have the element of surprise, nor did he have a weapon that could harm his enemy, but he didn't care. If he was going to die then he'd die on his feet, spiting the Authority as he'd always done. *Why?* His best friend had often asked him. *Because fuck them, that's why...*

He charged at Bloodletter and swung the machete at the man's head with all his might but the hunter caught the blade in his mechanized hand, and drew it aside, opening up Finn's chest for a killing blow.

"I'm gonna make this hurt..." Bloodletter hissed, pulling Finn close so that he could feel the heat of the man's breath on his face. "Make peace with your God, Brasa, because you're going to meet him soon."

Finn suddenly remembered the shock glove he was wearing, and he clicked the switch to send electricity coursing through the wires, and through Bloodletter's exoskeleton. The hunter cried out and Finn was suddenly released. Seizing his chance, Finn rammed the electrified glove into Bloodletter's mouth, sending incapacitating jolts of electricity into the man's body. Current coursed through Finn as well, and he was thrown clear, the glove still clenched between the prosecutor's cracked, blood-stained teeth. For several seconds, neither of them could move, until the power cell gave out and the paralyzing shock subsided. Finn turned his head toward the prosecutor, almost afraid to look, then his racing heart stopped beating. Bloodletter was not only still alive but the man was staring straight at him with a look of pure hatred and venom.

"Brasa!"

Electrical burns had ravaged the hunter's face and jaw, twisting the cry into something demonic and unearthly. The hunter then tore his crossbow from the stow on his armor and leveled it at Finn. A bolt was loosed but the prosecutor's hands were quivering and the dart flew wide. Gumming a curse, Bloodletter reloaded, and Finn tried to escape, but his body had endured too much. Legs shaking, he at last managed to stand and puff out his chest, hoping to meet his death with at least some dignity. Bloodletter was also back on his feet, steadying the crossbow with both hands, and this time Finn knew that the bolt would land true.

"Any last words, scum?" Bloodletter hissed.

"Fuck you…" Finn said, defying the Authority with his last breath.

But the trigger wasn't pulled. Instead the razor-sharp blade of a machete was thrust through the hunter's neck from behind, showering the snow at Finn's feet with hot blood. The prosecutor staggered forward and grabbed Finn before falling on top of him. The man tried to speak but all that came out of the hunter's mouth was his own blood, thick and treacly like Bloodletter's voice had once been. There was still hatred behind the man's eyes, then there was fear, and then nothing at all. Trembling, Finn shoved the dead body away like it was a year-old cadaver raised from the grave and struggled to his knees. Then he saw Owen, machete in hand and blood dripping from the edge. His friend looked he'd just been in a bar brawl, and the smug expression on his face suggested he'd won.

"We got him!" Owen said, his smile lighting up the night sky. "We did it!"

Then his friend was jolted, as if he'd been punched in the throat, and his face contorted. The smell of cooked human flesh wafted past Finn's nose, and Owen dropped dead where he was standing, smoke rising from a deep laser burn in his back.

"No!" Finn roared, rushing to his friend while Corbin Driscoll stood just a few meters away, shivering with adrenaline.

Finn pulled himself on to Owen's body and pressed his ear to his friend's chest but he heard nothing but an aching silence. Tears streamed down his face as he looked into Owen's glassy eyes and thumped his chest, desperate to restart the man's big heart, but what he'd once considered an inexhaustible wellspring of goodness had in an instant been reduced to ash by laser light.

"I'm sorry it had to end this way," Corbin whispered, his hands trembling. "But there can be only one winner, and it's going to be me..."

Finn stopped hammering on his friend's chest and looked Corbin in the eyes. Despite the worker's brutish mass, all he saw was a scared little man. He got to his feet and stood tall, with his back to Owen. He couldn't stand to look at his friend's corpse any longer.

"Do it then you back-stabbing piece of shit," Finn snarled. "You deserve to win. You're going to fit in with the golds just fine."

Finn could have rushed Corbin but he didn't. Owen Thomas, a man he'd known all his life, and who he loved as a brother, was dead, and without him he had no-one. Without him, what was the point of going on? Corbin raised the laser rifle and aimed it at Finn's heart, or what remained of it. The man considered saying something more, but like the coward he was, Corbin couldn't even summon the bravery to look him in the eyes when he pulled the trigger. Then nothing happened.

Corbin cursed under his breath and squeezed the trigger

again and again but still the weapon didn't fire. Hands shaking even more violently, he tossed the rifle aside and pulled a knife, before coming at Finn with the blade angled toward his throat. Instinct took over, and Finn caught Corbin's wrist and wrestled the man to the ground, before shaking the knife free. Tears clouded his eyes as he rained down blow after blow after blow onto the man's face, until his knuckles were broken and split and he could no longer tell the difference between Corbin's blood and his own. Even then, he kept punching until exhaustion overcame him. The next thing Finn knew, fireworks were exploding above the crucible, and the roar of the crowd had grown so fierce that they could have heard the cheers on Nimbus. Finn took one last look at Corbin's face, puffy and red, a mass of bludgeoned flesh that no longer even looked human, before clawing himself back to Owen and lying in the snow at his friend's side.

"I'm sorry," Finn said, the words barely a scratched croak in his throat. "I'm so sorry, Owen…"

Fireworks continued to scream into the night, exploding in a rainbow of color. There was white, red, green, purple and even a silvery-chrome, but in amongst them all was gold. Gold, the color of greed and oppression. Gold, the color of cruelty and violence. And gold, the color that Finn Brasa was now destined to become.

25

FROM CHROME TO GOLD

FINN FELT hands grasping under his arms and around his waist, then he was forcibly pulled away from Owen's body and guided a few steps away. Medics tended to the worst of his wounds, binding his bleeding knuckles and spraying his cuts and bruises with healing accelerants and antibiotics. He felt the prick of needles piercing his skin, but Finn remained numb to everything going on around him, and simply let it happen. He didn't know who had manhandled him and he didn't care. In that moment, his entire universe was a patch of frozen earth a few meters away, where the body of his only friend lay in the snow.

Finn could hear people shouting his name but he ignored them until the roar of whirling rotors shook him from his stupor. A squadron of aircars landed inside the crucible, joined soon after by a convoy of ground vehicles. Workers in orange overalls disembarked and began hastily assembling a stage, while medical staff in gold uniforms reverently carried away the body of the dead prosecutor and loaded him into a waiting ambulance.

Owen, however, merited no such respect. Still dissociated from the world around him like an out-of-body experience, Finn watched as they stuffed his friend inside a plastic sack then tossed him into the trunk of a ground car, like trash being collected from the sidewalk. He desperately wanted to intervene, to make sure his friend's remains were treated with dignity, but he couldn't move and he couldn't speak. He wasn't even sure how he was still breathing. Then, as if to add insult to injury, the body bag containing Corbin was dumped beside Owen's, and the trunk was slammed shut.

"Mr. Brasa?"

Finn heard someone talking but it was distant, like an echo.

"Mr. Brasa? Finn Brasa, sir?"

A man appeared in front of Finn, standing so close that it was impossible to ignore him. He was young, no older than seventeen Finn reasoned, and had yellow hair to match the gold piping on his uniform.

"I'm Prosecutor's Assistant Pritchard," the man continued. "If you'll please follow me."

The man was smiling warmly at him, as if he were a host in an Authority-sector restaurant and was about to lead Finn to his table. The ground car containing Owen's body drove away, and Finn suddenly realized that he'd rather be anywhere else on the planet than where his friend had been shot and killed.

"Where are we going?" he asked, still scarcely aware of what was happening.

"To the ceremony, sir," Pritchard replied, sounding surprised that Finn didn't know. "You won the trial, sir. Do you know how rare that is?"

The young man's voice was difficult to hear over the continued cheers erupting around the crucible, and the applause that he was receiving from golds, oranges and whites as he was led on autopilot toward the stage. The Regent of Spacehaven was already waiting for him, surrounded by hovering drones that were filming the man from multiple angles and beaming his image to streets and Recovery Centers all across Zavetgrad. Pritchard continued to speak as Finn climbed the stairs onto the stage, followed closely by prefects, though for the first time in his life, the authoritarian police officers were not threatening him with the prospect of violence but instead applauding him too.

"People of Spacehaven and all of Zavetgrad, we have witnessed a momentous occasion!" the Regent began, pontificating into the camera lenses like a preacher. "We all know the Trials to be an extreme test of fortitude, but above all they are a test of justice, so that we can be assured of the guilt or innocence of our convicted offenders." The Regent extended a hand toward Finn and he felt his heart race as if he had been singled out for execution. "Here stands Finn Brasa of Metalhaven, an innocent man, vindicated inside this very crucible!"

There was more clapping and the cheers were amplified through the TV screens hovering over their heads to a volume that shook the stage and made Finn's head hurt. The Regent then approached him, smiling with a paternal-like pride that was sickening in its insincerity. He took a step back and bumped into a prefect, who rather than club him unconscious with a nightstick, merely laughed and apologized for getting in his way. Then something was placed over his neck, but instead of a garotte or a noose, it was a medal.

"I award Finn Brasa the Justice Medal and elevate him from chrome to gold!" the Regent bellowed. Cheers rang out again but somehow they now sounded fake, as if he'd heard the same roar of applause before. "You knew Finn Brasa as a worker from Metalhaven's Yard Seven. That man exists no longer!" The Regent stepped aside and gestured to Finn with gushing pride. "Here stands Prosecutor Brasa of the Authority, and our newest gold!"

The words bounced around in his head like a laser beam ricocheting off the wall of a mirrored room. *Prosecutor Brasa... Our newest gold...* Then the Regent was in front of him again, and despite his freezing body, the proximity of the aristocrat made him somehow feel colder.

"It seems that we underestimated you, Mr. Brasa..."

The switch in tone from lovable showman to imperious tyrant was immediate and shocking enough that it caused Finn to take notice. The Regent was no longer smiling at him and he felt threatened. The drones had turned away to film the assembled revelers, while the prefects now stood with their hands wrapped around the handles of their nightsticks, watching for any sign that Finn might turn on their master.

"But make no mistake, Mr. Brasa, while you may now be a gold, you are *not* one of us," the Regent continued. "Step out of line and I will have you executed. There will be no trial. But accept your new position, embrace it, and fulfil your new role as prosecutor, and you will receive all the spoils that come with your newly-elevated status."

Finn was struck dumb but while fear had been his first emotion, anger was his second, and rapidly overtaking both of those was a bubbling hatred that threatened to overwhelm him. He clenched his fists, despite the pain of his broken knuckles sending shockwaves through his body and was about to strike the Regent when the ground car ferrying Owen's body to the crematorium passed through his field of view, and his rage vanished like melting snow. By the time the ground car had gone, so had the Regent, escorted off the stage by his prefects. Then Pritchard, with his easy smile and golden hair, appeared again to lead him away. There were chants of "Brasa! Brasa! Brasa!" as he neared the edge of the crucible and was shown to a waiting ground car, but the song gave him no comfort. Instead of shouts of admiration, all he could hear was Bloodletter yelling his name into the night sky like the howl of a hungry wolf.

The ground car set off and Finn found that Pritchard was with him in the back seat, still smiling like he was having the time of his life. Up front were two prefects, one of whom was driving, but unlike every other ground car that Finn had ever travelled in, there was no cage separating the rear compartment from the cabin. The streets of Spacehaven flashed past, and drunken revelers were spilling into the street. The hovering TV screens were now showing replays of the trial's final moments, focusing on Finn beating Corbin to death with his bare hands. Then the vehicle entered a tunnel or a garage and emerged in front of a pristine building with the emblem of Zavetgrad above it.

"We're here, sir," Pritchard said, opening the door and stepping out.

"Where?" Finn asked.

The man ducked back inside the car and smiled. "At the Law Enforcement Hub, of course, where you'll begin the next part of your life."

Finn wanted to ask more questions but Pritchard was

gone. Then his door was opened and he saw that a number of officers had lined up to meet him. One of them was Captain Withers, and as Finn climbed out of the ground car, he also saw the craggy face of Captain Viktor Roth, Head Prefect of the Reclamation sector.

"You bastard! ..." Finn snarled, breaking into a charge and landing a wild haymaker on Roth before any of the prefects could stop him. "You did this! They're all dead because of you!"

Finn went to strike the captain again but was restrained by several people, including Pritchard. He tried to fight the men holding him but he was too weak.

"Careful, now..." Roth said, using a handkerchief to wipe blood off his chin. Finn realized that it was his blood from his broken knuckles rather than Roth's. "I'm willing to let that slide on account of your recent ordeal, but don't push me."

"Fuck you," Finn said, spitting on the ground by Roth's feet. "As a gold, I can say that now, right?"

Roth shrugged. "There is no law against the use of profanity by a gold, no," the officer admitted. Then the man's eyes sharpened. "Still, it would be wise not get on my bad side, Mr. Brasa. Golds are not above the law, especially not fake golds like you."

Captain Roth then nodded to Captain Withers and withdrew, with his prefect supervisor and entourage close behind. Captain Withers remained and the woman was smiling, though it appeared to be out of genuine amusement, rather than to foreshadow any cruel intent.

"You've got some balls on you, I'll give you that," Captain Withers said. "But I'd take heed of what Viktor said. It wouldn't do to arrest the Hero of Metalhaven on the day of his great victory, but Viktor holds grudges, and he never lets go of them."

"I couldn't give a shit about your boyfriend," Finn answered, bitterly. "And don't pretend you're suddenly my friend now that we're both shiny and gold."

His comment wiped the smile off Wither's face, and she appeared genuinely offended and even hurt. Status was the key currency amongst the golds, and Finn had been propelled to the top of the tree, at least for now. For him to have rebuked Wither's friendship was a slight and one he felt certain he'd regret.

"It seems that you're not very good at making friends, Mr. Brasa," Captain Withers replied, her tone laced with the more familiar spite. Then she smiled again and it sent a shiver down his spine. "And not very good at keeping them either…"

The cruel reference to Owen was like a knife in the gut, constantly being twisted one way and then the other. Withers rejoiced in her victory for a few seconds, enjoying his heartbreak, then proceeded to carry out the duty she was there to perform.

"By order of the Regents of Spacehaven and Metalhaven, you are hereby acquitted of all charges," Withers began, while working her C.O.N.F.I.R.M.E. device to make the order official. "You are also hereby transferred from Metalhaven to the Authority sector, under the jurisdiction of the prosecutors, and raised in color from chrome to gold." The officer gestured to a waiting skycar, gleaming under the harsh floodlights in the landing area. "This will take you to your destination, where you will receive medical treatment before beginning your training."

"My training as what?" Finn asked, aware that Pritchard was hovering just behind him.

"As a prosecutor, of course," Withers smiled. "I, for one, look forward to your first trial. I'll be betting heavily on your claiming the first kill."

Finn snorted and shook his head. "Maybe you should murder 'Viktor' in a crime of passion and get yourself sent to trial. Then, I promise you'll be my first kill."

Withers puckered her lips but bit back whatever response was fighting to leap off her tongue and stepped back. Finn grasped that this wasn't because she'd struggled to formulate a comeback, but because his threat had genuinely intimidated her.

"Good luck, Prosecutor Brasa."

Withers saluted him, a gesture of polite deference that Finn never thought he would receive from anyone, let alone a Prefect Captain, then turned on her heels and marched away.

"This way, sir," Pritchard said, seeming to materialize out of thin air right in front of him. "Your skycar awaits."

Finn followed the young man, though the stim was wearing off and the effects of his injuries made progress slow and painful.

"Don't worry, we'll get you fixed up at the training barracks," Pritchard said, still smiling, as if it were not possible for him to do otherwise.

"Why do you keep calling me, sir?" Finn asked, easing his aching body into the flying vehicle. The question seemed to stump Pritchard, and he had to think hard for answer.

"The honorific, 'Sir', is simply how one addresses their superior," Pritchard finally answered.

"And that's who I am now?" Finn asked, curious to

understand the dynamic of their relationship. "I'm your boss?"

"Yes, sir," Pritchard smiled. "Technically, I am your valet or personal aide, if you prefer."

Finn burst out laughing but it quickly descended into a fit of wheezes and strained coughs as every muscle in his body complained loudly at him.

"I'm sorry, sir, did I offend you?" Pritchard asked, afraid for the safety of his new job.

"No, you didn't offend me," Finn sighed. "In fact, I don't think you have it in you to offend anyone."

The skycar took off and Pritchard remained mercifully silent. Several minutes elapsed though despite the lack of distractions, Finn found no solace. The image of his dead friend was etched into his mind, and no matter how hard he tried, he couldn't get Owen's face out of his head. Eventually, weariness proved to be his ally and he found himself drifting in and out of sleep as the vehicle hummed softly toward its destination.

"It really was incredible what you did back there," a voice said, jolting Finn out of his semi-slumber. He looked at Pritchard, though his valet hadn't spoken the words, and instead the voice had been projected over the cabin's intercom. "I've never seen anyone stand up to a prosecutor like you did."

Finn sat up and realized that it was the pilot of the skycar who was speaking to him. From the design of the man's flight suit, he was obviously a gold, though not a prefect.

"I was sorry about your worker buddy, though," the pilot continued, despite Finn not having answered him. "That guy

Corbin was scum. I've never been happier to see an offender get what was coming to him."

Finn almost threw up but he managed to keep it together by staring at a line of rivets in the floor panel of the aircar. The pilot was oblivious to his nausea and suffering, and continued to speak as if they were old friends.

"I wonder what happened to those others though..." the pilot continued, wistfully. "The white from Spacehaven and your other friend from Metalhaven. Cora and Soren, I think they were called."

"Soren was not my friend!" Finn growled, frightening Pritchard and causing the man to shrink into the corner of the cabin.

"Hey, sorry," the pilot replied, taking his hands off the yoke and holding them in surrender. "But yeah, I get what you mean. He was a bastard too. Maybe even worse than Corbin."

Finn took a few deep breaths and managed to reign in his nausea enough to sit back again. Then something the pilot had said resurfaced in his thoughts.

"What exactly did you mean when you asked what happened to Cora and Soren?" Finn said.

The pilot shrugged and returned his hands to the control yoke, not that this mattered, since the man was looking at Finn over his shoulder, rather than watching the route ahead.

"It's just that the TV feed didn't really show what happened to them," the man replied. "It was around the time when you were inside the control center that the feed got patchy. We saw Bloodletter take out the smaller Metalhaven woman, Khloe, but it went all fuzzy when Cora and Soren were killed. They announced their deaths but it's just a shame we didn't get to see it. I was kinda rooting for the Spacehaven chick, so I hope she didn't suffer."

"I thought you golds would be rooting for the prosecutors, not the offenders," Finn said, surprised by the pilot's comments.

"Nah, there's no point, since they always win," the man replied, breezily. "The excitement comes from betting the long odds that someone will survive."

Finn snorted and shook his head. While the pilot had perhaps meant well, he was clearly oblivious to how distasteful his comments actually were. Regardless of who he was rooting for or betting on, he was still watching people die for sport. He then wondered what would have happen if he told the pilot the truth, which was that Cora and Soren had escaped to Haven. Then he remembered the Regent's warning and the pieces fell into place. If he opened his mouth then he'd be gone quicker than a Nimbus rocket, and most likely so would the pilot and Pritchard, so he held on to his deadly secret, at least for now.

"They got knocked through a door and fell a full level into the basement," Finn said, mixing truth with a lie. "They were killed instantly. Cora didn't suffer, though I hope that Soren did."

The pilot laughed. "I hear you on that one!" he exclaimed. "But I'm glad the Spacehaven lady didn't suffer. That's something, I guess."

An alarm rang out inside the cockpit and despite it not sounding particularly urgent, it still sent a shiver of fear down Finn's spine.

"It's okay, we're just approaching the prosecutor barracks,

that's all," Pritchard said, sensing Finn's discomfort. "Look, you can see it just there."

Finn looked out of the window and it was only then that he realized they were flying over the central Authority sector. It was like a slice of the Nimbus Space Citadel on an otherwise desolate and dead planet, with gleaming buildings, lush green gardens, and tranquil azure canals. Then he saw a large open square, and another set of buildings that were more practical in nature, though no less resplendent in their architectural beauty.

"That's where we're going?" Finn asked.

"Yes, sir. That's your new home."

The skycar circled the complex, while the pilot chatted with a controller on the ground, speaking in acronyms and jargon that Finn didn't understand. Then the vehicle descended sharply and touched down in the square. The doors were opened but this time Pritchard didn't get out.

"Are you not coming?" Finn asked.

"Not yet, sir," his valet replied. "I need to gather your new personal effects and take care of some administration relating to your accommodation and bank account."

"Bank account?" Finn said, unsure whether he'd heard his valet correctly.

"Yes, sir, as a gold you obviously need money," Pritchard answered, still smiling. Finn had read about currency on his illegal data device, and it sounded like chits to him, but instead of just one thing, you could exchange currency for anything of value. "It won't take me long. Just step on to the tarmac and your instructor will be out soon to greet you. Then I'll see you again later, once I've taken care of these matters."

Finn saw no reason to argue so slid out of his seat and stepped away from the skycar. The door closed and the vehicle took off again, like a giant golden ladybug. Finn watched it disappear over the horizon, his mind racing in a dozen different directions.

"You made that a lot harder than it needed to be."

Finn spun around and saw a woman standing on the tarmac a few meters away. She was wearing a close-fitting uniform, like an armored version of his ragged jumpsuit, but in a jet black with gold piping and matching overcoat. The hood was pulled up and only then did he noticed that it was snowing in the Authority sector.

"Made what harder?" Finn replied.

The hood was thrown back and Finn didn't know whether to run away or charge at the woman and wrap his hands around her neck. He ended up doing neither and just stood with his mouth agape.

"Follow me, Prosecutor Brasa," said The Shadow, Elara Cage. "Your training starts now."

26
A NEW NAME

Elara Cage turned her back on Finn and began walking toward the barracks building as if the events of the last few hours hadn't happened. He remained rooted to the spot on the icy asphalt parade ground, struggling to process the fact that he was not only a prosecutor himself but that his trainer and mentor was a woman who had recently tried to kill him.

Or had she?

Finn closed his eyes and struggled to remember the events inside the crucible but he was tired and emotional and he couldn't be certain if his memory of The Shadow was faithful to what had really happened.

Was she trying to kill me, or did she save me?

A scene played out in his mind as vivid and as visceral as if it were happening to him all over again. He and Owen were on the run from Bloodletter and a wrong turn had suddenly found them cornered and at the sadistic killer's mercy. Elara Cage then appeared, her chameleonic armor reducing her appearance to little more than a shimmering blur, but instead of killing him and his friend, the hunter threw her grenade at her co-prosecutor instead, before vanishing like a delusion of fantasy.

But it could have been a mistake... Finn thought, arguing with his own memories. *She might have botched the grenade throw and ducked into cover to spare herself from the blast without knowing she'd missed?*

If that had been the only instance when Elara Cage had seemingly spared his life then Finn might have believed his own argument, but the truth was there had been another occasion, and it was one that was much harder to refute.

"I don't want you!" Elara Cage had yelled at him, her roundel dagger pressed to his throat. *"Stay out of my way!"*

Finn's mind was at war with itself and he felt like he was being torn in half. One side of Finn Brasa was urging him to see reason. It made no sense that this prosecutor – this murderer – had intentionally spared his life. *Why? For what purpose?* he asked himself, but his fractured mind had no answer. On the other side there were the facts of what had actually happened, no matter how implausible they seemed. And the fact was that The Shadow, Elara Cage, could have killed him twice and had chosen not to.

"Are you coming?" Elara said, suddenly realizing that Finn hadn't moved from the spot on the asphalt where he'd alighted the skycar.

"Are you a Metal?" Finn asked.

There were a thousand questions whirling around his mind like a tornado but those four simple words encapsulated them all. Elara regarded him for a second then retraced her steps, placing her feet perfectly inside the footprints that she'd already left in the snow, like a prowling cat.

"Yes, I'm a Metal," Elara replied, with surprising openness, considering the weight of the secret it revealed. "The first to escape Zavetgrad were all from Metalhaven. There was a revolt, more than a hundred and twenty-five years ago now. It almost brought down the Authority but like vipers they sunk in their fangs and clung on to power." The woman paused and pointed up to the ever-present shadow of Nimbus in orbit above them. "That's why Nimbus is so important to the golds," Elara continued. "It's a place where the Authority can be safe from people like us. Or at least that's what they think."

"What happened to the workers who revolted?" Finn asked.

"About a hundred of them managed to steal skycars and escape across the Davis Strait," Elara explained. "They established Haven, but those revolutionary workers of Zavetgrad paid a heavy price in blood. That's what Metal and Blood means, Finn. It means that Haven exists because of the courage and sacrifice of hundreds of workers like you and me, all chromes from Metalhaven who shed blood in the name of freedom."

"But you're a prosecutor?" Finn said. Elara's revelations had rocked him to the core but it was those two dangerously conflicting facts that stunned him most. "How can you be a Metal and also a gold who murders people in the name of the Authority?"

"I've saved far more than I've killed."

"That's not an answer," Finn said, frustrated that Elara was evading the question.

"There are no perfect answers, Finn. No easy choices. I do what I have to." Elara took a moment to think then narrowed her jewel green eyes at him. "But that's not the question you really wanted to ask me, is it?"

Outwardly, she appeared calm, and Finn could see that she was unarmed, but everything about her screamed danger. From her piercing green eyes to the way her long, slender body moved with a serpentine grace, she evoked the primal fear of a venomous predator.

"Then tell me, what do I really want to know?" Finn replied. Though he was afraid, his natural reaction was always to challenge, not withdraw.

"You want to know why I didn't kill you," Elara said, humoring Finn. "And more than that, you want to know why you alone were singled out for that honor."

"Honor?" Finn said, repulsed by how the woman had phrased her answer. He stepped toward her but every movement of his broken and bleeding body felt like torture. "Don't talk to me about honor. There was nothing about that charade that was honorable, least of all your part in it. I watched you murder Linden and Parker with my own eyes. Where was the honor in that?"

Finn had closed the gap between himself and The Shadow and he realized that his fists were clenched. Elara had adjusted her stance and become like a coiled viper, ready to strike should Finn lose what little self-control he had left.

"Don't presume to know me," Elara replied. Her voice was steady but the threat was clear. "You have no idea what I sacrificed to become the thing you know as The Shadow."

While outwardly calm, Finn could feel the rage radiating from Elara like a smoldering ember, threatening to ignite the world around them.

"I don't give a shit what you sacrificed, or think you

sacrificed," Finn snarled, stepping closer still so that the heat from Elara's body enveloped him. "All I know is that I saw you kill innocent people for sport, while letting others die at the hands of Bloodletter. A murderer is all you are, nothing more."

Finn watched and waited for a response but still her emerald eyes didn't so much as flicker. He wanted a reason to attack, so he could beat her bloody like he'd done to Corbin, but his instincts were screaming at him that Elara wasn't his enemy, and he couldn't understand why.

"And what about Skye?"

The mention of the woman from Stonehaven caught Finn completely off-guard, and suddenly he was back in the crucible, pressing the electrician's knife into her chest and watching the light leave her eyes.

"That was different," Finn said, stepping back and going on the defensive. "That was an accident."

"And was Corbin Driscoll also an accident?" Cage replied, tilting her head to one side.

"That was..."

Finn stopped himself, realizing that The Shadow had lured him into a trap, but he couldn't think of a word that hid the ugly truth of his act, so he left his answer hanging in the air like a poisonous gas.

"You were going to say, 'natural justice', or perhaps self-defense?" Elara answered for him. It was as if she could read his mind. "But we both know it was more than that."

"Maybe it was both of those things," Finn said, his voice wavering ever so slightly, but he knew it was a lie, and Elara shattered his feeble attempt at deception as easily as breaking thin ice.

"You killed Corbin because the bastard deserved to die, and that ruthlessness is something you'll need to harness," Elara said, still without emotion. "But you also stood up to the Authority, even before you entered the crucible, and you helped others freely, even when it put your own life at risk. That sort of selflessness is rarer than you think, and whether you believe it or not, that makes you special, Finn Brasa. It makes you Metal."

"A Metal like you?" Finn laughed in her face. "I know your story, 'Iron Bitch of Metalhaven', and we're nothing alike. You won your trial by murdering your co-workers like slaughtering animals. If becoming Metal means being like you then I don't want it."

"No, we're nothing alike," Cage hissed, and for the briefest moment, Finn thought she was going to hit him. "You're right about me. The crucible made me into the monster you see now, but I can't change what I am. I can never be redeemed. All I can do, in some small measure, is atone." Elara pressed her fist to Finn's chest above his heart and in his weakened condition the force of her push almost knocked him over. "The crucible changes people, Finn," the woman continued. "It was designed to set us at each other's throats, to show the people of Zavetgrad that there is no solidarity amongst the worker class, and that all they can rely on is the unwavering steadfastness of the Authority." She pushed harder and Finn had to fight to stay standing. "But it didn't change you. Your strength was already there, unbreakable from the start. That makes you special."

Finn took half a step back and the woman's fist slid from his chest and fell to her side, though her fingers remained clenched.

"Don't presume to know me, either," Finn hit back. He was angry at Elara though he couldn't be sure why. "You talk like I'm some sort of noble freedom fighter, but I'm not. I'm just a fool, mad at the world and too stupid to listen to those who warned me where my arrogance would lead."

"You're right..."

Not for the first time, Cage had said something that stopped Finn in his tracks and forced him to listen.

"Before the trial, you were like a spoiled child throwing a tantrum because the world wasn't fair," Elara continued, venting some of the anger that she'd so far so skillfully managed to contain. She huffed a laugh and suddenly she was looking down on him. "Arrogant doesn't even begin to describe it. You were reckless and not just with your own life." Now it was The Shadow who advanced, coming so close that she could have sunk her teeth into his neck had she wanted. "And it was that recklessness, not me, not Bloodletter, and not the Authority, that is the reason why your friend is dead."

Finn's fury suddenly exploded like an atom bomb and his fists flew, but even enraged he was too weak and too hurt to fight The Iron Bitch of Metalhaven. She blocked and dodged and let him punch himself out till he could no longer stand. Collapsing onto his knees, he pressed his hands into the snow, which melted and turned red with the blood leaking from his torn flesh. The fight had gone out of him and all that was left was the crushing reality of what he'd done. He wished the torment would end but no matter how much he willed it, his heart continued to beat strongly, forcing him to face the truth. Owen's death was his fault. He might not have pulled the trigger but he had put his friend and brother on the firing line.

"You should have saved him, not me!" Finn cried, his tears diluting the blood and turning it pink. "He was ten times the man I'll ever be. He was honest and good, despite everything this fucked up city did to drag him down. Owen was the one you should have brought here! Why didn't you save him?!"

Elara exhaled slowly and the weight of her breath seemed to drag her down, like it was an albatross around her neck. She crouched beside Finn and for a moment he wondered if she was going to offer him a comforting touch, but instead she remained coiled and vigilant.

"Not everyone can be saved, Finn, at least not yet," Elara whispered. "And while the guilt you feel will never leave you, it doesn't have to break you, either. You can use it. I'll show you how."

"I won't become a prosecutor," Finn said, his vision still blurred by tears. "I can't kill people in the crucible just so that others can be saved. I can't be like you. I won't."

The Shadow then offered Finn her hand. He wiped away his tears but hesitated, afraid of the path the woman might lead him down if he took it.

"If you listen and do as I say, then you won't need to become like me," Elara said. "My path is fixed, Finn, but you can be something much more. Something better."

"What does that even mean?" Finn asked, still hesitant and afraid.

"All in good time..." Elara replied. "First, we must get your wounds treated, and you need time to rest." She held her hand closer, almost touching his. "Please Finn. You have to trust me."

Finn wiped away the remains of his tears, streaking his face with blood in the process, then finally took Elara Cage's hand, and allowed her to pull him up. Her grip was strong. She was strong. The crucible had made her so.

With Elara still guiding him, Finn lugged his tired body across the courtyard to the door of the barracks block. There was a canvas bag on the floor in front of it, similar to the one Finn had found inside the flame pit. Elara guided his hand to the wall so that he could prop himself up, and without her steadying influence, he almost collapsed. Then his new mentor opened the bag and removed a metal can that was charred on the outside, as if it had been struck by lightning.

"Here, I thought you might want this back," Elara said, pressing the can into Finn's trembling hand. "He was a complication inside the crucible. One I hadn't foreseen."

Finn shuffled so that he could rest his back to the wall then turned the object over in his hands. Suddenly, all his aches and pains were gone.

"Scraps!" Finn cried, tears again welling in his eyes, though these were tears of happiness.

He continued to inspect the robot but while the machine was intact, the crossbow bolt that had rendered him inoperative had destroyed his power cell.

"All the tools you need to fix him are in your room," Elara explained. If his joy at being reunited with his robot had moved her in any way, she did not show it. "And anything else you require, you only need ask."

Finn laughed and scrubbed the wetness from his face, conscious that he'd now cried twice in front of the infamous prosecutor, which ran contrary to her opinion of him as being strong.

"Thank you for this," Finn said, nodding to the broken machine.

"As a gold, you don't have to hide him anymore," Elara said, moving the now empty bag aside and grasping the door handle. "As a gold, there are many new opportunities available to you. Opportunities to train and to learn the skills you'll need to survive, both here and eventually beyond the city's boundary fences."

Finn pushed away from the wall and stood tall, feeling stronger. Finding Scraps, broken but fixable, much like himself, had invigorated him.

"By beyond the city's boundary fences, do you mean that I'm going to Haven?" Finn asked.

"Eventually, yes," Elara answered. "And if all goes well then who knows, maybe you'll reach even further than that."

Finn frowned and Elara pointed skyward to the Nimbus Space Citadel, as omnipresent in space above them as the moon and the stars. It was more than just a symbol of the Authority's iron grip over the people of Zavetgrad – Nimbus *was* the Authority. And if the workers of Metalhaven, Stonehaven, Seedhaven, and all the other sectors, were ever to be free, then Nimbus had to fall.

"All in good time," Elara added. She turned the handle and inched open the door to the barracks block before pausing. "From this moment on, you must not refer to me as Elara Cage, at least not in public. In this place, I am only The Shadow and you are my apprentice.

"Do I have to call you sir or ma'am?" Finn replied. He was being flippant but the unwavering sternness of his mentor's expression told him that it wasn't a joking matter. "Seriously?"

"I know you have a problem with authority, but now that

you know what's at stake, I trust you can swallow your pride?"

Finn straightened his broken back and nodded. "Yes, ma'am."

Elara opened the door fully and Finn could see the silhouettes of other prosecutors and apprentices inside. He couldn't make out any of their faces but he knew one thing for certain, which was that none of them were like him.

"Am I still Finn Brasa in there or do I get a prosecutor name?" Finn asked, suddenly nervous.

"You will be given a prosecutor name in time, but you already have a new name," Elara replied. "It's a name that people are speaking in the streets and Recovery Centers all throughout Zavetgrad, and I suspect already in the halls of Haven too."

"What is it?" Finn asked.

"Hope," Elara Cage said. "You are metal and blood, Finn Brasa, and your name is hope."

The end (to be continued.)

CONTINUE THE STORY

Read about Finn's adventures as an Apprentice Prosecutor in book #2 of the Metal and Blood series, Prosecutor of Metalhaven. Available from Amazon in Kindle, paperback and audiobook formats, and in Kindle Unlimited.

ALSO BY G J OGDEN

Sa'Nerra Universe

Omega Taskforce

Descendants of War

Scavenger Universe

Star Scavengers

Star Guardians

Standalone series

The Aternien Wars

The Contingency War

Darkspace Renegade

The Planetsider Trilogy

G J Ogden's newsletter: Click here to sign-up

ABOUT THE AUTHOR

At school, I was asked to write down the jobs I wanted to do as a "grown up". Number one was astronaut and number two was a PC games journalist. I only managed to achieve one of those goals (I'll let you guess which), but these two very different career options still neatly sum up my lifelong interests in science, space, and the unknown.

School also steered me in the direction of a science-focused education over literature and writing, which influenced my decision to study physics at Manchester University. What this degree taught me is that I didn't like studying physics and instead enjoyed writing, which is why you're reading this book! The lesson? School can't tell you who you are.

When not writing, I enjoy spending time with my family, playing Warhammer 40K, and indulging in as much Sci-Fi as possible.

Printed in Great Britain
by Amazon